S0-BDP-538

ENTER MRS BELCHAMBER

ENTER MRS BELCHAMBER

Elizabeth Cadell

Thorndike Press
Thorndike, Maine USA

This Large Print edition is published by Chivers Press, England, and by Thorndike Press, USA.

Published in 1996 in the U.K. by arrangement with the author's estate.

Published in 1996 in the U.S. by arrangement with Brandt & Brandt Literary Agents, Inc.

U.K. Hardcover ISBN 0–7451–3946–9 (Chivers Large Print)
U.K. Softcover ISBN 0–7451–3956–6 (Camden Large Print)
U.S. Softcover ISBN 0–7862–0601–2 (General Series Edition)

Copyright © 1951, 1979 by Elizabeth Cadell

All rights reserved.

The characters in this book are entirely imaginary and bear no relation to any living person.

The text of this Large Print edition is unabridged.
Other aspects of the book may vary from the original edition.

Set in 16 pt. New Times Roman.

Printed in Great Britain on acid-free paper.

British Library Cataloguing in Publication Data available

Library of Congress Cataloging-in-Publication Data

Cadell, Elizabeth.
  Enter Mrs. Belchamber/Elizabeth Cadell.
    p. cm.
  ISBN 0–7862–0601–2 (lg. print : lsc)
  1. Large type books. I. Title.
PR6005.A225E53 1996
823′.914—dc20   95–43626

ENTER MRS BELCHAMBER

CHAPTER ONE

Mrs Belchamber had managed, without much effort, to keep herself to herself all the way from Paris. By employing her usual deterrents—a gaze of piercing dislike, a twitching of the nostrils as if scenting unpleasantness and, in extreme cases—as when the stout Frenchman had attempted to enter the carriage at Perrier—drawing back her head and looking like a cobra about to strike, she had secured seclusion. And space. Her suitcases were on the rack, but her coat, her travelling rug, her books and papers were disposed upon the three vacant corner seats, while her crochet bag, her flask and her travelling handbag of expensive make, occupied the middle ones. She was very comfortable. If the French had only known how to build trains that made less noise; if the French children in the adjacent carriages were less in evidence, and if the deplorable public sanitation of the French was brought into line with English standards, she would have gone as far as to say that she was enjoying her journey.

She looked at her watch, saw that it was five o'clock, and decided to pour herself out a cup of tea at the next station, when the excessive swaying peculiar to French trains would cease

1

and she would not be forced to waste any of the excellent tea she had made herself before leaving Switzerland. She put out a bony, beringed hand and took up her crochet bag, into which she had slipped some of her favourite biscuits.

The train slowed and then stopped and she lifted the *pince-nez* hung round her neck and placed them on her nose in order to read the name of the station: Les Hautiers-sur-Mouelle. Pretentious, to say the least, she reflected, for a place which was no more than a third-rate market town. It was a pity she had not been able to go by the boat train; it would have flashed by all these drab little stations and given them no more notice than they deserved.

Some tea. She hoped that the flask, which was unfortunately of Swiss make, would have kept the tea reasonably hot. Her English flask had outlasted innumerable foreign ones, but had unfortunately been broken just before she left Montreux. She was about to unscrew the top of the Swiss substitute when she paused, noting with displeasure that a large group of people had gathered at the door of the carriage with the obvious intention of entering.

This, she felt, was gross impertinence. They could see plainly, if they only looked, that she was an elderly Englishwoman travelling alone and just about to take her tea. To be thrust upon, to be invaded—for this had the appearance of an invasion—was intolerable.

2

Mrs Belchamber put the biscuits back in the crochet bag and prepared her first line of defence—the stony stare.

This had no effect. A stout Frenchman with a red beaming face gave her a rapturous smile and threw open the door, letting in a shaft of the pleasant spring sunshine.

'*Voilà!*' he exclaimed to the chattering, gesticulating companions crowding behind him. '*Mais voilà!* An empty carriage with nothing but an English lady and plenty of room. But see!'

'But see!' exclaimed an excited woman, pushing him aside and giving the glaring Mrs Belchamber a friendly bow; 'but see, here is plenty of room for everybody.'

'But see!' shouted two more Frenchmen, poking their heads inside. 'Here they will be comfortable.'

Mrs Belchamber understood French imperfectly; in her forty years residence on the Continent she had found that English did perfectly well; but she did not need to hear the dreadful truth; her eyes told her that some, if not all, of these entire strangers proposed to foist themselves upon her. She made a last protest by seizing the door of the carriage and banging it firmly, leaving the intruders outside, but two more stout men threw it open again and, with an excited burst of speech and charming smiles, ushered in two small boys in French sailor hats, a smaller girl in a modified

3

version of the same headgear, three suitcases, a small tin box, a large toy boat, a cardboard box smelling of cheese and apples, several overcoats and, finally, a larger suitcase. Mrs Belchamber's effects were treated with reverence, and the two men, who had now been joined by two women, begged that she would not disturb herself. If she would but allow this to go in this place—so!—and that in that place, and the other—so!—in the other, then all would be comfortably disposed. All would arrange itself; all would march.

Mrs Belchamber sat in her corner, her bony frame rigid and withdrawn. She saw the last piece of luggage stowed neatly, and realized that the two women, in chorus with the crowd outside, were bestowing vociferous farewells on the three children. To her bewilderment, the two stout men also appeared to be taking their departure, and a wave of horror swept over her; the three sailor hats were travelling alone.

She looked the three over; yes, they had an unmistakable air of having travelled, a calmness and self-possession which showed them capable of undertaking journeys unaccompanied. No doubt, thought Mrs Belchamber, shuddering, they would eat cheese and apples for the next hour, sail the toy boat up and down the corridor, shatter her peace as completely as they had shattered her privacy and be collected, at the next Hautiers-sur-Mouelle, by as noisy a band of friends and relations. They would take their possessions and go, and she would be left with the memory of the cheese and apple.

The train doors began to close, the farewells grew louder; the guard came up, and with the complete lack of attention to duty which Mrs Belchamber had noticed in French officials, joined the party for a brief exchange of views, plans, family history and mutual compliments. Finally, he raised a small horn to his lips and seemed about to blow upon it the rude noise which served as a signal, when the group parted and a tall young man, with a brief, pleasant nod of farewell that embraced every member of the party, stepped into the train, shut the door firmly and, without incommoding Mrs Belchamber in any way, arranged the three children at the window in the best position for making their final salutes. The trumpet blew, the train moved, the children waved and the cries of the farewell committee died away in the distance.

Mrs Belchamber found, with deep relief, that the newcomers were silent. She had not heard one word from the children; they had smiled, their eyes had twinkled, but, beyond a murmur or two of farewell, they had said nothing. She studied the three of them as they took their seats, and decided that their mother might just as well have saved herself trouble and had one child instead of three, for—apart from their size and the fact that the girl's hair was somewhat longer than the boys'—she could not detect the smallest difference in them. There was the elder boy—he might have been ten, with a brown skin, brown hair, and large brown eyes. There was the younger one; about nine, brown skin, brown hair, and large brown eyes. The little girl, she thought, would be about seven; brown skin, brown hair and large brown eyes. They looked typically French, and so did those ridiculous hats, but it was pleasant—if surprising—to find that French children could behave with English calm.

Mrs Belchamber's eyes went to the young man, and she experienced a distinct feeling of shock. She had already gained an impression of height unusual in a Frenchman, and now she could see why; he was not a Frenchman. He was as unmistakably English as the children were French. He had it written all over him— Mrs Belchamber read it with pride and pleasure—all the hallmarks, all the solid, the reassuring signs. Eton and Oxford. A splendid product of a splendid race. Nobody—except, perhaps the Norwegians—would have the effrontery to claim to be able to produce a finer physical type. The first—Mrs Belchamber bit into a biscuit and brushed away contemporary history with the crumbs—the first in the world. She looked the young man over with unabashed scrutiny and wondered what he was doing with three French children. Tutor, probably. But they were too young—and he didn't somehow, look like a tutor, though he was obviously in charge of them. It was a piquant combination—the tall young Englishman and the three self-possessed little French children. It would be interesting to know ... but of course it wouldn't do to ask. It wouldn't be the thing. It wouldn't be the thing at all.

'Friends of yours?' she inquired of the young man.

Christopher Heron paused in the act of sorting tickets and rested a pair of cool grey eyes upon the stranger. He sensed rather than saw a rich old lady—one got the impression of plain but good clothes, good luggage, general well-being. He mistrusted the look of her; she had a disagreeable expression and a long thin nose with a sharp point which he did not care to have thrust into his affairs. He placed her as one of a type which considers its own good breeding sufficient cover for a display of bad manners.

He answered her laconically, and went back to his sorting.

'Relations,' he said.

Mrs Belchamber flushed with anger, and the three children looked at her with calm interest. She glared back at them, but her curiosity was stronger than her anger. If information was withheld in one quarter, she could get it elsewhere. She looked at the elder boy,

7

assembled her French and addressed him.

'*Quel est—er—votre nom?*' she inquired.

He took his time in replying—it was plain, thought Mrs Belchamber angrily, that he didn't know his own language.

The answer came, at last, in halting but correct English.

'My name is Robert,' he said. He pronounced it with the English ending, and went on to introductions. He indicated first the younger boy, and then girl. 'This is my brother, Paul, and this is my sister, Josette.'

Mrs Belchamber stared at him.

'You speak English very well,' she informed him.

He gave her a short, un-English bow.

'Thank you,' he said.

'I, too, speak English very well,' said Paul.

'*Moi aussi*,' said Josette.

'That,' explained Robert, 'is because we are English.'

'That is true. I am English,' corroborated Paul.

'*Moi aussi*,' said Josette.

There was a pause. Three pairs of brown eyes were fixed upon Mrs Belchamber, but she was a little bewildered by this accommodating response; information was not always so easy to extract. Out of the corner of her eye, she saw the Englishman stirring restlessly, and hastened on with her questions before he could divert the children's attention.

'Where are you going?' she inquired. 'To England?'

'Yes,' said Robert.

'To England,' said Paul. 'I have been before.'

'*Moi aussi*,' said Josette.

Christopher leaned back and closed his eyes. To England. He thought with relief of the journey's end—though it was not to be quite the end. It was a pity to be taking the three of them to a London flat, especially in April, but it was all the home he had at the moment and it would have to do until he found a more suitable one. Perhaps it would have been wiser, when he heard of the fire, to have postponed coming over to fetch the three of them, but the arrangements for transferring them permanently to England had been long and elaborate, and he had felt it best to stick to the plan.

They had been, he remembered, singularly unmoved when he had told them the news. It was not easy to guess what they were feeling— that, perhaps was the English side of them— but he had expected Robert, at any rate, to show some emotion at the thought that the home of his ancestors stood in ruins, blackened and gutted. But Robert had made a practical approach to the situation.

'The Castle, it is burned?' he had asked.

'Yes. Not the walls, you understand, because they're stone, and very thick, but

9

the inside ...'

'All of the inside?'

'Yes. The Keep, and the Chamber—and I don't know how much you remember—you were such a small boy when you saw it.'

'Yes. But I remember it very well. And my mother showed us pictures sometimes—afterwards, when we came back to France.'

'Yes ... I suppose she did. But I'm afraid there's no hope that you'll ever be able to live in it again.'

'It cannot be made again?'

'You mean the damage repaired? No. You see, it would mean a great deal of expense, and another thing—'

He had hesitated. It was not the time to explain that an erection which had, for the last six hundred years, been considered a blot on the landscape, had at last been, if not totally, then partially removed. It was not the time to enlarge upon its history, which had been an ignoble one. It was better not to dwell on the fact that—since its erection in 1059 by Robert FitzHeron and his brother Ribald, Piershurst Castle had stunned anybody with an eye for beauty or line. William the Conqueror, looking round for Saxon manors to confiscate for his own adherents, had reined in his horse, given one look at Piershurst and crossed it off the list of awards. After the anarchy of Stephen's reign it had been placed on Henry II's black list of unlicensed castles ordered to be destroyed, but the King's advisers had felt that justice would be better served by allowing the notorious eyesore to stand as a perpetual punishment to the district. It had resisted sieges and survived assaults; it had seen countless Herons born and buried. Paul Heron, the sixth Earl of Piershurst, had been the last to live in it; before his son, Robert, the seventh Earl, could be brought over from France to take up his residence at the Castle, it had come at last to disaster. The seventh Earl was homeless.

Christopher turned his head and studied the seventh Earl. A nice little boy. A nice trio, in fact. This, his third meeting with them, had confirmed him in his previous view that they were, as children went, extraordinarily little trouble. He had not yet come to any conclusion about the wisdom of transplanting them to England, but it had been their mother's wish, and he had liked her enough, and had sufficient trust in her judgement, to fulfil his promise to her. She had displayed great sense throughout her difficult marriage, and had an instinct for doing the right thing: Christopher hoped that this would turn out to be the right thing.

He listened to the children's polite answers to the questions of the sour old woman opposite, and smiled to himself; she would extract something, but not a great deal of their history, for it was a complicated one. A troubled one, but those who had been most troubled were now at rest. The bitter feeling had passed; the new generation remembered little of the old quarrel, and cared less. Christopher himself—the only one who might have felt a pang at the sight of the three children—felt nothing but liking. If he felt regret, it was not for himself, but for the blow that his mother had received.

He had been brought up as heir to the Earldom of Piershurst. Until he was fourteen, he and his widowed mother had lived at the Castle with his uncle, who was an elderly bachelor, quiet, scholarly, almost a recluse. He had gone to Aix-les-Bains for a cure and, to the incredulous astonishment of all who knew him, returned with a French wife. Christopher, home for the summer holidays, remembered his mother's face, stony with rage, when the news reached her. She had not waited for the Earl's return; she and Christopher had left the Castle, and he had not seen Piershurst again until he looked upon its blackened and gutted ruins.

He wondered, sometimes, at his own calm acceptance of the fact that, if his new French aunt bore a son, his own chance of becoming the seventh Earl was gone. He had faced the prospect without any great sense of loss, but to his mother it had been a shattering blow, and one from which she never fully recovered.

The couple were left severely alone; at the end of a year hope began to revive; there was as yet no heir.

The following year, a son was born, and the year after, a second. After the birth of the third child—a girl—the Earl took his family to France and settled them in a house near his wife's home in the Pyrenees. It was here that Christopher, some time later, had, on an impulse, interrupted a holiday tour and paid them a visit.

He had been prompted by nothing more than curiosity; he had been the centre of the family quarrel, but it had raged round him without arousing any feeling other than that of embarrassment at the thought of his bald and elderly uncle as a father of infants, and an instinctive shrinking from a woman who was presumed to have married for a title.

He was nineteen when he first saw his aunt and the children. He went for a day and he had, to his mother's chagrin, spent six weeks with them. He had always liked his uncle; he liked even more his mature, sensible wife; he grew to love the atmosphere of the big, rambling house and the happiness in it. He could even find pleasure in teasing his fat little brown-eyed cousins and listening to their prattle—half French, half English.

He went back the following year after the death of his mother, and it was the last time he was to see his uncle. At his death, Christopher went over and brought his aunt and the children to England for a visit; it had not been unsuccessful, but she had decided to go back to France, and it was then that he had promised her that, if anything happened to her, he would bring the children to England and act as their guardian.

He was now fulfilling his promise. But what had been a smooth plan had now developed a great many hitches. The Castle had been their destination and the Castle was in ruins. Thérèse, the children's old nurse, had been coming with them, and with her Monique, her daughter; these two were to have taken charge of the children, but Thérèse had met him with a woe-begone countenance: Monique was ill—it was not much, moaned Thérèse, but she had a fever and it was necessary to wait until it passed before they travelled. They would follow—when Monique was better, they would follow.

So he was on his way to London with three children. Well, that was all right, he reflected. He wouldn't attempt it in any other circumstances, but these three had a capacity for keeping their heads. He supposed that they gave one another a sense of security: while they were together, outside events did not much affect their world on its firm tripod stand. They knew him well; they had been to England before; Thérèse and Monique would turn up in time; by Easter he would have found a house; all was well.

He studied the three children with satisfaction; it was obvious that they were

14

enjoying the journey, chatting in a friendly manner with the thin Englishwoman. In between her sharp questions, Christopher learned something about her. Belchamber, widow, by all appearances rich, aggressively English in theory but inclined to the Continental in fact; had been, before her marriage, one of the Melhamptons of Melhampton, owned a large house there and had given it, fully furnished, to a committee engaged in forming homes for aged gentlefolk—on condition, Christopher gathered, that she was to occupy the best suite for the rest of her life. The committee, he reflected, probably imagined, from her age, that she was on her last legs and that the best suite would soon be available for somebody else; when they saw her, they were going to get a shock, for this was the type that lived to be centenarians. He, personally, would give her twenty more years, and he was glad that he was not to see her for any of them. The late Belchamber must have had a time.

Christopher looked from the thin, sour face to the rosy cheeks of the children. There they were, perfectly at home and with nothing uprooted, nothing transplanted about them. There was nothing to worry about; the past was past and the future would look after itself. The day was warm, the seat deep and soft...

He awoke to find his charges gone and the old lady's eyes fixed upon him with a look of

15

grim expectancy. Though he had felt nothing, he had a suspicion that she had awakened him in some way, and the thought made him angry.

'Well?' she snapped.

He gave her his characteristic cool, unruffled glance. A large young man, he was not given to undue haste or effort, except in the field of sport; he disliked fuss or over-emphasis, and he liked to do things in his own way in his own time. This acid and interfering old lady seemed to want to alter this pleasant state of affairs, and he watched her warily.

'Well? Aren't you going after them?'

'After them?' Christopher raised an interrogative eyebrow.

'Those children,' she reminded him sharply. 'They went out.'

'So it appears,' agreed Christopher pleasantly.

There was a pause.

'Well,' said Mrs Belchamber finally, 'aren't you going?'

'Going?'

'Going after them. You're in charge of them, aren't you?'

'Yes, I am,' said Christopher, with an emphasis on the pronoun that made the old lady flush angrily.

'Suppose they fall out of the train,' she demanded. 'Who's to stop them?'

'If you saw three children preparing to fall out of a train,' said Christopher

16

conversationally, 'wouldn't you try to restrain them?'

'Certainly. Most certainly I would. But—'

'Anybody would,' said Christopher. 'You mustn't have any anxiety. The train is full; the windows are in full view; somebody will see them and stop them.'

He closed his eyes.

'And what,' he heard her ask angrily, 'are you going to do to prevent them from annoying other passengers?'

Christopher looked at her in concern.

'Did they annoy you?'

'No, they didn't but—'

He looked relieved, but said nothing, and the old lady looked at him with her lips screwed together in distaste.

'Do you mean to tell me,' she asked, 'that you're going to make no move to see that they're not getting into any trouble or annoying people?'

'They won't get into any trouble,' said Christopher, 'because there are so many kind people about—you for example—who are at hand to avert disaster. If I go out and see they're annoying people, I shall only be giving myself a great deal of unnecessary trouble, because if I see that they're annoying anybody, I shall have to take steps to stop them. If I don't know, you see, I needn't act.'

'Oh, really?' The sharp nose was curled in contempt. 'Then all the other passengers must submit to annoyance just because—'

'If children annoyed you,' inquired Christopher, 'what would you do?'

'I should stop it at once. But—'

'That is what everybody—every sensible person, like yourself, will do. And remember, if anybody has any complaints, I am here—' Christopher stretched out his legs more comfortably—'I am here to receive them.'

He closed his eyes with a well-feigned air of a man on the point of repose. The pretence was too good; he heard the old lady's voice through a pleasantly softening mist; in a few moments he was fast asleep.

CHAPTER TWO

Christopher awoke to find the carriage empty, and wondered, as memory came back, if the old lady was following in the wake of the children. The passage of a steward down the corridor informed him that dinner was being served; he speculated as to whether his fellow-traveller was dining and whether she had taken the children with her.

He went slowly along the swaying train and found the quartette seated at a table for four, old and young eating with equal avidity. Christopher paused as he came up to them, but there was no vacant seat near, and the waiter, shooing him forward politely, indicated a seat a little distance away. Christopher continued his staggering, zigzag progress, steadied himself at a table for two and was about to take the seat facing his party, when a stout man approaching from the other side seated himself, obliging Christopher to sit with his back toward the children. He felt a little annoyed, and gave his table companion a cold glance, which became colder when he saw that the man was stout, bearded, foreign-looking and obviously took his meals seriously; he was already tucking a napkin into his waistcoat and looking down the menu with absorbed interest. Looking at the bulge under the napkin, it was clear to Christopher that he had been studying menus with equal seriousness for a great number of years. There was a lot, he reflected, in this race business. Look round now, at this little lot; the English gazing out of the windows, or looking discreetly at their fellow passengers, or eating their food normally; the French leaning over their plates and getting down to it. Look at the couple opposite— patently French, and looking as though nothing in the world mattered except wiping up the last morsel of gravy—disgusting exhibition. The woman looked—

'George,' demanded the woman in the most English of accents, 'catch that waiter's eye, will you?'

Well anyhow, thought Christopher,

somewhat shaken, this fellow opposite was the real thing. A nice language, French, when you could reel it off without getting tangled up in the subjunctive. Perhaps when this fellow'd finished reeling off his order, he'd give someone else a look at the menu.

At this point Christopher, looking round to borrow one from another table, saw something which made him forget food and Frenchmen. A blonde; her make-up needed to be toned down, perhaps, but one couldn't have everything. A delicious pair of lips, a roving eye—two, in fact—a tender little nose. She was looking at him, and he read with delight the signs. If she was going to do the crossing, England was going to be a very much brighter place. In a pleasant haze of anticipation, Christopher allowed the waiter to translate the menu and place some food before him. Drawing his gaze away reluctantly from an inviting smile, he brought his attention back to his table, and saw with astonishment that he was not the only man who had let his thoughts wander. The Frenchman opposite, far from bending over his food, was now sitting bolt upright—as bolt upright as his curves would allow—and staring with glazed eyes into the distance.

Well yes, thought Christopher, a blonde like that spoke all languages. It was interesting to find that this, after all, was the stronger of a Frenchman's two interests. This chap had completely gone off his feed; in fact, he looked as though he'd seen a ghost. His small brown eyes had a filmy look; his beard was quivering; one hand was plucking at the napkin. He was a bit aged for this sort of thing, Christopher reflected—he must be at least fifty. Or perhaps his twin passions, meeting thus, had—

But how, wondered Christopher suddenly, could he have seen the blonde? She was directly behind him, screened by a shoulder-high partition; he himself could just get a clear view, but unless the Frenchman had leaned out of his seat, screwed his body round—an unlikely feat for a body of that rotundity—and turned his head the wrong way, he could not have seen her. He had obviously seen something startling, for his fork still lay unheeded upon his plate. There was, perhaps, an equally ravishing something in his line of vision; eagerly, Christopher turned to find out what it was.

The tables behind him, he found, were all now completely empty; there only remained Mrs Belchamber and the three children, and Christopher saw, with an astonishment bordering on the incredulous, that it was upon Mrs Belchamber that the Frenchman's gaze was riveted. It was the sight of Mrs Belchamber that had caused him to show this extraordinary emotion.

Astounded, Christopher allowed the blonde to pass without a glance and half-turned in his

21

seat to look once more at the old lady, trying to discover something about her that could account for this effect on an elderly, matter-of-fact-looking Frenchman. Mrs Belchamber, unconscious of the scrutiny, was looking at the waiter with a commanding air and holding up first one and then three fingers. One bill was hers; the other would be paid by that gentleman there—that one—

Turning to point a lean forefinger at Christopher, Mrs Belchamber encountered the dazed stare of the Frenchman beyond him. For a moment there was no sign of recognition in her glance; then Christopher saw the look of incredulity and the odd, mottled pallor that overspread her skin. The next instant she had turned away; she had risen and was shepherding the children back to their carriage; reached the door, acknowledged the waiter's bow with a curt nod, and vanished.

That was interesting, thought Christopher. She knew the fat Frenchman. And the Frenchman was—yes, he was going to leave his food; he had signalled to the waiter, crumpled his napkin, left an assortment of franc notes on the table and was off in pursuit.

Christopher thought for one moment of following him, but two considerations restrained him: one was his hunger; he had not eaten for some time, and if the crossing was bad, who knew when next he would taste food? And there was no reason why he should interest himself in the affairs of people he had never seen before and would—shortly—never see again. The old lady, he considered, was a tough customer and could manage her own business more than capably. Being pursued down a train corridor by a stout Frenchman was the last thing Christopher would have planned for her, but she could doubtless deal with him; the situation had its piquancy, and at any other time might have been worth following up—but there was enough, now, on his plate. Reminded thus of his food, Christopher finished his meal, paid his bills, but retained sufficient interest in Mrs Belchamber's affairs to avoid lingering over his coffee. He walked back to his carriage, pausing to light a cigarette. As he raised his head, he saw a little way ahead the stout form of the Frenchman; he was standing outside Christopher's compartment, in the door of which, calm, upright and unmoved, stood Mrs Belchamber. In contrast with her tall, lean figure, the man's shortness and bulk had an air of caricature—the full curve of his body seemed to flow abruptly into the absurdly short, pointed legs. From his agitated shoulders, the impassioned movements of his hands, Christopher guessed that an argument was in progress, and it was clear that Mrs Belchamber was determined to keep it from the ears of the children. She saw Christopher approaching and, raising an imperious hand, indicated to her companion that the interview was over. Turning her back upon him, she marched with as much dignity as the movement of the train would allow into the carriage; turning once more, she cut short the Frenchman's volubility with a curt sentence.

'It's no use chattering away at me,' she said coldly. 'I don't understand what you're talking about.'

The door closed behind her with a decisive click; Christopher, coming up to it, put out a hand to open it once more and murmured an apology to the Frenchman, who was in the way. He looked at Christopher, hesitated a moment and then spoke appealingly.

'*Pardon Monsieur—pardon—vous connaissez Madame?*'

Not on your life, reflected Christopher with relief, and smiled at his questioner.

'Sorry,' he said aloud, stepping into the carriage. 'No *comprendo. Verstehe nicht.* No French.'

He closed the door. Certainly his French wasn't up to Sorbonne standard. But there were one or two things he did understand, and he had heard enough of the argument to give him food for thought—if he wanted it. But he didn't want it; his life was full of his own problems, and if a stout elderly Frenchman pursued a thin elderly Englishwoman down a train corridor claiming relationship, it was no business of his. It was curious—*he* said he was, and *she* said he wasn't. Well, she ought to know, after all. All the same, concluded Christopher finally, he didn't understand it all.

The only thing he did understand, quite positively was that nobody would call Mrs Belchamber *Maman* unless they had some reason to.

CHAPTER THREE

Josette was asleep, leaning heavily on Christopher's shoulder when they reached the port. They had been running, for the past hour, in mist that had thickened to a heavy, swirling fog, and the train was a good deal behind schedule. The sunshine in which they had started out was far behind them; there was rawness and an unwelcoming sharpness in the air. After a glance at the tired little form drooping against him, Christopher got down her thick overcoat and wound a scarf round her neck. As an afterthought, he stuffed her hat into a case and wound a length of the scarf round her head. He would put her into a berth on the boat and let her sleep during the crossing.

'One thing,' announced Mrs Belchamber, watching his preparations, 'there's no wind. No wind, no waves.'

Robert regarded her with a disappointed air.

25

'The sea'—he held out two hands, the palms flattened—'it will be so? The ship will not rock?'

'No. And a good thing too,' said Mrs Belchamber. 'We've got enough trouble with darkness and fog and raw April air. We don't want any more. Come along now, like a good boy, and get me down those things.'

Christopher noted, with apprehension, that she had attached herself to his party. He could scarcely refuse her his help in getting her luggage on to the platform and finding her a porter; after this he made a brief farewell and hurried away, only to hear her sharp order to the porter:

'Now follow that gentleman—there. *Cet monsieur*—that one. *That* one, my good man. *Cet.* Don't you understand *cet*?'

The porter understood; Christopher heard his heavy breathing at his shoulder. Encumbered as he was with the children, he could not hurry on and put a safe distance between himself and the old lady following determinedly. He looked round hopefully for a sign of the stout Frenchman, but he appeared to have vanished; there had been no sign of him since the dining-car incident, and Christopher concluded, regretfully, that he had got off the train before it reached the port. There was nothing to distract Mrs Belchamber from her obvious determination to make one of their party.

She made it clear, on the boat, that she expected him to attend to her comfort. She chose a site on the deck and stood on it, with the children, until Christopher had got berths, paid the porters, arranged the luggage and returned to announce that all was ready. He watched her go with Josette to the cabin which the two were to share, noting with apprehension her grandmotherly, proprietary air.

The crossing was calm, but slow. Robert and Paul remained on deck with Christopher, pacing slowly to and fro, their hands thrust deep into pockets in imitation of his, their steps lengthened to his stride, their sailor hats, somehow, secure on their heads. Christopher studied the hats and, leaning against the rail, came to a decision. He looked down at the two faces, upturned in expectancy.

'You know,' he said, 'those aren't English hats.'

'They are not?' inquired Paul, in surprise. 'Ursule said that they were. She said—'

'Well, they're not quite,' said Christopher. 'And you are, after all, English boys and you want to look just the same as all the other boys when you get there—when you get home.'

'What hats do they wear—English boys?' asked Robert.

'Well, when they get a chance, they don't wear any hats at all. At school, they wear caps. When you're older, you'll wear a hat like

27

mine—but not until you're about eighteen. But you won't need these hats you've got on, so what I think we ought to do is—'

He paused, having been about to say chuck them overboard, but this was somewhat abrupt. He glanced overboard and waited.

Robert put up a tentative hand and felt his hat. He was, Christopher saw, getting the idea. Paul took his off and looked at it with obvious affection.

'Thérèse said that we were to look after these, because they cost so much,' he said.

'It is a pity,' said Robert, 'to waste them.'

'Yes,' agreed Paul. 'Henri and Pierre could wear them. They liked them very much, when they saw them. We could say we are finished and we could send them.'

Christopher saw that the end of the hats was not yet.

'Well, go and put them into your cases,' he said, 'and you can send them back to Henri and Pierre some time.'

They nodded obediently and went below, and Christopher stared after them moodily. Perhaps he had, after all, undertaken this charge somewhat too lightly. None of the three children looked as well or as cheerful as they had done when they started out; the boys had shadows under their eyes and Josette ... he didn't like the flush on her cheeks. That dinner on the train hadn't been exactly planned for children's stomachs; he had offered her some

28

hot cocoa when they had come aboard, but she had refused it.

He turned and stared into the fog; in less than an hour they would be in England and the rest of the journey would be straightforward. His car was waiting; all they had to do was get into it and drive up to London; his servant, Merrow, a family man, would have the children in bed and tucked in and they could sleep it out; Thérèse and Monique would arrive in a few days and resume their responsibilities. All that remained, after that, was choosing schools and finding a home—not a Castle this time, but a house large enough, and with land enough, to give the children space and freedom throughout their childhood. Space was the great thing. Room to move; woods and water and hills—there must be hills. He might marry, if he found anybody special; he might even have children of his own, though three was enough to go on with.

The two boys joined him once more, and together they stared out into the thickening mist. Their fellow-passengers passed to and fro, and some stared curiously at the tall, good-looking Englishman with the two little French boys. Christopher's face wore a worried frown not often seen upon it; he was thinking that unless the fog lifted, he would find it impossible to drive up to London.

The steamer nosed its way into the harbour; Robert and Paul hung over the side, peering as ropes were flung and the ship edged up to the jetty. Christopher went below to rouse Josette, and was met by Mrs Belchamber. She had put on a long, old-fashioned tweed coat and he noticed that, in spite of the long journey, her tight grey curls under the stiff black hat were as neat as they had been when he had first seen her. Not a hair was out of place. Her manner was more than ever proprietary.

'I've been looking at that child,' she said. 'She's caught cold. She ought to have been in charge of someone who knows something about children.'

'Well, she will be, soon,' said Christopher, abruptly.

He went into the cabin and roused Josette gently, and found the old lady at his heels.

'See what I told you?' she said. 'She's got a nice heavy cold. Children can't stand this sort of junketing unless they're in good hands. And we'll be lucky if we get up to London tonight in this blanket.' She shouldered him aside. 'I'll stay here with her,' she told him, 'while you get all the luggage looked after.'

Christopher gave her a long look of suspicion. He was tired of her company; he was bored by her carping and her acid comments. He thought her disagreeable and entirely superfluous, but he was beginning to realize that shaking her off was not to be the simple process he once imagined it.

'I think you'd better see about your own

things,' he said coldly. 'I've got enough on my hands with three children and our own luggage.'

'I'll stay with the children,' said Mrs Belchamber, returning stare for stare. 'You go along and get seats in the train.'

'I don't want seats in the train, thank you,' said Christopher. 'I'm not going by train.'

She seemed, for a moment, almost disconcerted.

'Not?'

'No. My car's here. I'm driving up.'

'In this fog?' She gave a snort. 'You can't see a yard in front of you.'

It was true, but Christopher, ignoring the remark, applied himself to the task of wrapping Josette up again in her warm scarf. She sat passively on the bunk, and he noted uneasily her heavy eyes and listless air.

'That's what comes of going to sleep and letting them wander up and down draughty corridors on trains,' said the old lady. 'Now perhaps you'll develop a sense of responsibility.'

It was better, it was safer to ignore her. Christopher lifted Josette and set her gently on her feet.

'Come along,' he said gently. 'You can stay with Robert and Paul until we go ashore.'

She slipped her hand into his and he led her outside; the old lady followed close behind. Christopher took no notice of her; his mind

31

was busy figuring out the best plan of action.

He had not thought of fog or delays; he had imagined the three children tucked up long before this on the back seat of the car, the luggage stowed behind and the car racing smoothly to London. He had not anticipated this check, and he was shocked at the heat of Josette's small hand resting limply in his own. Children's temperatures rose when they had colds; she should be warmly in bed.

His spirits lifted a little when they got into the customs-shed, for Mrs Belchamber, to his infinite relief, was claimed. A thin, middle-aged woman in spectacles and a tweed cloak had come to meet her.

'You are Mrs Belchamber?' she said, after glancing at the labels on the luggage.

The old lady turned her grimmest look on the newcomer. Christopher moved aside to dissociate himself from the altercation which he knew was coming.

'I'm Mrs Belchamber—yes.'

'How nice to see you. I was asked to come and meet you.'

'And who asked you?' demanded Mrs Belchamber, drawing her long coat more closely round her.

'The Committee.' The tone was pleasant, but firm; there was not a little of the schoolmistress about the manner in which the newcomer sought to sweep her charge in the required direction, and Christopher saw Mrs

32

Belchamber's nose sharpen in preparation for battle. 'The Committee. They are so grateful to you. We have your suite all ready, and Lord Harver has asked me to say that he will be coming over in a week or two—and then we shall be able to get all the papers signed and the deeds transferred. You don't know how extremely generous we all think you. Such a beautiful house—and we've got it running quite smoothly already, and everybody is looking forward to seeing you. Have the Customs finished with you?'

'They haven't begun with me,' stated Mrs Belchamber flatly. 'And I didn't ask anybody to send anybody to meet me.'

The newcomer lost none of her determined amiability. If she was on the Committee for disposing of old gentlefolk, thought Christopher, she was probably used to cranks. He felt very grateful to her; she was going to remove what had looked like becoming a permanent fixture. The Belchamber was leaving.

'Shall we,' cooed the Committee, 'get through as quickly as we can? We don't want the London train; ours is the branch line.'

'Ours is nothing of the kind,' said Mrs Belchamber. 'And I shall get through in my own time, and nothing will induce me to travel in that hearse that goes meandering all through Kent and Surrey. I know where my own house is, thank you. I don't need any Committee to show me the way, especially the wrong way. I shall go up to London, as I have always done in the past, and I shall stay the night at my usual hotel and I shall travel down to Melhampton comfortably in the morning. I've never used that branch line, and I'm not going to begin now. Don't let me keep you.'

Christopher was relieved to see that the Committee's smile remained fixed. He swung his cases on to the Customs counter with a double satisfaction; he was freed of his incubus, and the incubus now had an incubus of its own. He had great faith in the Committee, who looked extremely efficient; it would have the old lady on the branch line and meandering through Kent and Surrey in no time at all. His mind reverted to his own problem.

He could not drive up; visibility, which here was about twenty yards, was, he was told, nil in the London area.

He could send the children up by train and telephone Merrow, and Merrow could meet them and take them to the flat. But after a glance at Josette, he rejected the idea. He would stay with the children and decide whether to go up to London with them and come down for the car tomorrow—or stay at a local hotel for the night.

On the whole, the last seemed the most sensible plan. It would cover everything; they would all have a comfortable night and drive

34

up in the morning. But a night in an hotel, with a feverish chill...

Christopher watched the official chalk marks appearing on the cases, and heard the porter's inquiry.

'London train, sir?'

He felt suddenly desperate. He was tired; he had left England two days ago and the past forty-eight hours seemed a nightmare of trains, stations, charges, formalities, meetings, a babel of tongues, farewells, promises. The fog was an unnecessary, a spiteful obstacle at the end of his journey. He didn't want to go on the London train, but it seemed as though there was nothing else to be done, and nowhere else to go. A feeling of frustration gripped him.

He shook it off and turned to answer the porter, and, as he did so, it flashed upon him that there was, indeed, somewhere to go. He felt relief sweeping over him, and a sense of pleasure and anticipation. Of course there was somewhere to go! He laughed aloud—a short sound of relief, of restored energy and a shedding of care and anxiety. Yes, there was somewhere to go. Not fifteen miles from here was a house perpetually open to him; where he would find shelter for as long as he wanted and a welcome, the anticipation of which warmed him as he stood in the damp mist-hung customs-shed. Of course there was somewhere to go!

He would go to Scotty's.

CHAPTER FOUR

Scotty was not, and made no claim to be, a Scotsman. His surname was Linden, but his friends, if they ever knew it, had forgotten it. Wherever he went—and he was seldom in one place for long—he was introduced, known and remembered simply as Scotty.

He had been one of four children whose mother, for some reason best known to herself, had christened them Violetta, Dorothea, Wilhelmina and Maximilian. These cumbersome labels had been shaved by their contemporaries to Vi, Dot, Bill and Thanks-a-Million, and this last Scotty remained until the night following a dormitory feast following a school pageant, when he had wakened his companions with horrid screams and informed them that Mary, Queen of Scots was sitting at the foot of his bed.

His father had been a successful business man, and at his death, Scotty had inherited a good deal of money. He was a young man of simple tastes and inexpensive habits, and there was no fear that inheritance would be dissipated by riotous living. Scotty, moreover, was of an industrious disposition, and anxious to invest his money in a career that would give him exercise and profit at the same time.

He bought a fruit farm in Warwickshire; this

venture failed, as did, subsequently, a chicken farm in Yorkshire, a sheep farm in Cumberland and a cattle ranch run—Scotty said—on American lines in the Scottish Highlands. He had then decided to try mixed farming in Kent, and now, after four years, was—to the surprise of his friends—still trying it.

Though Scotty was older than Christopher by about four years, the two men were lifelong friends; Christopher had seen and deplored every project save the mixed farm, which he had never visited. He had thought the scheme a foolish one, but he felt thankful, now, that Scotty had refused to take his advice, and had come to live near the old town of Grenton. A drive of little more than fifteen miles and he and the children would be in a comfortable old farmhouse, safe with Scotty.

He freed himself gently from Josette's small, hot hand, and issued instructions to Robert.

'Don't move,' he said. 'I've got to see if the car's here—then I'm going to ring up a friend. All right?'

'Yes,' said Robert. 'All right.'

The car was here; Christopher tipped the mechanic who had brought it from the garage, and made his way to a telephone. Thumbing anxiously through the pages of a directory, he found the L's and looked down the list. Scotty was not among them.

Cursing at the delay, Christopher lifted the

37

receiver and dialled Inquiries. The double buzz sounded and went on sounding, but those on duty, reflected Christopher savagely, were obviously busy with their own affairs.

This was going to be a long job. He had no doubt of finding Scotty ultimately; Scotty's interests were all centred on his farming and he was always to be found on his own premises. But the night was getting older—and colder; Christopher's hands were chilled inside his leather gloves, and he decided that it would be wiser to get the children settled comfortably in the car before he woke up the telephone exchange.

The children were where he had left them. The crowd in the customs-shed had thinned, and he could see his little group, isolated; a rather desolate-looking and abandoned-looking little gathering when seen from afar, but revealing more cheerful aspects as Christopher drew nearer. Two porters, speaking sketchy French, were engaging Robert and Paul in conversation; Josette was taking little interest in the proceedings, but looked up at Christopher, as he joined them, with such tired relief and thankfulness that he felt, for the first time, the full extent of the responsibility he had so lightly undertaken.

He took Josette's hand firmly in his and, after a moment, stopped and swung her into his arms. She settled in them with a little sigh, and put a hot cheek against his shoulder.

'Let's get going,' said Christopher. 'I'm going to tuck you all up in the car while I telephone to a friend to say we're on our way. Ready?'

Everybody was ready. The two porters were joined by two volunteers, and Robert and Paul were settled warmly on the back seat of the car, while Christopher wound Josette into a travelling rug and placed her in front beside the driving seat.

'There!' he said. 'I'll be back in a minute and then we'll be off.'

'To where, off?' inquired Robert politely.

'To a farm. To a nice farm where you'll see cows and things. And pigs, perhaps.'

Both boys smiled; slow, attractive smiles that scarcely moved their lips, but lighted up the large, beautiful eyes.

'I like the cows,' said Robert.

'I like them, too,' said Paul.

Christopher waited for Josette's corroborative murmur, but it was not to be heard; stooping, he saw that she was asleep. Again he felt a pang of uneasiness and apprehension, and, closing the doors, raised a hand in salute and hurried back to the telephone. On his way he passed Mrs Belchamber and, unable to avoid her, gave a brief bow and hastened his steps. There was not, he saw, any increase of cordiality between her and her escort, who was looking much less assured than when she had borne down upon her charge. They were, he guessed, on their way to the train, and he realized that the Committee must have had its way, for the London train had gone. The Belchamber would, after all, go meandering all through Kent and Surrey.

Something—he never afterwards decided what—made him pause and turn for a moment to get a last glimpse of the stringy form. Now that it was being finally removed from his life, he could afford to look at it with feelings softened by the ever-increasing distance between them. He smiled to himself, and was about to go on his way when he caught sight of a figure standing between two officials; a short, bulky figure engaged, once more, in earnest argument. Christopher stood for only a few seconds before a sense of self-preservation bore him away, but during those seconds he looked keenly, and realized several things: the Frenchman was trying to explain something— his unpremeditated visit to the country, guessed Christopher. More, his explanations involved Mrs Belchamber, for all three were looking at her, and Christopher knew, from the increased rigidity of her back view, that she had observed the little scene. An impulse—a sudden, terrifying impulse swept over Christopher; an urge to place himself between the old lady and her pursuer. He saw himself going back, involving himself in the affairs of entire strangers; with a wrench, he pulled himself round and hurried on to the telephone box. He must be mad, he reflected; he didn't even like the old lady; and Heaven knew he had enough troubles of his own...

The telephone exchange seemed not much more alert than before, but painfully, perseveringly, Christopher extracted from a waspish operator the information that there was, indeed, a Linden E. living at Lower Grenton.

'It's in the book, if you look,' she said tartly.

'It's not in *my* book,' said Christopher. 'Can you tell me the number, please?'

'It's in the book, printed. Did you look under the L's?'

'Yes, I did. What's the number, can you tell me?'

'It's in the Elwing area,' stated the operator. 'Grenton comes in the Elwing area. It's no use looking in any other area if you want a number in Elwing area, is it?'

'Not in the least,' said Christopher. 'Now if you'll just give me the—'

'What area were you looking in?'

Christopher ground his teeth and glanced down at the book.

'Elwing area,' he said. 'District number—'

'Well, then it's in there, plain as plain. It don't do to call Inquiries if you don't need Inquiries. It's there for all to read. Lind, Linden A., Linden E. It's all there, if you look.'

Christopher, willing to be convinced, flipped over the book and ran down the L's once more.

41

'There is,' he stated slowly and with much more emphasis than he had yet used, 'no Linden E. in this book. Now will you very kindly give me the—'

'You're lookin' at the L's?'

He gritted his teeth.

'I'm looking at the L's. I'm looking at the Elwing area. I'm looking at the January issue. I'm looking at the—'

'Ohhhhh! Well, naturally, if you look at *January*! If you look at January, when it stops in March and the new April book comes out, then what choo expect? Grenton wasn't in the Elwing area, not in January, and then it was changed, see?'

'I see,' said Christopher. 'May I have the number now?'

'Yes, you can. If you'd said you were looking in January, instead of wasting my time, I could have told you before. The number's Grenton four-two-four. Want to be put through?'

'Please.'

He waited through a series of buzzes, squeaks, a jumble of voices and, finally, a jarring whirr that pierced his ear and made him wince. At last a man's voice came through with a thick, country intonation.

'There's no answer from four-two-four.'

Christopher hunched himself against the instrument in desperate appeal.

'Try again, will you? It's a farm—I'm sure they won't be out.'

42

'I knaow it's a farm. I knaow, it's Mr Linden's farm. He waon't be out, no—not out of the farm, like, but he'll be outside, most likely.'

'Not at this time of night, surely?' pleaded Christopher. 'It's urgent. Could you try him again?'

The man tried again. There was no answer. Something like panic began to creep over Christopher.

'Doesn't anybody live with him?' he asked. 'Isn't *anybody* there?'

'Nao. He lives alone, does Mr Linden. But I tell you what—I'll ring through to Mrs Garcia.'

'Garcia?'

'Yes. She works for Mr Linden, and she lives with her sister at the Post Office at Lower Grenton. When anybody wants Mr Linden bad, I rings up the Post Office and they tells Mrs Garcia and she blows for him.'

'She—?'

'She blows for him. She can't keep running over, you see. She keeps a horn, like, and when she blows it, he can hear it, and he knows he's wanted on the phone urgent like.'

'Well, for God's sake ask her to blow and blow hard,' besought Christopher.

He waited, picturing Mrs Garcia and her horn, and while he waited the operator explained that at first Mr Linden had been summoned by whistle. This, however, had also

43

summoned the local constable, who had twice risen from his bed on false alarms. Thereafter, Mr Linden had bought a horn and given it to Mrs Garcia.

Scotty would, reflected Christopher, a gleam shining through his anxiety. He probably bought two horns—one for Mrs Garcia to summon him and the other for him to summon the cows. Scotty would do just that sort of—

'Hello,' said a voice, and Christopher squeezed the receiver to his ear in ecstasy.

'SCOTTY!' he shouted. 'Where the hell were you?'

'Good Lord—it's Chris!' exclaimed Scotty in mild surprise. 'Go away and ring later—I've got a cow calving.'

'I'm coming over, Scotty,' said Christopher. 'Is that all right with you?'

'Over? Over here? Well, come on then—what's keeping you?'

'I've just got over from France, Scotty, and I wanted to make sure you were there.'

'Where else would I be?' demanded Scotty. 'I live here. I work here. I'm not a ruddy architect, like some, free to chase all over the Continent. I have to milk cows twice a day. Come on and give me a hand.'

'I'm coming. But—Scotty—'

'Well?'

'I'm not alone.'

'That's all right,' said Scotty equably. 'Bring her too.'

'Don't be a fool. Look—I've got three children.'

A rift appeared in Scotty's equanimity.

'You've WHAT? *Three!* Good Lord, you weren't even married last time I saw you!'

'I'm not married. I—'

'*Not?* I say,' protested Scotty, 'you have been going it.'

'Listen, will you? They're not mine. I—'

'Well, whose are they? Hers?'

'They're nobody's. They're my cousins. You know—my uncle's—'

'Oh! You mean little Lord Fauntleroy and his brother and sister?'

'Yes. It's a long story, Scotty, but I've got to get them into shelter, and quick. We've just landed from France, and they're cold and tired and one of them's got a temperature.'

'Well, well, well,' commented Scotty. 'I always thought you were the kind of fellow who kept out of trouble. Well, bring 'em along, bring 'em along. How're you coming?'

'I've got my car here. Can you put us all up? Have you got room?'

'I've got *rooms*. There's nothing in 'em except beds, but we'll fix something up. There's nothing to eat except cheese and nothing to drink except milk.'

'How do I get out to you?'

Scotty told him, and Christopher, after repeating the instructions, banged the receiver down and made hurriedly for the car. Six miles along the London road, turn sharp left, keep on for three miles and turn right at the fork, resisting the temptation to take the road marked Grenton. On till you struck The Thatched Inn and then past it, a sharp turn to Lower Grenton along a narrow lane made entirely of potholes—'don't mistake it for a road, old fellow, but keep on it until you see a four-square building blocking the road. That's it.'

An hour's careful driving through the fog. Christopher beat his gloved hands together to warm them and broke into a trot to restore his circulation. He reached the car and whistled a soft little air, wrenching the door open. There was Josette, still asleep, and in the back, the boys dozing—

The tune died on Christopher's lips and he stared open-mouthed. On the back seat, bolt upright between the two boys, sat Mrs Belchamber.

There was a pause. After two attempts, Christopher managed to speak.

'I don't quite—'

'This looks,' admitted the old lady grudgingly, 'like an intrusion. But I should be glad of a lift up to London.'

'I'm not going to London,' broke in Christopher brusquely.

Mrs Belchamber glared at him angrily.

'My good young man,' she said, 'you told me distinctly that you were driving up. You said

46

quite clearly that—'

'I changed my plans,' said Christopher. 'I didn't see any necessity to inform you.'

'Inform me? But you completely misled me! You gave me to understand that—'

'I'm so sorry,' said Christopher, 'but I'm in a hurry to get off. A friend is waiting for us. If you'd very kindly—'

'There are cows,' said Robert, rousing.

'And there are pigs, too,' said Paul, sleepily. 'It is a farm.'

Christopher leaned over and opened the back door, holding it open politely for Mrs Belchamber. She made no move to alight.

'I don't want to be impolite in front of the children,' began Christopher, grimly, 'but I'd be very grateful if you'd allow me to get off.'

'And what do you expect me to do?' inquired Mrs Belchamber. 'The London train has gone, long since. The next one is somewhere near midnight. Am I to sit in this place in the fog until midnight?'

'The lady who came to met you will—'

Mrs Belchamber's black hat waggled with triumph.

'Her? She's gone. I gave her the slip.'

'I wish I had your technique,' said Christopher. 'Goodbye.'

'You can shut that door,' said Mrs Belchamber flatly. 'You've got me into this scrape and now you've got to get me out. I lost the London train through that bullying

47

creature they had the impertinence to foist on me—she thought she was going to get me on the other one. But I decided to drive up with you, and I gave her the slip. I didn't come to my age without knowing how to protect myself from interference. I hope she enjoys looking for me on the train. And I hope she'll be able to invent a plausible story to account to them for my disappearance. And now tell me, if you please, what we're going to do.'

Christopher looked round him. It was going to be difficult enough to drive as it was; if he had to go round looking for somewhere to put this leech-like old woman, he would find himself befogged, stranded with three cold and hungry children. They, after all, were his first charge; he must find them warmth and comfort, and what happened to the Belchamber was none of his affair. She had entered his car uninvited, she must go wherever he cared to take her.

There was one other point to be settled, however. She had not been entirely frank about her evasive tactics. She had not mentioned the Frenchman. Christopher chose a sentence carefully and delivered it with a certain force.

'I saw your son on the station,' he said abruptly. 'Didn't you?'

Her steady stare, far from wavering, became so glacial that Christopher felt it in his bones. Her nose, directed straight at him, seemed about to pierce like an arrow. Her lips barely moved as she spoke.

'My—?'

Christopher summoned his courage.

'Your son,' he repeated.

'I have no son,' said Mrs Belchamber with complete finality.

Christopher gave up without further struggle. Without a word, he got into the car, swung into the road and headed North.

'Where are you going?' inquired Mrs Belchamber, after a few moments.

'To a friend's farmhouse. I don't know what it's like, and I don't particularly care; all I know is that there'll be room for us all. If it isn't up to your standards of comfort, it won't be my fault,' said Christopher coldly.

There was no reply. He heard the three occupants at the back shuffling themselves into more comfortable positions. He drew Josette towards him until her head rested against his shoulder; then he concentrated on the difficult drive ahead of him.

The inn ... So far the road had been fairly good. Now the sharp turn ... now they had reached the potholes. Peering out, unable to see more than a few yards ahead, Christopher crept on. The car lurched and swayed; nobody spoke, and he concluded that the boys had fallen asleep. The lane became a cart track and suddenly, round a blind, difficult bend, they saw the lights of a house. The small light dancing before them must be a torch. Christopher edged on through the swirling whiteness, and the torch gleamed straight in front of them. He stopped, and a bulky form loomed through the mist. The car door was wrenched open and a voice boomed out of the night.

'Well, well, well, you made it! Good to see you, Chris, old son. Half a mo'—I'll direct you.' Scotty banged the door, stood on the footboard and piloted Christopher into a huge barn lit by two hurricane lamps. 'She'll do here,' he said, stepping off and opening the car door once more. 'Now come on out and let me have a look at you.'

Christopher found the boys wide awake, and Mrs Belchamber looking about her with her sharp glance. He gathered the sleeping Josette into his arms, and she roused a little, looking at him with heavy eyes.

'It's all right, my sweet, we're here,' Christopher told her. 'You'll soon be nice and warm in bed—Scotty, we're one more. This is Mrs Belchamber. She missed her train.'

'How d'you do. Any friend of Chris's, etcetera, etcetera,' said Scotty. 'Come on, now—follow me. Come on, you two little fellers—you can give me a hand with the luggage. That's it—steady on, now. Avast! Heave-ho! Yo-ho-ho and there she goes! What muscle, what muscle, what hustle and bustle, what fussle and tussle and Moses!

what muscle!'

Scotty had the suitcases out in a line; Robert and Paul were doing something to help, but they were finding it impossible to keep their eyes off the huge figure swinging out cases and booming out a hearty welcome. In the uncertain flickering light Scotty did, indeed, look a fearsome figure, and it was clear that Mrs Belchamber's expression, as she took in details of this appearance, was growing more and more grimly disapproving.

Scotty was six feet two, broadly built, with limbs that looked—and were—of enormous strength. He was dressed in a pair of dark blue dungarees, with a shirt that had once been white; his feet were encased in waterproof boots, into the top of which he had tucked the ends of his trouser legs. Mrs Belchamber's eyes travelled to his face, as she scanned the sleepy eyes, the large, sensual-looking mouth, Christopher could see that she was drawing conclusions which were to prove as fixed as they were erroneous.

She was not, he knew, the first to be misled. Scotty was a perfect model for the popular conception of raffishness. Men, meeting him for the first time, placed their womenfolk behind them and prepared to protect them from the worst forms of assault. Women waited, some fearfully, some hopefully, for a demonstration of the evil passions which were written, for all to read, on that loose mouth and in the lazy, unexpectedly blue eyes. There was, however, no demonstration; Scotty's sole injury to women lay in his neglect of them.

It took adults some time to realize that, like a book, Scotty was not to be judged by the cover. Children, reading nothing in his face but indolent kindness, got at once on to terms of warm friendship. The light in the eyes of Robert and Paul showed clearly the beginnings of hero-worship, but Mrs Belchamber's look of wary distrust deepened. Scotty, attributing it to embarrassment at having come uninvited, increased his efforts to put her at her ease.

'Now we're all here,' he said. 'We'll take the luggage you want, and fetch the rest in later. Now *atteniong! En avang*! I see I've got to polish up my *ici ong parle Français* for all you little Frenchies. March! Fall in and follow me! Madame, your servant. If I jostle you with a suitcase or two, it will not be in malice. I would not wound the friend of a friend. In line! One, two, three—left, right, left, right, mind the beam, left, right. Now we're in the stackyard— the broad heavens above, the white mist around, and cow-muck below. *Atteniong aux pieds!* Madame, madame, I *told* you—but don't worry. It will remove itself when dry. Through the yard, up to the door, throw it open. Madame, ze kitchen. A humble roof, and not entirely rainproof, but look at that whale of a fire!'

Christopher had already looked; he had

pushed a large Windsor chair before it and had settled Josette comfortably. Now he straightened and looked at his friend.

'Food,' he said.

Scotty led him to a cupboard.

'Cheese, like I said,' he answered, throwing open the door. 'Cheese and bread—not much bread, but fresh—more or less. Mrs Garcia brought it only yesterday. You savvy Mrs Garcia, who toots on the horn? She does my work. Butter—in there, in that bowl. And there's milk—gallons of it. And cheese, like I told you. I make it. And eggs—*les oofs*. That's all. There ought to be a lot more *oofs*, but the hens won't lay them in the places appointed. But we've enough for now, I trow.'

'All right—bread and cheese and eggs and milk. Bedrooms?'

'Six. *Eins, deux, tres, quarto, cinco*, six. That's not counting the two attics where the rats romp. Go and inspect, old son.'

Christopher looked round the great kitchen. The fire blazed; over the mantelpiece were two oil lamps which shed a soft glow over the room. The furniture consisted of some wooden chairs, two large cupboards and an enormous deal table. There was a sink in the corner, but no taps; two buckets of water stood beside it.

'No hot-and-cold,' said Scotty, following his glance. 'But a well and a pump. Those two young Frenchies'll have us watered in no time. Eh, you two?'

53

Robert and Paul, gazing up at him, gave long, blissful sighs. How warm, how friendly was this England, now that one had got out of the fog! One could not see now, but one could hear, and the sounds were entrancing; the deep moan of a cow and the high snuffle of a bull. Geese, disturbed, were protesting near by; dogs were barking and there was the stamp-stamp of hooves in a stable. When this white curtain of mist lifted, when the black curtain of night was swept aside by the sunlight, how much there would be to look at!

While Christopher looked and the boys listened, Mrs Belchamber's sharp nose investigated the smells. Farmyard and manure and something more—yes, that unspeakable smock hanging on a peg on the door. Milk had dried on it, soured on it and now stank on it. Her nose lifted in disgust, Mrs Belchamber walked to the door, lifted the offending garment between a fastidious forefinger and thumb and, opening the door, dropped the smock outside and closed the door firmly.

'There are healthy smells,' she said, looking Scotty in the eye, 'and there are unhealthy smells.'

She walked past him and out of the room, obviously on her way to inspect the accommodation. Scotty looked after her with admiration.

'Old war horse,' he commented. 'Are you guardian to her as well as the others?'

54

'No. Never met her before we got on the train today, and can't shake her off. Let's give these kids something to eat, Scotty—and then into bed. They're played out.'

'Supper,' said Scotty. 'Now then, you two, while we're getting something to eat, you go and get your things off and find a room to put 'em in. Get yourselves out a couple of nightshirts or else you'll be like the old lady who fell into the Amazon without her pyjammers on. Look out there—I'm going to put this pan on the fire and make some omelettes. *Les omelettes—comprenez?* Chris, old son, busy yourself getting that little Sleeping Beauty ready for bed. Then we'll find a bed to put her in.'

Mrs Belchamber returned, her expression grimmer than ever.

'Scarcely any furniture,' she reported. 'No gas, no electricity, no running water, no bathroom.'

'No wireless,' added Scotty, 'no—'

'No bedclothes, no amenities, no window curtains.'

'No television,' chanted Scotty, 'no croquet, no diabolo, no—'

'And no sanitation,' ended Mrs Belchamber, grimly.

'I'll show you,' said the contrite Scotty. 'You should have *asked*! Out here and across— here's the torch,' he continued, leading the way. 'Don't mind the geese. If they go for your legs, you must overlook it and get your own back at Christmas. You're staying for Christmas? There's the door. No lock, I'm afraid, but the geese always give plenty of warning. They—'

'Give me the torch,' said Mrs Belchamber, snatching it. 'This serves me right.'

Supper was eaten round the huge table. Mrs Belchamber, her black hat still firmly on her head, carved great slices of bread and buttered them thickly. Scotty made omelettes, light and golden, and put steaming jugs of hot milk on the bare board. Robert and Paul ate like hunters, but Josette, leaning against Christopher, merely sipped some warm milk and fell into a restless doze. Mrs Belchamber eyed her uneasily.

'That child isn't well,' she said. 'You oughtn't to take her out of this warm room into those vaults of bedrooms. She'll catch her death.'

'We'll light fires,' said Scotty, spooning out helpings of cream cheese and flicking them, with a jerk of the wrist, on to outheld plates. 'We'll light great, big, roaring fires and warm the old bones of the homestead.'

The old bones were not long in warming up. The fireplaces were old-fashioned, but efficient; Scotty brought up wood and coal, lit fires and propped the mattresses round them to air. He produced from somewhere threadbare blankets, and to these were added all available coats, rugs, anything that could serve as bed covers. The boys were put into a room next to one allocated to Christopher; Mrs Belchamber walked from room to room choosing one—to judge by her sniffs—by the smell. She would, she said, have Josette in with her, and Christopher, surprised, but not disposed to argue, carried Josette upstairs and tucked her into her bed, which was pushed as close to the fire as possible.

Under the glow of lamps, in the warmth of the big, leaping fires, the household settled gradually into some kind of order. Christopher sat by Josette's bed until her eyes closed, and then, gently freeing his hand, tip-toed along the corridor to look in at the boys. They lay under a miscellaneous assortment of covering, warm and rosy, but wide awake.

'They want a nightcap,' commented Scotty, walking in to inspect them. 'I'll give them one. Would the old lady like anything before she turns in, Chris?'

'I'll see,' said Christopher.

He turned and walked back along the corridor and raised his hand to knock gently on the door. Softly though he touched it, it gave way a little, and Christopher's eyes fell on something placed on a chair just inside the room.

He stared at it for a moment, and then slowly identified it.

It was Mrs Belchambers' black hat.

Fastened to it on each side was a bunch of neat grey curls.

Christopher, with the utmost caution, withdrew. He went downstairs to the kitchen, and presently Scotty joined him. He was carrying a bottle, and he set it carefully on the table before Christopher.

'What's that?' asked Christopher.

'Brandy. Very old, very rare, very precious. I keep it in the cupboard on the landing and only use it in the gravest emergencies,' said Scotty. 'It's the last of my father's stock. And a splendid sedative. One teaspoonful and those two lads up there asleep like cherubims.'

Christopher stared at him.

'Good Lord! You mean ... you gave Robert and Paul ...'

'One teaspoonful, in warm milk. We'll dispense with the warm milk,' said Scotty. 'Pass your glass.'

CHAPTER FIVE

Christopher opened his eyes to see sunshine flooding the room. He glanced at his watch and saw that it was half past seven, and, with a jerk that freed him from his assortment of bedclothes, got out of bed and, walking from one to the other of the two large windows, looked out, getting a fair idea of the extent and position of the farm.

It was not large. The lane, curving more like a river than a road, narrowed as it reached the farm, and the farmhouse looked, to the approaching traveller, as though it blocked further progress. The lane merely wound round the house, however, and went on its way towards the village of Lower Grenton.

The first gate visitors came to when approaching from the town of Grenton, or from the main London road, was the wide and usually open one giving on to the farmyard. Entering this, and going through a smaller gate, callers found themselves in a stackyard with a view of the kitchen door, through which entrance could be obtained with ease. Those who scorned the kitchen approach gave themselves a great deal of trouble by walking farther along the lane as far as a small iron gate which they might assume was the front entrance; if they could open it, they found themselves walking up a narrow, nettle-grown path to the front door, which had large panels of plain glass and gave an interesting view of the broad staircase and a bare hall. The knocker was an imposing one in the form of a sheep's head, and looked as secure as a fortress until it was touched, when it came off and rolled into the creeper growing round the doorstep. The bell—large white porcelain knob of the Pull-me variety—came away at the first tug. The few visitors who got so far, now stood looking round them helplessly until they read signs which proclaimed that the door had not been opened for years, after which they went round, sensibly, to the farmyard and found their way once more to the kitchen door.

Beyond the stackyard, Christopher, looking out, saw the barn in which the car had been left; he could see its gleam in the deep shadows. The cowsheds, long and low, came next, beyond were stables, empty pig-sties and a fold with half a dozen calves among whom moved, incongruously, two French sailor hats. Christopher wondered how long they had been moving out there; since dawn, probably.

Looking across the fields, he saw, about two miles away, a low wooded hill and the chimneys of a large house; beyond was Grenton. The scene was open and peaceful and Christopher saw that Scotty had, as always, placed himself in one of Nature's loveliest settings. On this spring morning, with a last faint touch of mist to soften outlines, the countryside had an enchanted air.

He brought his eyes back from the distance to study the farm buildings; they were all in excellent repair, neat and newly painted. The prudent farmer waited for his profits and put them into his stock and buildings; Scotty looked after the buildings and hoped that the profits would look after themselves. This was by no means a model farm, but the layman might be deceived by its air of well-being. The paint was fresh, the animals had an air of deep content, the chickens, ducks, geese, guinea fowl, kittens and puppies moved placidly about the place; Scotty himself, appearing for an instant in the doorway, looked as though he had not a care in the world.

Christopher turned from the window and pulled on his clothes hastily. Moved by an urgent desire to know how Josette had passed the night, he opened his door and walked down the corridor towards her room. As he did so, the door opened and Mrs Belchamber came out.

Early as was the hour, she was fully dressed, and on her head was the stiff black hat. Her suit hung in uncreased folds round her bony, angular figure; her grey curls were as tight as ever. He greeted her briefly and spoke in an undertone.

'How's Josette?'

'Ill,' said Mrs Belchamber. 'She's been coughing all night, and you have to get a doctor to come and see her. She's caught a good, thorough chill.'

Without answering, Christopher went past her into the room, seeing as he crossed the threshold that Scotty had left a large bucket of coal and some firewood outside the door. The fire was still burning in the bedroom; he realized that Mrs Belchamber must have kept it going during the night.

Josette was lying with her head towards the blaze; as Christopher came in, she turned and gave him the ghost of a welcoming smile. He sat gently on her bed and took a hot little hand in his.

'How are you, Josette?' he asked gently.

She coughed—a hard sound that brought Christopher's fears rushing back.

'Thank you, very well,' she said.

'How do you *feel*?' asked Christopher.

'She feels perfectly well,' said Mrs Belchamber sharply, from behind him. 'But she's tired—naturally, after such a long journey—and she's got a headache. Now you just get off that bed and go and get a nice sensible doctor, and he'll give her a nice pill and make her well in no time. Now go on.'

Christopher sat still, sizing up the situation. He was in a farmhouse with bare rooms, without running water or the more civilized type of sanitation. He had on his hands a sick little girl, two small boys and an overbearing stranger. He must get away as soon as possible, shake off the old woman, get the boys to his flat and put Josette under professional care. He felt anger, but no return of the panic that had gripped him the night before. He resented finding himself in such a situation, but he felt completely able to deal with it. He patted Josette's hand and laid it for a moment against his cheek.

'I'll get a nice doctor-man to come and see you,' he promised, 'and then you'll soon be well.'

'Where is Paul?' inquired Josette.

'Paul? He's outside with Robert, where you'll soon be—playing with the baby cow and the baby chicks—the *poulets*—and the geese. Now tuck that hand in and keep warm and I'll go and fetch someone to make you all better.'

He tucked her in, rose and followed Mrs Belchamber out of the room.

'I'm afraid,' he said, 'that you had a disturbed night.'

'Naturally I did,' said Mrs Belchamber. 'But somebody has to look after the children. It's a good thing I was with her to keep the fire going and see she was warm. I suppose you slept without stirring.'

Christopher admitted, reluctantly, that he had.

'Naturally,' said Mrs Belchamber. 'Now about breakfast. Do you suppose your peculiar friend has taken any steps to get us any?'

Christopher thought it unlikely. His experience told him that Scotty provided a warm welcome, simple food and ample fuel and then went outside to get on with his work, leaving his guests to fend for themselves. If they wanted him, he argued, they knew where to find him.

Going downstairs in the wake of Mrs Belchamber's poker-straight back, Christopher found a large fire burning in the kitchen, but no preparations for a meal.

'I told you,' said Mrs Belchamber. 'Nothing. For the past thirty years and more,' she informed him, 'I've been able to order my morning tea and take it before I rose. I—'

'You should have gone off on the branch line,' said Christopher abruptly and then, remembering that she had watched over Josette during the night, he spoke more gently. 'I'll go out and see Scotty and find out about a doctor. That's the most important thing. The breakfast can wait.'

Mrs Belchamber gave a snort.

'When those two boys come in, starving, in an hour's time, ready to eat the table, tell them that breakfast can wait!' She gave him a venomous glare. 'If there exists a more irresponsible man than you anywhere, I have yet to meet him.'

Seven-thirty in the morning was not the time for an argument. Christopher opened the wide, heavy kitchen door and stepped outside.

The air was cold, but soft. Geese arched their necks and ran, hissing, towards him; hens cackled and pecked round his feet. He heard voices in the cowshed and made his way towards the building, stumbling over three small puppies as he went. He unlatched the upper half of the cowshed door and pushed it open, looking in upon a scene of great tranquility. The cows were munching contentedly; Scotty was milking a cow, and Robert and Paul were looking on entranced.

'—and that one's the mother of that heifer I showed you outside—remember?' Scotty was saying. 'Moss Green, she's called. This is Green Farm and so I call 'em all greens—that one's Olive Green. Full of temperament, she is. There's Lime Green and Sea Green—that end one. Fetch that barrow up, one of you, and that spade, and you can start cleaning up. Hallo there, Chris, old son.'

Christopher watched the two boys as they shovelled busily, staggering under heavy loads and finally pushing the reeking barrow along the bumpy stone floor of the cowshed and out through the far door.

'Useful pair,' commented Scotty. 'Chic hats, too. How're things indoors?'

'Not too good. Scotty, I've got to have a doctor.'

Scotty got off the milking stool, lifted it and a foaming bucket of milk and lumbered down the narrow shed.

'Josette bad?'

'Yes. She's caught a chill or something, but she's coughing and she's got a temperature—I don't like it. Who's your doctor?'

Scotty emptied the milk into a large churn and leaned against the whitewashed wall.

'A doctor,' he said slowly. 'Oh dear, oh dear. Oh, dear.'

Christopher frowned.

'Come on, Scotty,' he urged. 'I'm worried.'

'The best one here,' said Scotty slowly, 'is

Doctor Curtis. But I don't—'

'Well, will you ring up, or shall I?'

'Her,' corrected Scotty gloomily.

'What?'

'Her. It's a her. Doctor Stella Curtis. But I don't—'

'Well, will you ring her up, or shall I?'

'Oh—you,' said Scotty decidedly. 'Definitely you. If I ring her up, the chances are a hundred to one that she won't come.'

'Won't come out? Don't be silly—she'll have to come out. If there's illness—'

Scotty opened the door and rolled the churn outside before he spoke again. All his movements were slow and deliberate and Christopher, watching him, felt the slackening of speed, of tension, that his meetings with Scotty always brought. Here there was no rush or hurry; the cows set the pace. Now they were being let out, across the cement yard, across the stackyard and into the larger of the two orchards. It was no orderly procession; the animals knew where they were bound and Scotty let them take their own time in getting there. They trailed, halting to inspect every object in their path; they stopped to drink in the trough; they crowded close to Christopher, nuzzling him, and put their heads down threateningly at the tumbling puppies. Robert and Paul, flushed, manure-splashed, came into the yard and smacked encouragingly at passing flanks. By the time the herd had passed beyond

66

the gate of the orchard, Christopher's impatience had evaporated; when Scotty returned to his side, he was ready to continue the discussion at his friend's pace.

'Well,' said Scotty. 'About this doctor.'

'Yes. I'd like to get her along soon, if I can. I'm grateful to you, Scotty, for taking us in, but although I never mind roughing it on my own, this isn't the place to nurse sick children. I'd like to get these kids off as soon as I can.'

'If you get those two boys off this place, I'll be surprised,' said Scotty. 'I've got me two new hands. Four to be precise. Those two young Froggies have worked like dock hands all the morning. Funny thing about them—English children usually stand and watch how it's all done, but those two—there's something practical about the French—they didn't do much staring; they just got behind me and pushed, as it were.'

'Quite so. The doctor—' said Christopher.

'Well—yes. You observe about me a certain reluctance?'

'As well as I can observe anything before eight in the morning—yes,' admitted Christopher. 'What's the matter with her?'

'Nothing. Nothing at all,' said Scotty. 'But she doesn't like me.'

'Well, I'm not going to hold that against her. What's her number?'

'Four-eight-two. You'd better explain that this is nothing to do with me—it'll give her

67

more confidence. You see—'

'Well?' said Christopher.

'Well ... she doesn't understand me, that's what it is,' explained Scotty. 'She doesn't realize that I like my animals better than I like most humans—or, if she does realize it, she doesn't share my preference. The first time I ever rang her up was one of those mix-ups you can't explain afterwards. You see, the vet's number is eight-four-two, and how any man in a state of anxiety can be expected to differentiate—Always beats me how expectant fathers don't get the wrong number and call in the vet.'

'You called her in mistake?'

'It was winter, and snowing, and I hadn't settled in, and the cowsheds were leaking and my best cow was dying on me. Winter Green. I don't know to this day what I said, or what she said, but I rang up what I thought was the vet's number and the doctor came out here, all through the blizzard, thinking she was going to deliver a Mrs Wintergreen who was in the throes. It was very awkward.'

'Very,' admitted Christopher. 'But hasn't she had time to forget it?'

'She might have had, but there was another unfortunate business one night, when a couple of tramps—gypsies came in to help themselves to my gun—I'd been shooting and they saw me cleaning it when they went by earlier in the day. Well, the dogs went for them and the two men

68

held 'em off and made rather a mess of a pet collie of mine—Clover—the one over there. I heard the noise, and came out, but they didn't hear me coming, and when I saw what they'd done to Clover, I forgot myself and made a nasty mess of the two of them. When I'd worked off a bit of steam and saw what they looked like, I thought I'd better get Dr Curtis out to patch 'em up. While I was ringing her up, the two birds pulled themselves together—how, I shall never know—and upped and offed. They must have thought I was ringing up the police. I hunted for them and then tried to stop the doctor from coming out, but she'd started. She was on her way—three in the morning, and winter, of course, and snowing, naturally. If I could have run myself over to provide a patient for her on her arrival, I'd have done it, Chris, for sure, but out she came, and I had nothing to show her but my knuckles. So you see, she's put me on her black list. If you want her out here, you'll have to make some soft, persuasive noises over the telephone.'

'Four-eight-two.'

'Let her have another hour in bed, if it isn't too urgent,' advised Scotty. 'She'll be all the sweeter, and we'll be all the fuller.'

Christopher went inside to see the black hat bent over the large, old-fashioned range. There was a tattered cloth on the table and some battered spoons and forks. Mrs Belchamber straightened and looked irritably at Christopher.

'This peculiar friend of yours,' she began, 'hasn't he any possessions?'

'Possessions?'

'Doesn't he own anything besides cows?' demanded Mrs Belchamber. 'He has no spare sheets, no spare blankets, no silver or glass, no presentable spoons and forks, knives without handles, saucepans without lids and buckets without bottoms. If I'm to cook on a stove that a self-respecting savage would consider out of date, then I must at least have something to cook *in*. And I must have something to cook *with*. I could find only two eggs—with all those hens making all that clatter out there, why should there be only two eggs? And I shall want some milk.'

Christopher took the largest jug he could find and filled it from one of the churns in the dairy. Inquiring about eggs, he was informed by Scotty that there were scores of eggs, if only one knew where to look for them.

'The hens lay,' he said, waving a hand in a wide circle. 'But they choose out-of-the way little corners each day so I really can't say where they lay. Find the Earl and his little brother and tell them to go on an egg-hunt. They ought to fit a couple of dozen into those musical comedy hats they're sporting.'

Robert and Paul found egg-hunting an enchanting game; Mrs Belchamber found egg-cooking less amusing. She provided, however, a breakfast solid enough to satisfy the keenest appetite, and served it with acid comment.

'That range,' she told Scotty, 'hasn't been cleaned properly for years. Didn't I understand that a woman comes to work for you?'

'Mrs Garcia,' said Scotty. 'What's on that plate?'

'French toast. If you don't like it, you can cook yourself something you do like. What's that disgusting smell?'

The disgusting smell was tracked down to Robert's and Paul's shoes, and the meal was interrupted while the boys removed them and placed them outside the door.

'And yours,' said Mrs Belchamber, glaring at Scotty.

'Mine don't come off,' said Scotty. 'This isn't at all bad, this egg-and-tomato brew. My woman,' he went on, his mouth full, 'comes at nine. I make my own breakfast when I'm alone, that is—and she clears it up and cleans up generally and then cooks me a midday meal and leaves a bit of cold supper in the cupboard before she goes.'

'Well, judging from the state of this place,' said Mrs Belchamber, '"cleans up" is a gross overstatement. What time is the doctor coming?'

'Any time now,' said Christopher. 'He's a woman.'

71

'Oh,' said Mrs Belchamber non-committally.

He finished his breakfast, went upstairs and sat on Josette's bed, rubbing one of her hands gently and murmuring comforting sentences from time to time, and soon he heard footsteps and Mrs Belchamber's thin, precise soprano mingled with contralto under-tones. He rose, and Mrs Belchamber ushered in the doctor and took up her stand at the foot of the bed. The doctor put her bag down on the table, smiled at Josette and advanced to the bed, and Christopher saw that she was young—not more than twenty-six or seven—strong build, hard and muscular and with a firm jaw that made Christopher understand the dangers of bringing her out on wild-goose chases.

The examination was brief; the doctor tucked Josette up again, closed her bag with a snap and gave the patient a reassuring smile.

'You'll be fine,' she said. 'We'll soon have you out there milking all the cows.'

She went downstairs, Mrs Belchamber leading the way. Christopher, glaring at her back, wished that there was some way of making the doctor understand that the old lady was an interloper, without the smallest right to be present, with not even the most distant of relationships to justify her proprietary attitude. She swept the doctor into the kitchen and faced her.

'Well, what?' she inquired abruptly.

72

'Measles,' said the doctor.

There was a pause of blank surprise. Mrs Belchamber recovered before Christopher.

'I told you so,' she said. 'I knew it. You can always tell.'

Christopher, trying in vain to frame a sentence that would express his sentiments towards her without shocking the doctor, heard the latter putting a question.

'Has there been any sort of contact, do you know?'

'None, so far as I know,' said Christopher. As he spoke, the words of Thérèse rushed to his mind. Monique, who had a fever; Monique, who had been with the children until the day they left . . . 'Well, yes,' he said. 'I think perhaps there was—but I didn't know.'

'I said so from the beginning,' put in Mrs Belchamber.

Christopher remembered that he had, in his childhood, played a game in which, brought in to meet relations he disliked, he had pretended to himself—often with great success—that they were not there. It was years since he had felt the need to protect himself by these childish tactics; he had, in growing older, learned more effective methods of avoiding uncongenial contacts—but in Mrs Belchamber he had met something outside the usual range of limpets. He stared at her, trying to make himself realize that it was not yet twenty-four hours since he had first set eyes on her. Now she stood, erect

73

and sour, her sharp nose bored deep into his affairs, her whole attitude one of long familiarity with him and his family.

'How long were you intending to stay here?' inquired the doctor.

'I only came for the night,' said Christopher. 'We landed late last night in that fog, and I didn't think I'd get up to London.'

'That where you live?'

'Yes. I was taking the children—temporarily—to my flat. But now ... Can I get a bed in a nursing home anywhere near?'

'What d'you want a bed in a nursing home for?' demanded Mrs Belchamber. 'That child will be far better here.'

'Here?' Christopher stared at her, astounded. 'Here? How on earth can we keep her here?'

'Why can't you?' asked the doctor. 'Nice airy room she's in up there; healthy spot, lots of good milk and eggs and butter when she's convalescent.'

'This place isn't exactly fitted out with all the conveniences,' pointed out Christopher.

'Certainly it isn't,' said Mrs Belchamber, 'but this isn't the time to worry about yourself. You've got a sick child up there and she'll want careful nursing, not carrying from nursing home to nursing home. She needs a good fire in her room, peace and quiet and constant watching. That's all. She won't notice any lack of home comforts for a little while.' She turned

74

to the doctor. 'Will she?' she demanded.

'She'll be all right here, if there's someone to nurse her,' said the doctor. 'But it'll be uncomfortable, I dare say, for the rest of you.'

'You can leave it to me,' said Mrs Belchamber. 'Do we have to send in for the medicine?'

The doctor wrote a prescription, tore it off the pad and handed it to her.

'Get that and follow the directions,' she ordered. 'I'll be out again tomorrow. What about those two boys out there? Any symptoms?'

'Not so far,' said Christopher, 'but I suppose it's only a matter of time.'

'Not necessarily. Well—I'll be here in the morning,' said the doctor, taking up her bag.

Christopher saw her to her car, walked back into the house and found Mrs Belchamber, standing in the middle of the kitchen, waiting for him. They faced one another, and she waited for him to speak.

'You've been very kind,' said Christopher, with as much cordiality as he could command, 'but there's no need for you to stay on and make yourself uncomfortable. Your friends will be anxious about you.'

'Let them,' said Mrs Belchamber.

'I can drive you to the station any time, and—'

'I'm not going to any station. I'm going to stay here and see that that poor child is

75

properly looked after. I don't care very much for children—or animals—but I like to see them in good hands. And I don't consider yours good hands. You're proposing to put that child into a nursing home and—presumably—take the two boys to London, where they'll both develop measles in a stuffy flat, while you go out and look for more nursing homes for them. It won't do, let me tell you, my good young man. The sensible course is to let them get it all over here. If it were winter, I wouldn't dream of proposing it, but this isn't winter. This is spring, and the two boys can run wild out there with your peculiar friend and ruin all their clothes, but it'll keep them out of the way, and keep them healthy and exercised, which is more than they'd be in a stuffy London flat.'

'I see,' said Christopher. 'And the cooking? And the cleaning? And the nursing?'

'I shall do the cooking. From the look of this place, I wouldn't dream of allowing that visiting woman to touch my food, or the children's. I shall see her when she arrives this morning, and I shall make her understand that she has got to clean the place and keep it clean. Your peculiar friend must keep us supplied with coal and wood; and you will have to see that I have an adequate supply of fresh water, and you will have to do the shopping. There are several things I shall want.'

'Look here,' said Christopher, when he

could speak. 'I—'

Before he could say any more, there was an interruption. The door of the kitchen was thrown open and the figure of a woman appeared on the threshold.

'Garcia's the name,' she said, entering.

The two women faced each other, their lips setting more tightly as they made their inspection. Mrs Belchamber saw what she had expected—a strong, muscular figure, garments that could not, by any stretch of imagination, be called fresh and clean; a bold, defiant expression. Mrs Garcia saw a lady of the type she recognized as genuine; the type, moreover, that Mrs Garcia had lately held firmly under her strong thumb, the type that had to be taught that slaves were no longer available on the English market; the type that Mrs Garcia most loved to subdue.

The silence lengthened, and tension grew and at last became explosive. Mrs Belchamber straightened her shoulders and looked at Christopher.

'You may go,' she said firmly, 'and leave us alone.'

Christopher went.

CHAPTER SIX

Mrs Garcia was a short, sturdy woman of about forty, whose face, with its high cheek bones, brown skin and fine brown eyes, was sufficiently foreign to give those who saw her, and heard her name, a distinct shock when the unmistakably Cockney accent came to their ears. When on a visit to relations in London's dockland, she had met and married the dashing Garcia, to whose other charms was added the name José. The couple moved from place to place, finally coming to live with Mrs Garcia's sister, who was in charge of the little sub-post office of Lower Grenton. José was employed as handyman at Grenton's largest hotel, and kept the lion's share of his earnings for himself; Mrs Garcia had, at first, augmented her mouse's portion by taking in plain sewing, but the speed with which her sister's family increased made home life more and more disturbed, and, finally, the changing status of domestic helpers little by little opened to her a sphere in which she could exercise the latent bullying that had failed to quell her volatile husband. She made a careful selection from the vast new field of employers, fixed her wage, dictated her terms, gave slatternly service and left without warning at the first hint of criticism. She was, she explained, sensitive, and took things to heart; if some people didn't appreciate what she was trying to do, there were plenty of others who would.

At the farm, with the uncritical Scotty, she had found a billet that suited her very well. She knew his movements, and was able to get in a good many restful hours while Scotty was working out of sight. She put her feet up comfortably on the stove, and applied herself to thinking out methods by which she could lure her husband back to a post which offered him less opportunity to exercise his charms. José was notoriously successful with the chambermaids, and had, on more than one occasion, so far forgotten his matrimonial obligations as to take temporary lodgings in the town. From these adventures he returned to his wife, who explained to her friends that his wandering ways were due solely to the fact that their union had never been blessed. The touch of little hands, she explained, would have kept him at home. Her flowery phrasing had earned for her a deep respect among her own circle, who felt that anything served up with such style must be worth listening to.

Nobody ever knew what effect the flowering phrasing had had upon Mrs Belchamber during that first interview. Scotty, informed by Christopher that it was being held, waited for Mrs Garcia to sweep by him, pausing only to inform him that she was leaving for ever. No Mrs Garcia appeared, however; when next seen, she was sweeping the stairs—a task she had not performed since her first day at the farm, when she had done it to show how much dust her predecessor had left on them. She was then seen scrubbing the kitchen and informing all who passed that she considered it her Christian duty to put aside her feelings and work herself to the bone for the poor little mite lying on a bed of sickness upstairs.

Scotty accepted this explanation without comment, as he did the news that his house was to be used throughout the nursing of one or more cases of measles. All that was required, in his opinion, was space, and there was plenty of space.

'You can spread out, you know, Chris. No need to huddle in two or three rooms. If you look round, you'll find four bedrooms on that floor and two on the next level and then two attics—roomy ones, with a lot of light. Make good studios.'

'Who the devil,' inquired Christopher irritably, 'wants studios? I'm not running down your hospitality, Scotty I've had too much of it all these years to expect anything but where in Christmas is all your stuff?'

'Stuff?'

'Stuff. Furniture, effects, cutlery, china, linen, silver. Where's all the stuff your father left you? What's become of all the stuff there used to be in that whacking great mansion you were brought up in? Where's it all gone?'

'Oh, I see what you mean. My stuff,' said Scotty, pausing in his task of cleaning the stables. He wiped his hands on the back of his trousers and considered the matter. 'A lot of stuff is in crates and boxes in the feed-store over there. A lot of—'

'Well, why the hell don't you unpack it and spread it about? Every time I've stayed with you since you started this farming life, there's been less and less in the way of bodily comforts. That first place of yours was comparatively luxurious. Then you moved—'

'That's just it—I moved,' said Scotty. 'I kept moving. The first move—from the ancestral home to my first farm was easy. I had no stock—just household goods, and the removal company just lifted them out of one place and arranged them in the other. It was a nice job. But the next time I moved, I had cows to transport, and a couple of young bulls, and three—no, four—horses and all their paraphernalia, so the household part of it was a bit overlooked. I got into the way of leaving things packed up, and I've found it much less trouble, I must say.' He paused and looked at Christopher with a puzzled air. 'Have you ever seen,' he inquired, 'what happens to stuff if you leave it about a house untended? It's extraordinary—you'd never believe! It does the most unexpected things. Silver, for example, gets spots all over it. Black spots. Some things turn quite a different colour. All your kitchen stuff gets covered with fungus, and so do your books and lamp shades and what-all. If my father saw some of that Sheffield plate he was so fond of, he'd turn in his grave, he would really, Chris. So you see,

81

it's cheaper, in the long run, to leave the stuff in boxes and just get along with the essentials.'

'You haven't got the essentials.'

'Well, what's essential for one isn't necessarily essential for a couple of others, is it?' pointed out Scotty, reasonably. 'For myself, I'm comfortable enough. After all, I'm only indoors—awake, that is—a couple of hours a day, and all I want then is food and a fire. When it comes to nursing measles, I grant you I'm a bit short of commodities, but if you're in need of anything special, just say the word and I'll get out the van and pop along into town and ship it back for you.'

'We'll be all right,' said Christopher. 'At least, the Belchamber says we'll manage. How can I go about getting rid of her, Scotty?'

'Rid of her? What's the idea of getting rid of her? I thought she was permanently attached to you, or to the children. If she's going to nurse the little 'un through measles, what do you want to get rid of her for?'

'She gives me a kind of hunted feeling,' said Christopher. 'And there's something sort of... well, fishy about her.'

'Fishy? The old girl?' Scotty was plainly incredulous. 'You must have got it wrong, old son; she's like the Bank of England—ancient but sound. She reminds me of my great-aunt Mildred, who was a pillar—repeat, pillar of virtue.'

'I didn't say there was anything definite,'

said Christopher, 'but wait till you hear. A fat sort of Frenchman sat opposite me when I was having dinner on the train, and when he saw Mrs Belchamber he looked as though his eyes were coming out of his head. He gave every sign of having had a hell of a shock.'

'Well, that's not surprising,' said Scotty. 'A lot of foreigners feel like that when they catch sight of these elderly Englishwomen. There is something about them, after all—they don't really look human, in the wide sense, if you follow me. They—'

'He chased her up the corridor,' said Christopher, 'and called her *Maman*.'

Scotty's reaction to this was gratifying. He stared incredulously at Christopher and seemed for some moments unable to speak.

'He called her which?' he asked finally.

'*Maman*. She brushed him off and we saw no more of him during the journey. Then when we landed, he appeared, arguing with a couple of officials—I'm quite certain he didn't intend coming over to England, and all he appeared to have in the way of luggage was a brief-case and a smallish bag, but all I can tell you is that the Belchamber *saw* him—and ten minutes later, there she was hidden in my car, having given the slip to the Frenchman and a woman who'd come to the boat to meet her. You wouldn't think it to look at her, Scotty, but she's obviously on the dodge.'

'But...' Scotty appeared to be sifting the

evidence—'but didn't you ask her why she was leaving sonny behind?'

'She said he wasn't her son.'

'Eh?'

'She said she hadn't got a son.'

'She did? And you're quite sure he called her Mommer?'

'Perfectly sure.'

'Well ... I'm inclined to think she must be,' said Scotty, thoughtfully. 'What I mean is, who—what man would call her Mommer unless he had to?'

'Well, that's how I feel too,' said Christopher. 'So you see, she must be dodging something. There's a big meeting at this house of hers—they've got a lot of papers for her to sign in connexion with this house she's handing over. The place is running—I mean it's full of what they call decayed gentlefolk, all settling down there on the assumption that they're in for life. If she doesn't sign the papers and give them legal possession, how are they going to feel?'

'Perhaps she's going to stay here until the day of the meeting,' suggested Scotty. 'That'll give her time to shake the Frenchman off.'

Christopher looked unconvinced.

'I hope you're right—but I don't like it, Scotty. When you come to think of it, I drove off with her—a rich, lonely old lady. It looks bad if anyone works it out on those lines. Suppose they come after her? They can't leave

84

things as they are, can they?'

'They'll find her eventually,' said Scotty. 'They'll make inquiries at the port and start from there. But it'll take some time, and in the meantime look how useful she's making herself. She's got an awful lot of energy, Chris, for an old bag of bones of that age. What would you say she was sixty? seventy? eighty? I like that Continental cooking she did this morning. After four years of Mrs Garcia—'

'Well, that's what I was coming to. The Belchamber proposes to do the cooking and the nursing too, and if she attempts it, she'll be the next on the list of patients. We need a nurse, Scotty, and I thought of asking the doctor about sending one out, if there was one to send out, but what nurse would undertake the job under these camping conditions?'

'Nurses,' said Scotty, 'are very devoted women. They—'

'Yes, yes, yes. But the Belchamber and the Garcia are enough in themselves—I can't see a professional swallowing them down with the primitive conditions. Isn't there a strong girl who'd come in for a few hours a day and sit with Josette?'

Scotty pursed his lips.

'Can't think of any off-hand,' he said slowly. 'If only Cress had been home, she—'

'Cress?'

'Cressida.' Scotty's voice was lowered to a reverent note. 'But she isn't due yet. She only comes at the beginning of every month and—let me see—this is still April, isn't it?'

'End of. Who's this Cressida?'

Scotty walked to the nearest firm support—the stable door—before answering. Christopher saw that his eyes had taken on a far-away, dreamy look.

'You can't explain Cressida, Chris old son,' he said slowly. 'There are some things you can't put into words.'

'If she has that effect on you, and she's free, why don't you get her to marry you and come and unpack all your stuff for you and get it spread out into a decent home?' inquired Christopher.

'M-marry me? Cressida? Why, she wouldn't dream—she wouldn't—'

'Well, how d'you know until you ask?'

'I did ask,' said Scotty simply. 'I don't know how I screwed myself up to the point . . . how I had the appalling nerve, the—the brass assurance to dare to—to—'

'Well, what did she say?'

A long, long sigh came from somewhere in Scotty's depths.

'She didn't say anything,' he said dreamily. 'She just took my hand, and smiled gently, and shook her head. That was all.'

'Is she a nurse?' asked Christopher, returning to practical matters.

'A nurse? Cressida? No, she's—'

'Well, you proposed her for the job. What

other qualifications has she got, besides holding the patient's hand and smiling gently and shaking her head?'

'She took a nurse's training once—when she was younger,' said Scotty. 'But she broke down.'

'A broken-down nurse. Well, I think we can do without that one,' decided Christopher. 'Any other suggestions?'

'You don't understand, Chris,' said Scotty urgently. 'You don't know what you're talking about. If I thought for a moment that Cress was home ... but she always comes along to see me, almost the first thing, so she can't be here. But if she were, and if she didn't have to get back to London, she'd—'

'Oh, for Pete's sake, Scotty!' cried Christopher in exasperation. 'I've got a sick child up in the house and we need help. I mentioned a strong, useful woman and you dragged in one who broke down and who doesn't, in any case, live here. Why—'

'Her home's here, but she won't live in it, for reasons with which I entirely agree,' said Scotty. 'She comes down once a month, and just in the nice spring time—I can't tell you exactly when—she takes a fortnight's holiday.'

'So if she happened to be down here, and if it happened to be her fortnight's holiday, and if and if—'

'Quite so,' said Scotty. 'Life's full of ifs. I'm only trying to say that if you could get hold of

Cressida, you wouldn't notice. Go on up there, to the house, Chris,' he urged, 'and try. It's worth it. It's only a walk, after all. Walk up to Greensleeves and—'

'To—?'

'Greensleeves. The name of the house— look—' Scotty drew Christopher a few paces and pointed. 'Among those trees. This farm belonged to the house; I bought it, four years ago, from Cress's father. Greensleeves, Green Farm. The town used to be Greentown and got watered down to Grenton. Go on—walk up there, Chris, and say I sent you, and tell Cress, if she's there, that we've got measles and need a hand.'

'Seems a waste of time,' commented Christopher.

'See here,' said Scotty persuasively. 'You remember the time we were stuck on that glacier and I dragged you, foot by foot—'

'You saved my life,' said Christopher in a resigned tone. 'Every time you want anything, you bring that up. Go ahead. I'm listening.'

'I dragged you, foot by foot—'

'—round the last bend,' Christopher joined in the well known story, and the saga for two voices went on.

'—and I bandaged your broken head with my shirt and said: "One more corner, Chris, and they'll see us." I had a *feeling*, and I was right.'

'You had a feeling, and you were right.

You've got another feeling?'

'Yes, I have,' said Scotty, undaunted. 'I've had it all the morning. I've been feeling queer.'

'Perhaps it's what the Belchamber said about your personal hygiene. She put it rather strongly, I thought.'

'It's nothing to do with hygiene. It's a feeling that Cress is home. Chris, go up there, and see.'

'All right. All right, I'll go. We'll get this settled once and for all. Greensleeves—silly name for a house. Who named it?'

'I can't tell you, but you can't lodge a complaint,' said Scotty. 'They've been dead several hundred years. The house is empty—I mean, there's only the furniture and a caretaker and a gardener. You can go across those fields, and you'll come out at a lane that joins the road up the hill. Mind how you go through that far orchard—there's a bull in there, and he uses a pretty rush.'

'I see. Is that why Robert and Paul are climbing trees close by him?'

'That bull's got a good head behind those nasty horns of his,' explained Scotty. 'He doesn't waste his vitality chasing speedy little boys—he saves it up until he can pick on something your age, a bit gone in the wind. You don't look as hard as you used to, old son. How about giving up the architect's office and—'

'Thanks. See here, Scotty, can we do anything about losing those two French hats?'

89

'What—those?' Scotty gazed at the two boys' headwear in honest admiration. 'Why, you wouldn't take those off them, would you? They give just the right touch to the place. They charm. They cheer. With those in the cowshed this morning, I got an extra gallon out of every cow. Something frisky about them, I think. What on earth do you want them off for?'

'Well—they look so un-English.'

'Well, we keep getting that sort of thing,' said Scotty. 'I don't suppose William of Normandy looked particularly English, or William of Orange or old Hanoverian George. A couple more foreign-looking hats won't do the country any harm will it? You leave them alone.'

'All right—I'll leave them alone. See you later,' said Christopher, 'with or without the young woman.'

He went through the far orchard, keeping to the hedge and giving the bull a wide berth. The fields were damp underfoot but the air was fresh and dry. Christopher found himself squaring his shoulders and breathing deeply, and he realized, with a lifting of his spirits, that, in spite of this temporary setback, the problems which had beset him for the past two or three months were coming to an end. He had got the children to England; he liked them and knew that they liked him. They were young, happy and adaptable; the measles would be a merely temporary check on the way to his goal;

90

a home for himself and the three children. He had never liked his flat in town; it had been chosen, he remembered with some amusement, to afford his mother a convenient home on her visits to London. She disliked hotels, and Christopher had fallen in with her wish to take a flat which she could occasionally share.

He wondered, as he walked, what her feelings would be if she could see him now, with the three children—with Robert, against whom in particular she had nursed what Christopher had considered a senseless grievance. Once more he struggled against his feeling that she had shown, in the matter of the succession, a side of her character that had been less than generous. Circumstances, he knew, had combined to make the disappointment more than ordinarily bitter; her husband had been cheated of the title by death; it had been snatched from her son by what she peristed in referring, to the end of her life, as trickery.

Christopher's only regret in the matter was that he had been brought up at the Castle. He had once, in his eleventh or twelfth year, experienced a passing distaste at the thought that he was living under his uncle's roof and being brought up as his uncle's heir. What had prompted his feeling of unease, he could never afterwards guess, but he had spoken to his mother of the possibility of a separate home and she, surprised and puzzled, had pointed out that they were living at Piershurst at his uncle's express wish. Afterwards, when, burning with anger and humiliation, she had prepared to leave and make way for the hated Frenchwoman, Christopher knew that she had remembered his request and wished with all her heart that she had given in to it.

With a sigh, not for himself, but for her, Christopher went through the last field and along the lane and began the slow climb up the hill. With every step, he felt better; his lungs were filled with the finest air he had breathed for some time; Scotty was a grand fellow and they had had some wonderful times together; Mrs Belchamber's keepers would find her out soon and remove her; measles was something that almost every child had to go through; it was spring and he was strong and young—in another three weeks or so he would be twenty-six, which was a good age, neither callow nor calloused.

He came to the brow of the hill and found himself walking beside a high wall; the property was evidently larger than it looked from the farm. The wall continued for some distance, and then Christopher saw a small wooden door. He paused and considered for a moment; the wall stretched as far as his eye could see, but, if he went in by this entrance, he might come to the house by a short cut across the grounds. It was worth trying—if the door was unlocked.

The door was unlocked; Christopher closed it behind him and found himself in a thick wood. Following an ill-marked path, he came out on to a drive, which presently widened and wound through open parkland. He looked at the beeches with respect; they were magnificent specimens, tall, beautiful and of great age. He wondered what the house was like; judging by the size of the grounds, it was yet another of the mansions too large for present-day occupation. It was small wonder that the owners lived elsewhere. And it was small wonder that Cressida, if she had been reared in this atmosphere of ease, had failed to complete the arduous preliminaries of the nursing course.

The drive turned somewhat sharply. Christopher, absorbed in the wide view of the countryside opening before his eyes, followed the curve abstractedly, and so was totally unprepared for the sight of the house when he came upon it. As he came up to it, his steps slowed and finally halted. Entranced, he stood stock-still, gazing with a slowly mounting delight.

It was a perfect example of a fourteenth-century manor house. As Christopher stared at it, his gaze changed from that of enchanted spectator to one of professional scrutiny. Walking up to it slowly, walking round it, going back to re-examine some part of it more closely, he took in more and more of its absorbing detail.

He saw that it had been, originally, enclosed in high walls. These had been in some places lowered, in others removed; the moat had been filled up. The roof had mellowed to a warm, beautiful colour, and in one part, which had been restored and enlarged, he saw the faint purple and dull red of the bricks behind the thick creeper covering them. He stared at the battlements, the stone-mullioned windows with their delicate Gothic tracery; his eyes went to the massive towers with their buttressed walls. His professional interest now thoroughly aroused, he moved back a few paces to get a better view of the chimneys, which were built in pairs; he stood for some time admiring their beautiful proportions and elaborate decoration.

The plan centred round the great hall— Christopher guessed that it had once occupied the whole height of the house. The original stables and kitchens had been built round a quadrangle, and Christopher walked slowly up and down, studying the clean lines, the beautiful proportions, lost to everything but the loveliness of the buildings.

Another consideration soon struck him; the building's excellent state of preservation, and its neat and well-cared-for appearance. He knew, from what Scotty had told him, that there was a resident caretaker and a gardener, but the place had a fresh and welcoming air not often felt in houses which had been long unoccupied.

He walked along an alley of ancient yews and slowly drank in the atmosphere of Greensleeves. For atmosphere it had; he felt completely removed from the hurry and worry of modern living. The most unimaginative could not fail to feel, here, a sense of peace and well-being. The house and its surroundings told a long, unemphasized tale of wealth and power and rank. Here was strength, security and spaciousness. Hardy warriors had lived here, and gentle women. It was a home built to afford spacious comfort within and staunch defences without. It breathed nobility and a calm graciousness.

Christopher had a sudden longing to look at the interior, but one, two swift walks round the building disclosed no sign of either gardener or caretaker. Well, he could wait, he decided, turning from the house at last and making his way back to the farm. He would come back— yes, he would come back and get somebody to admit him. There were features of the interior it would be pure joy to examine. He would get hold of Scotty and see how much he knew of the history of the place. It was just like Scotty to send him up here without so much as a word about a jewel of a house like that one, without—

Christopher stopped abruptly, recollection flooding over him, and a realization of what he had come for. It seemed a trivial matter in the face of five hundred years of changing history, but he had measles to think about, and a nurse, and Clarissa. No, Cressida. Well, there had been no sign of Cressida, but as he was there, he might as well go back and raise a shout or two. The windows had been open; he would make a noise under one of them and this Clar—this Cressida might lean out and listen to his proposition. It was somewhat of a forlorn hope; if she had a fortnight's holiday, she was not likely to want to spend it nursing a measles case. But Scotty, below his unprepossessing exterior, was sound; if he said it was well worth trying, it probably was.

Christopher turned and walked with swift steps back to the house. He made his way round to the forecourt, paused and looked doubtfully from the open windows to the massive closed door. On second thoughts, he reflected, it might be better to give a good pull at that bell.

He moved towards it and paused. The door was opening. Christopher had barely time to wonder whether the caretaker was a man or woman when the heavy door swung slowly open. In the doorway, framed against the shadowy hall, stood a girl.

Long afterwards, Christopher was to remember that he had always given the girl of his dreams a small, fragile figure and hair the colour of his favourite dry sherry. She was to have had a delicate skin, a wistful expression and an unusual shade of violet eyes, preferably with long black lashes. He had sometimes made a swift sketch of her principal charms on the plan of a specially-designed house, or on a blotting pad in the middle of a letter to one of her less-favoured sisters. He knew, quite surely, the kind of girl he wanted, and would one day find.

The girl in the doorway was slim, but she was tall; her lashes were long and black, but the eyes below them were brown and their expression was one of coolness and detachment, which changed, as Christopher stood staring at her, to a question.

Christopher knew that he should state his business, and made an effort to remember what it was. She was coming out; she was moving out of that shadow into the sunlight. She was standing beside him, and her head came up to his shoulder.

The pause lengthened, and a small frown appeared on her smooth brow. The sight filled Christopher with despair, and he struggled to dispel the shadow of disapproval he saw dawning in her eyes.

'Good morning,' he said.

She bent her head, and waited. This was agreement, but scarcely co-operation. Her lips, he noted, were wide and curved and soft. He thought them so lovely that his despair left him and he was filled with an uplifting rush of happiness. He felt the sun warm upon him; what a day he rejoiced, what a lovely, lovely day and what a lovely house and what a—

'Are you Cressida?' he asked her suddenly.

'Yes,' said Cressida, and then, as he remained staring, saying nothing: 'Did you want anything?'

'Yes,' said Christopher. 'I came to—' He paused.

Cressida's gaze became cooler.

'Well?' she prompted. 'You came to—'

'To—Do you know,' said Christopher in a burst of confidence, 'I can't for the life of me remember.'

CHAPTER SEVEN

'But I told you!' said Scotty.

'You didn't,' said Christopher. 'You said nothing whatsoever about her. You harped nauseatingly on your own feelings, and said nothing to—to prepare me. You sent me over there and—'

'I said you couldn't put her into words,' said Scotty. 'Can you put her into words?'

'Certainly I can,' said Christopher. 'She's slim and beautiful.'

'So are lots of girls,' pointed out Scotty. 'If I'd said that, you might have walked up there a bit faster, but would it have prepared you?'

'Perhaps not,' admitted Christopher. 'Scotty, I can tell you this—confidentially. She knocked me right off my feet.'

'I knew she would,' said Scotty. 'Why d'you think I sent you?'

He was in the feed-store, filling a small, battered basin with a mixture of food for the cows. The basin filled, he walked through the yard into the adjoining cowshed, shook the mixture into a feeding trough, and went back for a further supply. Christopher followed him to and fro, his eyes on Scotty, his thoughts on Cressida.

'What did she say?' inquired Scotty after a time.

'She says she'll come. I put it rather strongly—I might have overdone the pathos a bit, but the facts, when you run through them, sound pretty heart-rending. I was surprised myself. Young man—me—with three orphans on his hands; home burnt down, child struck down by disease, desolate old lady clinging on for support. When you take it circumstantially, it would melt a harder heart than Cressida's.'

'Well, what did you arrange?'

'I'm going to walk up and fetch her after lunch and she'll spend every afternoon up here, helping where and how she can. Then I'll walk back with her after supper every night.'

'The hell you will,' said Scotty. 'Damn it, Chris, you can't horn in like this! I've got priority—I've known her for four solid years!'

'Then it's time you gave someone else a chance,' said Christopher. 'Incidentally, do you realize that, for three of those years, she's been living within a stone's throw of me in London? For three years we've walked the same streets. We've—'

'You're speaking,' said Scotty, 'of the girl I love.'

'Well, we've moved in the same orbit. I wish I'd used the car less and the Underground more. Her station's Green Park—and I've driven past it scores of times and never given it a second glance.'

'You should have feelings, like me. Didn't I tell you this morning that I had a feeling?'

'You did. I didn't like to ask her what her job was, Scotty—what does she work at?'

'She's a model.'

'A model? You mean a sort of—sort of artist's—'

'No, I don't. You're thinking of Trilby. Cress is one of those photographic models you see in all the women's magazines.'

'What makes you think I read all the women's magazines?'

'Pardon me,' said Scotty. 'Well, she's featured in other places, too. On theatre programmes; on cigarette advertisements; and in all those powder advertisements—you know, Florette or Laurette, one of those. Picture with Cress holding a baby in one hand and a supply of Florette powder in the other and the caption: "At two, or at twenty-two." You must have seen it. It's on all the buses.'

'You know that accounts for it,' said Christopher suddenly.

'Accounts for what?'

'The feeling I had when I saw her. I told you—she bowled me over, but I had a persistent feeling that I'd seen her before—somewhere. Something about her was familiar in some odd way.'

'There's nothing odd about it,' said Scotty. 'Her likeness is everywhere. She's what they call a free-lance model; that's to say, she doesn't belong to any specific company or organization; she's on her own. It took her a little time to get known, but she does all right now.'

'There's one more thing,' said Christopher. 'It sounds something of an anti-climax, but—'

'Well?'

'I don't know Cressida's other name.'

'Surname? Gray,' said Scotty. 'Spelt with an a. Her father's Major Gray—used to belong to one of the crack regiments, I don't know quite which, and sent in his papers when he inherited this house.'

'He inherited it?'

'Well, yes—I told you! That's how I came here. I met him up North when that ranch I was running packed up. I was throwing good money after bad—it cost me a lot, that place, Chris. Then I fell in with the Major. I don't quite know how. He said he'd just come into a manor house in the South, and offered me the home farm. So I bought it.'

'Without seeing it?'

'When I paid the money down,' said Scotty slowly, 'I didn't even know for sure that there was a home farm. The Major has a way—'

He stopped agape. Two small figures had made their way into the feed-store and were waiting politely for him to finish his sentence. Christopher turned to see what Scotty was staring at, and stood aghast, taking in the details of the two boy's appearance.

The sailor hats were still firmly on their heads, not fresh and neat now, but streaked with mud and manure. Their shoes were unrecognizable, covered with a wetter mixture of the same components; their faces, rosy and glowing, shone through a layer of dust. Their clothes were torn and flour-sprinkled.

'Well,' said Scotty on a long note. 'We ... el, look at that!'

Robert's teeth gleamed in his enchanting smile.

'We 'ave been up there'—he pointed a finger upwards towards the granary.

'So I see,' said Christopher gravely. 'And what brought you down?'

'The bell,' explained Paul. 'Madame has rung the bell for *déjeuner*.'

'She has rung it twice,' said Robert. 'We are to go inside, I think.'

'Well, I'll go inside with you,' said Christopher. 'Madame'll have a few words to say when you walk through the kitchen smelling as high as you do. How long'll you be, Scotty?'

'I'm through now. I'll come with you,' said Scotty. 'I'd rather face Madame behind a protective screen.' He tossed the basin into the barrow. '*En avang!*' he said. 'Something tells me that this is going to be a painful interview.'

They walked in procession to the door of the kitchen and waited until Scotty and the two boys had wiped some of the removable dirt from their footwear with the stiff broom standing outside the door. Christopher lifted the latch and, ushering the boys in, followed with Scotty. They stood, a little sheepishly, while Mrs Belchamber, standing stiffly by the table, ran her eyes over them.

The kitchen, Christopher saw, had undergone a complete transformation. The floor was scrubbed, the range had a gleaming blackness it had never known before; the grime had been removed from the sink, odd garments of Scotty's no longer hung here and there. There was a cloth spread on the table—a tattered cloth, but clean and white. On the stove were plates and dishes, and from the dishes issued a savoury smell that made hungry mouths water.

Mrs Belchamber still wore her stiff black hat and grey curls. Over her suit was a stiff white overall. She looked grim and unbending and almost startlingly clean. She addressed the company impartially.

'Lunch, while I am cooking it,' she observed in her grating voice, 'will be served at one o'clock. It is now a quarter to two. Will you two boys kindly go outside and remove your unspeakable shoes?'

Robert and Paul went.

'You, too,' said Mrs Belchamber, to a point above Scotty's head.

Scotty followed the boys. Christopher, left alone, put a question.

'Where's Mrs—what's her name—Garcia?'

'Mrs Garcia is upstairs, sitting with Josette,' said Mrs Belchamber frigidly. 'You remember Josette, perhaps? She is the little girl in your charge, who has measles. You will be surprised to know that she has had her medicine and a cool drink. Her temperature is down to a hundred and two. I've darkened the room to protect her eyes, and Mrs Garcia has kept a fire going. I don't suppose you are in the least interested in any of these details, but I feel it my duty to keep you in touch with what goes on in connexion with what are known technically as your charges. I expect no thanks. And you boys,' she went on, without pause, as Robert and Paul entered, 'you will both please go to the sink and wash your hands before sitting down to a meal. You will find a towel there, which I have produced out of my own luggage.

No splashing, please. Now your faces. Now dry yourselves thoroughly, and leave the towel for Mr Scott in case he should feel impelled at any time to wash. Sit here, Robert. Paul, you there. Mr Scott, will you kindly sit there and serve? We are eating casserole made of a chicken that I sent Mrs Garcia out to buy. I cannot provide lunch for five—since Mrs Garcia has already had her meal—out of nothing.'

The meal was cheerful, despite Mrs Belchamber's grim presence. Robert and Paul, seated on either side of her, gave an account of their morning's activities, and she heard them with a kind of severe courtesy, interrupting only to correct occasional errors of grammar, or to point out that the English did not wipe their knives and forks on a piece of bread and keep them for the next dish. Scotty ate voraciously, pausing only to compliment Mrs Belchamber on the excellence of her cooking.

'How you could let that woman'—she shuddered—'touch your food...'

'How d'you find her?' inquired Scotty. 'Does she do any work? I never saw her come or go and I don't know what she did while she was here.'

'You have only to look round,' said Mrs Belchamber, 'to see that this is the first time she has ever used a scrubbing brush. She is, without exception, the most slatternly creature I ever came across.'

'I say—you'd better not tell her that,' said Scotty. 'She'll resign in a body.'

'I have told her exactly what I think of her,' said Mrs Belchamber, 'and she has not resigned.'

Lunch over, the company dispersed. Scotty bestrode a bicycle, which had wheels, but no tyres, and went up to a distant field to open the gates and bring the cows in for the afternoon milking. It was decided, after a short conclave, that Robert and Paul might be allowed to visit Josette whenever they wished to.

'They've been with her all this time, and there's no point in keeping them away now,' Mrs Belchamber decided. 'If they're going to get it, let them all get it together and be done with.'

The boys crept upstairs quiet but jubilant, and Christopher faced Mrs Belchamber, feeling himself compelled to acknowledge something of his debt to her.

'You've been very kind,' he said. 'But you couldn't be expected to—as a matter of fact, we've got hold of a—well, a sort of nurse, who can come every afternoon and evening and give a hand.'

'What do you call a sort of a nurse?' inquired Mrs Belchamber.

'Well—she trained, in a way. She's a friend of Scotty's, and she's here for about a fortnight. I'm going along to fetch her now. Perhaps ... you may find her very useful.'

'When I've seen her, I can tell you. What is her name?'

'Miss Gray.'

'And her age?'

'I don't know—yes, I do. She's twenty-two.'

'Ah!'

With this monosyllable, uttered with great reserve, ringing in his ears, Christopher vaulted over a gate into the orchard, walked through it in happy abstraction and then roused to realities by the pounding of hooves close behind him, finished in a fine burst of speed and hurled himself over the far gate five seconds before the bull reached it.

He walked on more soberly. He was going to see Cressida and—to add the last touch of felicity—she had promised to show him round the house. She would stand with the sunlight coming through the tall, narrow windows and playing round her head. He would follow her up beautiful stairways and along a minstrel's gallery. He could think of no setting more suited to her than the beautiful, gracious house.

The door, this time, was open, and it seemed to him that it breathed invitation, and a welcome. He heard a movement inside, and was on the point of calling Cressida's name when he realized that the footsteps could not be hers; they were not light, but heavy and measured. Stepping back a pace, Christopher waited. The caretaker, perhaps...

The next instant, a man appeared at the door, saw Christopher and paused. He stood, as Cressida had stood, framed in the doorway and he made, Christopher realized, almost as perfect a picture.

It was not youth, this time, or fresh loveliness; but the man standing before him was as much a part of the scene as the girl had been. Everything about him, though Christopher with an artist's keen appreciation, fitted: his figure, his air, his quiet assurance. He was almost absurdly right the only possible lord for this lovely manor.

He was tall and handsome, with a rather long, clean-shaven face and close-dipped greying hair. His eyes, half-closed against the sun, had a faintly humorous look; his clothes were easy, without being informal. Christopher knew that, when he spoke, his voice would be pleasant and cultured.

They looked at one another for a moment, and then Christopher began.

'I'm afraid I—'

The man stopped him with an upraised hand and a whimsical smile.

'I know,' he said. 'You're looking for my daughter.'

'Yes, I'm ... You must be Major Gray,' said Christopher, adding to his own surprise, 'sir. You're—'

'I'm Cressida's father. She tells me she's going along to help nurse—a case of measles at

108

the farm.'

'Yes. I hope you won't mind,' said Christopher.

He was trying, as he spoke, to account for Major Gray's presence. Scotty had said that nobody lived here but a caretaker and a gardener, but—

'I came down from Town about an hour ago.' The pleasant voice broke into his thoughts. 'Look here—I don't know where Cressida's got to—won't you come in and wait for her?'

'I'd like to very much,' said Christopher frankly. 'I've been pretty keen to get in ever since I saw the house for the first time this morning. Houses,' he explained, 'are my job.'

'You're an architect?'

'Yes. Heron and Mayes. I'm the Heron, but I'm off duty for a few weeks, to settle a bit of family business.'

'Heron.' Major Gray repeated the name once or twice, softly, as though attempting to recall something. 'Heron ... I've met a Heron somewhere, at some time ... but it's gone, I'm afraid. Perhaps it'll come back later. Will you sit down, or would you like to look round?'

They were in the great hall. Christopher's eye went from the huge open fire hearth to the minstrel's gallery above, and then, with delight, to the characteristic open timbered roof. He withdrew his eye reluctantly and answered Major Gray's questions.

'I'd like to go round, if I may.'

They went round the house, Major Gray proving an interesting and instructive guide. The interior, Christopher saw, was as well preserved as the outside. Every room was furnished, even to silver and ornaments and, here and there, great vases of flowers. Major Gray moved slowly from room to room, pausing to point out items of more than ordinary interest.

'You'll know the date?' he asked Christopher, smiling.

'Edward the First, I'd say.'

'You're more or less right. It was begun in 1300 and finished in Edward the Second's time. It's not unique, of course—I've been over a good many houses that could compare with this one, but none of them, I think, were in as good a state of preservation—and none of them had as many of the original features. And there are some treasures among the furniture here, too, if you look.'

'I'm looking,' smiled Christopher.

'That bed, for example'—Major Gray stopped before a richly carved four-poster. 'Tudor—and the steps are interesting. I like the notion of climbing up three magnificently carved steps to bed. That table there is interesting, too. It's older than the house. Eleventh century—and so's the candlestick. Know what this is?'

'A ... isn't it ... shawm?'

110

'Quite right. Shawm. Instrument of the oboe family. That's genuine fourteenth century.'

Christopher, eager, absorbed, followed his host down to the beautiful hall at the end of the inspection, and drew a deep breath.

'Thanks,' he said. 'It was very good of you.'

'Not at all,' was the answer. 'It's a pleasure. I like showing people round—that is, if they've a good sense of values. It's a nice place; one can't afford to live in it under present day conditions—or perhaps I ought to correct that and say that I can't afford to live in it. But I come down here frequently in the summer, and sometimes people come down and I show them round. Foreigners, mostly. That's why I'm down today, as a matter of fact—I'm expecting a man and his wife at three o'clock. Swedish. Always surprises me how much they know about period stuff. This fellow's coming down to look at that arquebus—or arquebuse, or harquebus, if you prefer it.' Major Gray pointed to a gun on one of the walls. 'I was telling him about it and he asked if he could come down and look at it. He's got one—1530, he says it is, and he thinks this'll make the pair. Take it down if you want to. It's an interesting piece.'

Christopher walked across and took the gun down carefully. Major Gray came across and stood at his shoulder, running a finger affectionately along the barrel.

'See that serpent-shaped piece of iron? That
111

held the burning match. You press the trigger—so—and the match comes instantly to the flash-pan and ignites the charges in the barrel—there—through the touch-hole. They were used in Henry the Eighth's time—but not, of course, this one.'

He took the gun from Christopher and put it back in its place.

'Why not this one?' inquired Christopher.

Major Gray looked at him with an expression at once surprised and quizzical.

'Why? Because, my dear fellow, it isn't genuine, that's why. This man insists that it is, and nothing I can say will convince him that he's wrong.'

'But ... I can't pretend to be an expert,' said Christopher hesitatingly, 'but I know something about ... about old firearms. My uncle ... well, he taught me a good bit, and—well, if that isn't genuine, sir, it's an astonishingly good fake.'

'Of course it is. If I were a dealer,' said Major Gray, 'I'd have no trouble in calling that a genuine article and asking a pretty stiff price—but I'm not a dealer. If this fellow that's coming down today wants it, he can have it—but not if he insists that it's genuine.'

'But if it isn't—I mean, if he decides that it isn't genuine,' said Christopher hesitatingly, 'will he buy it?'

'I shouldn't think so,' said Major Gray. 'Why do you ask?'

'Because,' Christopher turned and looked up at the gun, 'well, if he doesn't want it, and if you'd sell it, I'd like to buy it.'

'You? What do you want it for?' asked Major Gray in surprise.

'I'm like the Swede—I've got a piece it would go with very well indeed.'

'A gun like that?'

'Not like that—no. Mine's a flint-lock, self-loading gun—as a matter of fact, it's genuine Charles the First. My uncle—well, it was left to me. That fellow up on the wall there would go awfully well in its company. How much'—hesitated—'how much were you going to let it go for?'

'I didn't want to let it go at all,' said Major Gray frankly, 'but you'll have more years in which to enjoy it than I shall. If you really want it, you can have it for what I gave for it.'

He named his price, and the two men stood for a moment, smiling at one another. Christopher felt a warm surge of liking for the man facing him.

'It's a deal,' he said. 'Thanks.'

'That was a swift bit of business,' commented Major Gray. 'I—' He paused and walked towards the door. 'I hear a car,' he said hurriedly. 'Will you forgive me? And I think, yes, I can see Cressida there—will you go and meet her?'

Christopher needed no second invitation. Following the direction of Major Gray's arm, he saw Cressida and went with long strides to intercept her. She saw him and waited for him, standing still and watching him as he came up and joined her.

'I've been with your father,' he said. 'Where were you?'

'I went into Grenton—there were some things to get. Some people are coming down to tea.'

He fell into step beside her and they turned in the direction of the farm. Looking at her from time to time, he could detect no likeness to her father, but she had the same ease and quietness of manner, and, on her, the little air of dignity sat prettily.

'Do you realize,' he said. 'that when I left you this morning, I didn't even know your name? I didn't know anything about you, except that when we get back to Town, we'll be practically neighbours. Let's make a dinner date,' he urged, 'for the night we get back.'

'I'll be back in a fortnight or three weeks,' pointed out Cressida. 'You'll be here indefinitely.'

'Why indefinitely?'

'Because one of the boys will wait until the very last day of the quarantine, and then go down with measles, and the other boy'll wait until the very last day, too, and then get them. Then Scotty'll get them, and then you.'

'Well, I planned to be home by the end of the month,' said Christopher. 'It's hard on you,' he added thoughtfully, 'leaving a house like Greensleeves to go back to London.'

'Why hard?' inquired Cressida in her cool, quiet voice.

'Why hard? Good Lord, wouldn't you give your ears to live there? Given the requisite staff, that is. Wouldn't you?'

'No,' said Cressida quietly. 'I wouldn't even give one ear.'

'Do you like London all that much?' asked Christopher curiously.

'I don't like London at all. I don't like any city, much. Except Paris. I didn't feel shut-in when I was in Paris, somehow. Do you like Paris?'

He ignored her obvious wish to change the subject.

'Why don't you like Greensleeves?' he asked again.

She gave him a little sidelong glance of annoyance, and spoke more coldly.

'I didn't say I didn't like it,' she said. 'I think it's beautiful. I just said I didn't want to live in it, that's all.'

He felt that this was far from all, but he did not persist. His curiosity was piqued; he could sense strong feeling behind the quiet words, but she obviously did not wish to pursue the subject, and he was content, for the moment, to drop it. She had not shown, as yet, any undue pleasure in his society; her manner was friendly, but in it there was none of the warm responsiveness he usually met when he showed his preference for a woman. He looked for a word to describe her detachment, and found to his surprise that it was wary. It was perhaps natural, he reflected, that a girl with so strong an appeal for the opposite sex should cultivate a technique for keeping them at a distance.

'I didn't quite explain about Mrs Belchamber,' he said.

'Mrs—?'

'Belchamber. She's the old lady, who for some reason has attached herself to my suite. She's making herself extraordinarily useful and I ought to be grateful to her, but she's got a grating voice and a hard face and one of those sharp, interfering noses. I think she's got some idea that I've abducted the children. They're nice children,' he added. 'You'll like them.'

He helped her over gates, kept her close to the hedge when passing the bull and found Scotty looking out for them.

'Cress darling, you do my eyes good,' he said. 'You go in, Chris, old son, and Cress can stay out here and talk to me.'

'I've come here to make myself useful,' smiled Cressida.

'Ah, please!' begged Scotty. 'I haven't seen you for a whole month, and it's seemed like years. Do you like Chris? He's big, but he's not as big as I am,' pointed out Scotty. 'He's got a better brain than I have, but not such a nice nature. He's strong, but he can't stand up to

116

me. He's—hey! where are you going?'

'Inside. I'm going to report for duty,' said Cressida.

'Well, then, I'll come with you,' said Christopher.

'No—I'll go alone. If Mrs—'

'Belchamber.'

'If Mrs Belchamber's as terrifying as you make her out, I'd better go and get it over.'

'Without protection?' said Scotty.

'Without protection. See you later,' she said lightly, and was gone.

'She's always doing things like that,' said Scotty gloomily. 'You look forward to her company and then find you haven't got it. It gives you a nasty, empty feeling. That old lady of yours, Chris, doesn't like me.'

Scotty was feeling a little sore. He had gone into the kitchen for something he had forgotten and Mrs Belchamber, waylaying him, had given him a pithy résumé of the conclusions she had reached about his person and possessions. She had used expressions which he had never before heard applied by a lady to a gentleman, and his ears were ringing with adjectives, the more complimentary of which were slovenly, unkempt, seedy, out-at-elbows, un-self-respecting, clod-like, and animal. He had been treated to a short discourse on the aims of education which were solely, he learned, designed to teach a man how to keep himself clean when he passed out of the

117

hands of the school matron. He had learned his place in Lower Grenton society, which ought to have been, but was not, one of leadership and example to those who ought to have been, but were not, looking up to him.

All this, from one who had come uninvited to his house, seemed to Scotty to be a little high-handed. He found Mrs Belchamber, indeed, something of an enigma. He considered that her appearance was, in its way, as unfortunate as his own, without being as misleading. But he had striven all his life to act in a way that would tend to counteract the effects of his unprepossessing exterior; he had tried to be gentle and courteous. Mrs Belchamber, as far as he could see, had made no such effort; her manners were as sour as her features; yet in spite of this, she seemed to him to exact from others, without effort, a great deal of service and co-operation, and from the children at least, a measure of affection.

'And you know what?' he said to Christopher, at the end of a recital of his humiliation, 'she's ordered hot baths all round. How can you provide hot baths in a place that hasn't got a hot bathroom? Monday, you and the boys; Tuesday, her first and then me; Wednesday, you and the boys; Thursday, her first and then me, Friday, you and the boys, and Saturday—what do you think? Me again! On Sunday, Godliness moves in and cleanliness moves out. Three baths a week!'

'How do you manage when you're by yourself?' asked Christopher.

'Me? Well, I manage, that's all. Every so often I yank the tin tub into the kitchen and give myself a rub-down, but it's a troublesome performance, one way and another, and I can't say I let the matter of ablutions weigh on me too much.'

'That's what the Belchamber said.'

'She told you, too? How does she know?'

'I hardly like to tell you. She said you were a disgrace to your upbringing.'

'What's my upbringing got to do with her?' demanded Scotty. 'I'm getting a bit tired,' he complained, 'of the way she sits in a far corner and screws up her nose when I'm in the room. There's nothing wrong with a good, healthy farmyard odour.'

'That's what she said, but she says she prefers it in a farmyard.'

'Well, on the whole,' summed up Scotty, 'I'll be glad when she's found and restored to her rightful place. Doesn't it strike you as a bit ominous that nobody's given any sign of looking for her yet? First thing you know, Chris, she'll be round your neck for life. Could you find time to tell her that my name isn't Scott?'

'Here she comes,' said Chris. 'Tell her yourself.'

Mrs Belchamber had opened the kitchen door and was addressing Christopher.

'We'd like you,' she said, 'to come in and help us move some furniture round.'

'Delighted,' said Christopher.

'And Mr Scott'—Mrs Belchamber fixed her eyes coldly on Scotty—'there's a bucket of slops here to be emptied.'

Scotty gazed at her, his eyes starting out of his head.

'A—a b-bucket ... What's wrong,' he asked getting his breath back, 'what's wrong with Mrs Garcia?'

'Mrs Garcia left, as usual, at three.' Mrs Belchamber drew in her chin. 'Do you expect me to do it?' she inquired.

'Well—no. But—but good Lord!' cried Scotty, 'do you mean that I—do you mean to say that I—me—a descendant of the Lindens, the son of Crusty Linden, the grandson of Portly Linden ... me, a limb'—his voice rose passionately—'a limb of a famous tree, a member of a family that can trace its ancestry right back to George the Fifth, do you mean to say I've got to descend to this?'

'Yes,' said Mrs Belchamber.

'Oh. All right,' said Scotty. 'If you say so.'

CHAPTER EIGHT

After Mrs Belchamber had interviewed Cressida and acknowledged, grudgingly, that

120

she might be useful, the household fell into a routine which became daily more settled. The doctor, calling each morning, pronounced the case of measles to be a mild one and, on each visit, examined Robert and Paul to discover whether they were showing any signs of the disease. They continued, however, obstinately healthy, the only change in their appearance being caused by the loss of the hats, which had fallen off when they had been climbing a tree. Fluttering down in the vicinity of the bull, they had afforded that animal half an hour's employment, at the end of which the hats looked, in Scotty's opinion, more un-English than ever.

Mrs Belchamber had assumed command of the household. She ordered furniture to be moved from one part of the house to the other, rummaged among Scotty's meagre store of linen to produce curtains for the sickroom; tattered sheets were patched, rugs brought down from the attic, plates and dishes rescued from odd corners and assembled in their proper place.

The house began to assume a lived-in air. The kitchen was now only used for meals during the day and for baths in the evenings, and had ceased to be the all-purpose chamber in which Scotty had once been so comfortable. The other rooms, not considered by Mrs Belchamber fit to be given the name of drawing-room or sitting-room, were known merely as the big front, the little front and the side room, and it was in the little front—a pleasant room with a pretty view over the fields—that the company assembled in the evenings. As it was directly below the sickroom, Josette could summon anybody at will.

The boys were seldom indoors. They paid regular visits to Josette and kept her informed of the arrival of every new calf, puppy, kitten, or chick, but the time that was not spent on the farm was now passed at Greensleeves. The caretaker and the gardener, an old couple who had been in the service of Cressida's mother, and who had come to England with Cressida four years earlier, were discovered to be what Robert called French-Swiss; they were delighted to talk their own language to the boys, and were soon on excellent terms with them; Robert and Paul were shown exactly what they could and could not do at Greensleeves, where they could and where they could not go, and they found the old house almost as exciting as a playground as the farm.

Mrs Belchamber issued orders, and everybody obeyed them, the children with a light-hearted air which proved that they stood in no awe of her, Cressida with quiet amusement, and the others—Christopher, Scotty, and Mrs Garcia—with varying degrees of unwillingness. Christopher's chief feeling was one of bewilderment at the hold that the old lady—a virtual stranger—had assumed over his affairs; Scotty was uneasy, for he was aware that when Mrs Belchamber had ended the cleaning-up process in the house, she was about to continue the process on his person. As for Mrs Garcia, she went about her new and augmented duties with a hypnotized air. Mrs Belchamber was something outside her experience; the brisk way in which she rattled off insults, the uncanny instinct she had for knowing what people were doing without seeming to observe them; above all, her fearsome determination to have everything in—and out—of sight cleaned, scrubbed, polished not only once, but over and over again was, Mrs Garcia considered, going too far, and kept her in a state which she described to Cressida as all a-twitter.

The sickroom was darkened to protect Josette's eyes; as her condition improved she found time hanging a little heavily on her hands, and Mrs Belchamber decided to read aloud to her now and then. The choice of literature was not extensive, for besides innumerable copies of the *Farmer and Stockbreeder*, Scotty's library appeared to consist of three books only—Ruskin's *Ethics of the Dust*; an out-of-date guide to Paris entitled, *On Foot through France, Part 3: The Capital*; and a small volume of commercial correspondence with the title, *Business Man's French*. Scotty, confronted with this feast for the mind, could give no account of the way in which any of the volumes had come into his possession, and explained that his own books were in the packing case in which they had been put when he had left his first business venture, the fruit farm in Warwickshire. Mrs Belchamber, driving him before her, stood over him while he hammered at the rusty fastenings of the packing case; when it was at last opened, it was found to contain the tropical kit which Scotty had bought before completing his arrangements to go out to an ostrich farm in Africa.

'That's half an hour wasted,' said Mrs Belchamber grimly, surveying a crushed Panama and several linen suits. 'Is that what you were going to wear for chasing ostriches?'

'Well, no. Those were for landing in Cape Town,' said Scotty, on his knees beside the case. 'The ostriches were up-country. It all fell through.'

'Ostriches!' sniffed Mrs Belchamber. 'Well, there's one thing, you find their eggs more easily than you can find the eggs these hens of yours lay all over the place. What's in that big trunk? Would that be the books?'

'We could try it,' said Scotty, panting in his attempt to get the trunk right-side up.

The trunk proved even move difficult to open than the packing case. Yielding at last to the combined efforts of Scotty, Christopher, Robert, and Paul, it opened to reveal several saddles and a miscellany of stirrups, brides, and bits.

'No books,' said Scotty, surveying the assortment. 'You can't read those.'

'Oh yes, you can,' said Mrs Belchamber. 'Oh yes, certainly you can. You can read bad packing, carelessness, laziness, shiftlessness, and dirt.'

'What—all that?' inquired Scotty, genuinely surprised.

'All that. And more. Well, you needn't open any more of that clap-trap, thank you. I'll use the books we've got.'

'They're not exactly children's literature, are they?' asked Christopher.

'I'm not looking for children's literature,' declared Mrs Belchamber. 'I don't want any of your Piggy-wiggy or Henny-wenny, thank you very much. If you're going to read children that kind of thing, all they'll do is stay awake and listen to it. I'm simply looking for something that'll send a child to sleep, that's all.'

The three available books certainly served this purpose. Cressida listened to the harsh, rasping voice and watched Josette's eyes fixed on the reader; from round-eyed fascination, they would change to an absent stare, and soon the lids would droop and the patient fell into a sound sleep.

'It's odd,' she told Christopher, walking slowly homewards across the fields. 'She's a dreadful person, in many ways, but she does

125

get things done. I think it's because she never gives any unnecessary order; she pushes everybody around, but never on unessential jobs. She's got a hawk's eye for anything that needs fixing, that's all.'

'You don't *like* her?' asked Christopher, incredulous.

'Well, it's fantastic, but I—well, I think I do. That is, I don't see how anybody could like her very much, but I like certain things about her. She's shrewd and clear-sighted and she's never afraid to say just what she thinks.'

'Why do you consider that a virtue? It's much harder not to say what one thinks—and much pleasanter all round, don't you think?'

'In a way—but look how useful it is,' pointed out Cressida, 'to have someone to tell Mrs Garcia all those home truths! If the old lady weren't here, we should all be squirming under the Garcia thumb!'

'Instead of the Belchamber thumb.'

'She gives me a lot of advice—Mrs Belchamber, I mean. She's warned me against Scotty, because she says you can see at a glance what kind of man *he* is when innocent girls are abroad. And she's warned me against you.'

'*Me?*' said the astounded Christopher.

'Yes, you—because she says you can't see at a glance. In other words, Scotty's villainy is obvious and yours is insidious.'

'Well, perhaps she's right. What do you think she's staying on here for?' asked

126

Christopher curiously.

'She hasn't, for the moment, anywhere to go,' pointed out Cressida. 'She gave up her house in Switzerland and sold all her things, so she's not keen on going back there. I think she'll go—eventually—to this house of hers at Melhampton, but I think she wants to give them all the trouble of finding her and apologizing to her for what she calls her schoolgirl reception. She says a detestable creature bore down on her when she arrived and treated her like a Third Form truant. Is that true?'

'Not quite,' said Christopher. 'There was certainly a woman there to meet her, and she certainly had a domineering touch, but there was more in it than that. Did Scotty tell you about the Frenchman?'

'Well—yes, but I . . .' Cressida hesitated.

'You thought I'd exaggerated?'

'No. I only thought you'd drawn the wrong conclusion. She's lived abroad for so many years—she must know a lot of foreigners. Her French is terrible, though she likes you to imagine she can reel it off, and I think the man was probably an old acquaintance—or even a creditor, though she doesn't strike me as the sort of person who runs up bills. I think you heard something out of context, and if you could fit it into the whole of that conversation they had, you'd find it made sense.'

'If there's nothing in it, why is she here?'

asked Christopher. 'I'm convinced that she was going off with the woman who came to meet her—until she caught sight of the Frenchman. Once she'd seen him, she decided to use my car to get away.'

Cressida was thoughtful for some minutes.

'If that woman was looking for her,' she said at last, 'and if the Frenchman was looking for her, they'd—well they'd—'

'They'd get together. That's what I think, too. They'll join forces, go back to this place at Melhampton, and send out a posse from there.'

'Well, then,' asked Cressida, 'why aren't you doing something? You know the address—or you can find it out from her luggage labels. You could talk to her about getting in touch with them.'

'I could—only it's so obvious that it's the last thing she wants. No,' there was a new note of decision in his voice, 'I'm going to let it stand, for the moment. I don't know why, quite—perhaps because she's pulling things together here and I'm afraid they'll fall apart if she leaves. We'll leave it, and if and when the police get here, we'll—'

'Police!'

'Well, yes—they'll have to use the police— unless they keep their own bloodhounds. When they catch up, she'll probably try to involve me, but I shall fall back on my obvious virtue and innocence.'

128

Cressida gave a little chuckle, and Christopher smiled in sympathy.

'What's the joke?' he inquired.

'Oh—nothing—except Mrs Belchamber. How can anybody look at her and think of her being chased by police and Frenchmen?'

'Frenchmen,' said Christopher, 'will chase anything, they tell me.'

They walked a little way in silence, and now and then Christopher turned his head and looked at the girl beside him. There was always something new to see, something new to learn—the way she moved her head, the way she smiled, the way she glanced up at him. She was friendly; she was even, in a sense, responsive—but it was not the kind of response he was looking for. Behind her quiet, easy manner was something he could not fathom—a touch of reserve, a hint of distance.

'Christopher—'

He looked down at her, a little unsteady at hearing his name on her lips.

'Well?'

'I want to talk to you about Scotty.'

'No—not now,' pleaded Christopher. 'Not just now, in the only time I can ever get you alone. We can talk about Scotty any other time.'

'Not when he's there.'

'Of course—why not? I've always talked about him when he's there; he'd like to be there; he'd like to listen. And I get you to myself so seldom! Let's talk about ourselves. Let's talk about what we'll do when we get back to Town. Let's talk about how we'll bring up Josette and the boys. Let's talk about the kind of house I've got to look for. Let's talk about you or even about me. Don't you want to know anything about me? Shouldn't you, before crossing the fields at night with a man you've been warned against, find out what sort of man he is? Couldn't you ask him what he thinks about all day and half the night? Or tell him what you think about? We've so little time, Cressida; how much of the day do I get you to myself like this? I want to know so much about you—and to know whether you could ever take any interest in me—in the man I am and the man I might, in good hands, become. Let's be together while we're together, please— won't you ... Cressida?'

The name was spoken like a caress, but her voice, when he heard it, was cool and unmoved.

'You're Scotty's friend—the first of his friends I've ever met, and his closest friend, and I wanted to talk to you. I'm worried about him.'

'Why about him? He hasn't got three orphans on his hands, one of them sick.'

'Didn't he, at one time,' asked Cressida, 'have quite a lot of money?'

'Well—yes,' said Christopher, giving way reluctantly to her gentle persistence. 'He did.

130

His father left him a packet. What he's done with it—specifically—I can't tell you, but he's got the quite erroneous idea that you can be a farmer just because you like messing about with cows and crops. Or perhaps that's inaccurate. I don't think he ever tried to be a farmer. All he wanted to do was to live this care-free, open-air life, without much responsibility—except to see the cows regularly milked—and without much hardship. Whatever you hear about farming being a hard life, I've never yet met a farmer that I'd call overworked. Long hours, yes—but such slow, pleasant unhurried hours. Did you ever know a farmer who couldn't stop and talk to you for hours at a time, or show you his stock and land, or who looked as played out as the average businessman does at the end of his day doubling down the platform and fighting for a place on the five-forty? They all tell you that they're close to ruin, and then run up to a steep figure for something they fancy at the cattle sale. They sleep well, they eat well and they live at a nice, steady pace. Scotty's one of the laziest men who ever breathed and he finds even that a trouble. This life was made for him. He falls out of bed just after five—a nasty hour in winter, admittedly but in five minutes he's in a cosy cowshed snuggled up against a warm cow. From then on, he does his round at his own pace, and finishes up at night with his muscles aching, but without any other sign of wear and tear. Now why are you worried about Scotty?'

'Hasn't he run through most of his money?'

'Probably,' said Christopher. 'I haven't asked him, but I will before I leave here. If he goes on long enough without making ends meet, he'll have to chuck it and live on an allowance—he's got some capital he can't touch, and some trustees he can't touch either. So you see he won't starve.'

'Couldn't you look into things for him while you're here?' pleaded Cressida. 'You're his greatest friend.'

'That doesn't give me any right to poke into his private affairs, does it?'

'Yes,' was Cressida's opinion. 'It does.'

'Well, I don't want to. His affairs must be pretty well mucked up. I could probably, having a business head, tell him which drain he's pouring money down, but I can't impose any kind of system. He doesn't work on any system. He wouldn't know what a system was if you showed it to him.'

'Well, I'd be less worried about him if I thought you'd at least talked to him while you're here. I feel, in a way, responsible. You see, he bought ... my father sold him the farm, and I'd feel better if it—if it paid better.'

'Scotty couldn't make anything pay,' said Christopher. 'You mustn't lose any sleep feeling that way about his affairs. What he needs more than an accountant is a good,

132

steady wife. Not a girl like you—you wouldn't suit him at all—but a strong, sturdy girl with a good head and strong muscles. Can't we find him one?'

'Not easily. We'll be in Town, and the strong muscles, as a rule, stay in the country, don't they?'

'It's a wife he wants,' repeated Christopher. 'We'll find him one.'

'Perhaps you can,' said Cressida. 'But I lead rather a busy life. Models don't have the easy job most people imagine, you know. Or didn't you know I was a model?'

'Scotty told me. It explained why I was so sure I'd seen you before. Oddly enough, I knew it wasn't *you* I'd seen, but your likeness. Somewhere—I don't yet know where, but I suppose it was looking down at me from a poster.'

'Hardly a poster,' said Cressida. 'The fashion pages—or the back pages. I'm on the kitchen page at the moment, with an apron and a rolling pin, making a Featherflake tart. It isn't my usual line, but it all helps.'

They had reached the last gate. There was only the lane, and then the road, and then the grounds. She would murmur her thanks, say good night and slip away and it would be fourteen—sixteen hours before he saw her again. There was so much he wanted to say, but he was afraid to say it. He had never before met a girl whose frown he had dreaded; he had

133

never before felt the need to pause before he spoke, to bite back a phrase which might offend. His treatment of girls, of women, had varied with the subject, but he had always felt himself possessed of the normal share of tact, of charm, of persuasiveness. This girl, with her quality of detachment, made him feel as though he were groping his way in the dark. The ground was familiar, but the light of his self-confidence had been extinguished. It was useless to call up his vanity, or to remember the ready response of other women. There was not yet, he felt with an increasing dejection, any sign of that kind of response from Cressida.

It was enough, for the moment, to snatch what moments he could. For the present, he would be content when she was beside him, with her shoulder brushing his and her hand occasionally touching his own...

He left her at Greensleeves and walked back the way he had come, dreaming, planning, rehearsing scenes in which Cressida, at last, looked at him with eyes in which he could read feeling similar to his own. He would—

'Where the hell,' shouted Scotty, 'did you get to?'

'We looked everywhere for you,' said Christopher.

'Don't lie.' Scotty clambered over a gate and came up indignantly. 'You waited till that calf was on the way and then you sneaked off, you treacherous cad, you. Cressida would never

134

play a low trick like that without your lying assurances that I wasn't able to come.'

'How could you leave that cow in her hour of trial? Bull or heifer?'

'Bull, of course. They're always bulls, blast them. What did you and Cress talk about?'

'We talked about you.'

'You're a barefaced liar. Did you get up to any monkey tricks? If you did, I'll make sure that nobody can ever save your life again. A fine friend,' sneered the defrauded Scotty. 'A fine return for what I did for you. I dragged you, foot by foot—'

'Well, you could have followed us,' pointed out Christopher.

'I couldn't. That cow behaved as though nobody's ever had a calf before.' He sighed. 'Oh well, I don't blame you. I'd have done the same in your place. That's a wonderful girl, Chris, old son.'

'Yes. She's—well, I—'

'Oh, I know what you think of her. I can give you the names of at least four poor fish round these parts who all feel just as you do—and I do. If a man's got any blood circulating in his system, he doesn't have to look at Cress more than once before he feels it all rushing up to his head. And you don't suppose she doesn't get a lot of attention in London, do you? Just because you didn't happen to run across her doesn't mean that the other three million fellows missed her. You just happen to have struck a lucky time when you can have her more or less to yourself, but when you get up to Town, you'll have to fall back in the queue. That's why you find me so big about this. If I thought you had any more chance than the others, I'd feed you to the bull, piece by piece. Mind you, short of marrying me, I don't think Cressida could hit on a better fellow than you.'

'Thanks. Tell me, Scotty, how often does her father come down?'

'The handsome major?' Scotty turned and walked slowly back beside Christopher. 'Oh, in the summer, quite frequently. He invites people down and then gets here in time to stand in that picturesque doorway exuding the well-known charm.'

The words jarred on Christopher, and he found himself, to his own surprise, speaking abruptly.

'I like him,' he said.

Scotty stopped in his tracks and stared speechlessly for a moment.

'But you—but you haven't seen him!' he said.

'Yes, I have. I met him when I went up the second time to Greensleeves to fetch Cressida. She wasn't about, and her father came out.'

'Ah!' said Scotty, walking on and speaking in an unreadable tone. 'And then what?'

'He showed me round. It's a lovely place, and he made it pretty interesting. He's got some good stuff there.'

'Ah,' said Scotty again. 'You think so?'

'I saw some of it. I bought a gun off him.'

Once more Scotty came to a dead halt and turning, stared at Christopher.

'You ... you bought a gun off him,' he repeated.

Christopher frowned.

'Well—yes. Anything wrong with that? Bit quick, I admit, but it happened to come up and we made a deal.'

'You made a deal,' repeated Scotty woodenly. 'He made a deal.' He threw his head back suddenly and gave a shout of laughter. 'He—made—a—deal,' he said choking. 'Oh Lord, did you hear that? He made a deal.'

Anger, slow but hot, rose in Christopher. He was not often angry, and he could not remember the last time he had been angry with Scotty, but the laughter, and something in Scotty's tone, sent the blood to his head.

'Shut up,' he said.

Scotty checked a burst of laughter and, taking a step closer, peered unbelievingly through the half-light, into Christopher's face. As he saw its stony expression, he sobered abruptly, and for a few moments there was silence. Then he spoke slowly.

'I said something?' he asked.

'Yes. No—you didn't. But—well, to tell you the truth, I enjoyed going round that house more than I can tell you, Scotty. Some people like one thing and some people like another, and I like houses. And I liked Major Gray. I thought he was a decent fellow, and if you're trying to tell me he's sold me a pup, you're wrong. He didn't try to sell me anything—I saw the gun and I asked if I could buy it. If anything, he went out of his way to tell me it wasn't worth much—at least, that it wasn't genuine.' He paused for a moment. 'But if you want to tell me anything about him, then go ahead and I'll listen. But—well—don't laugh before you let me in on the joke, that's all.'

Scotty thrust his hands into his pockets and hunched his shoulders in a gesture Christopher knew well.

'I slipped up,' he acknowledged soberly. 'I slipped up badly. I forgot he was Cress's father.'

'So did I,' said Christopher.

'You mean'—Scotty sounded incredulous—'you mean you like him—you like him on his own account?'

'Why not? He's a good-looking, decent chap.'

'He's good-looking,' acknowledged Scotty slowly. 'Perhaps he's decent, too. I suppose it depends which way you look at it.'

'Look at what?'

'And I forgot,' went on Scotty, disregarding the question, 'that it's four years since I bought something off him, and I forgot—and it'll do me good to remember—that he had the same effect on me, when I first saw him, as he had on you.' He reached over, extracted a case from Christopher's pocket and helped himself to a cigarette, waiting until Christopher produced a lighter. 'Thanks.' He walked a few paces to a tree stump and sat on it, elbows on knees, looking up at Christopher. 'Yes, I'd forgotten,' he said again.

'Why don't you like him?'

'Well, I didn't say I didn't like him.'

'All right, then, let's have it the other way. What's wrong with him?'

'I didn't say there was anything wrong with him. When I laughed, I was laughing because—well, in four years, if someone comes to you and tells you they've made a deal with Major Gray, you'll laugh.'

'All right, I'll laugh. Why?'

'Because,' Scotty's voice came through the semi-darkness, 'because that's how he lives—by making deals. A lot of people make their living by selling things. They set up a shop and get behind a counter and do all they can to get out of you more for their wares than they paid themselves. The more shop-window they can put up, the more they can charge you. They can even over-charge you. You can go into a stinking little hole calling itself Antiques and you can pay through the nose for something the proprietor picked up for a song. You've been cheated, of course, but, between the shopkeeper and the public, it's a game of do-me-down-if-you-can. Now this Major Gray

139

makes a living, and a nice comfortable living, by doing just what he did when you met him the other day. He gets you into his house—in your case you got in by chance, but he was there to receive the next visitors by appointment—and he acts the squire and shows you his treasures—all the heirlooms. Before you leave the house, you've persuaded him—and sometimes he takes a lot of persuading—you've persuaded him to let you buy something that's taken your fancy, or something he's brought—and oh! how subtly—to your notice. He won't live down here because it pays him better not to. He lives in his club in Town, and during the season, he keeps his eyes open for the rather special kind of tourist he needs for his purposes. They have to be a special kind; cultured, because only the cultured could appreciate to the full the beauties—inside and out—of Greensleeves. They have to have money, or he's wasting his time. They have to be, in a sense, connoisseurs and collectors. He doesn't invite them down. He talks, quietly and with a whimsical regret, about Greensleeves. He gives them date and period, and if they've any imagination, they can't help setting him against the background—and he fits. He completes the picture and makes it, to anybody interested in the English scene, perfect. Can they, they ask hesitatingly—they hesitate because they might be touchy, those dispossessed squires—can they by any chance ...? Well, yes, they can. Oddly enough, he's going down himself the next day to see his caretaker. If they care to drive down, he'd be delighted to show them over the house. They come, and they almost invariably make a deal. If they don't he doesn't press. He can afford to waste a day now and then. If you're here in August, you'll find him almost every afternoon at the open door, handsome, slipping faultlessly into place against the splendid English scene. And there you have it. He does what every merchant does—buys low and sells high. Whether his methods stick in your throat or not is something you decide for yourself. I just happen, in the most extraordinary way, to have found out more about him than most people know, so I suppose that makes me prejudiced.'

The voice ceased, and it was some time before Christopher spoke.

'You'd better let me have it all,' he said.

'There's not much. I bought this place from him—I told you—before I ever saw it. I'd have bought Greensleeves too, if he'd tried to sell it to me—but I think he'd decided, even then, how he was going to use it. I had a bit of a job finding the money—hadn't got the other place cleared up and I went to my trustees. They helped me out, but one of them—old-fashioned kind of chap—thought I'd been hypnotized to buy the place I'd never seen, and so he went to a lot of trouble to find out something about Gray. He found out where he has a lot of his fakes made, and who the people are who fix up the new to look even more convincing than the old. All interesting, and none of it criminal, of course. You can't be had up for selling copies as copies. And in my case—and in yours, of course, there's always Cressida to keep us from complaining.'

'What does ... what does Cressida think of it?'

'Cress? Well, it took her a bit of time to see what he was up to. She was in Switzerland when he inherited the place—she was brought up in a school in Lausanne. Her mother died when she was eight, and she didn't see much of her father, one way and another. She thought—when she heard about Greensleeves—that she'd have a home at last, but when she saw it, she gave up the idea. There was no money, only the house and its contents. She soon got to understand that it was being used as a kind of antique shop, and decided to get out and get a job. She tried nursing, as I told you—but she went at it too hard and it knocked her over. She had a hard time for a while, and then she was offered one or two modelling jobs, and she hasn't looked back since. She doesn't talk about her father and, so, of course, I don't. I often feel I'd like to find some kind, quick method of putting him out of the way, but that's only because I think he's let Cress down, not because I've any strong feelings about him myself. That gun you bought—you'll see another, and then another, exactly the same, hanging on that wall next time you go. You'll see it, and he'll know you've seen it, and he'll know that you know that—and so on and so on. He won't mind. He regards himself as someone in a legitimate trade; you're one of the customers and the deal's over and done with.' Scotty rose and ground out his cigarette. 'Well, that's the major. I hope you won't like your gun any less.'

Christopher made no answer. He would not, he felt, like his gun less, but his thoughts on the man who sold it to him were oddly mixed. He saw, again and again, the house and, standing before it, its splendidly fitting owner. He found it difficult and, to his surprise, deeply distasteful to have to adjust the focus in the light of the facts he had learned from Scotty; hearing them from anyone else, he would simply have disbelieved them. He was not inexperienced enough to resent having been taken in by appearances, but he knew that the afternoon had been one of peculiar pleasure, and that he had warmed to Major Gray in a way which he now looked back upon as extraordinary.

'Like biting into one of those perfect-looking cherries,' said Scotty, following his thoughts, 'and finding a worm inside.'

'I thought,' said Christopher, 'that he was a—a particularly nice fellow.'

143

'Who wouldn't?' asked Scotty. 'After all, he's a confidence man, when all's said and done, and who ever made a success of that job unless they could inspire confidence? Always beats me when women—and my life's getting so narrow that when I say women nowadays, you can take it that I mean Mrs Garcia—when women look at the criminal's photograph and say: "Well, fancy, with a nice face like that." Any fellow placed as Gray is, can sell off family pieces to visitors and tourists and make a nice little bit on the side, all tax-free, but it takes an artist to stage it as he does. And when you look at it, he gives pretty good value. I happened to see him selling an Australian couple one of those medals he does so well out of. Did he show you one? Well, he will. These Australians bought one for a stiff figure—it was supposed to have been one made during the Civil War, between 1642 and '46, by the famous Thomas Simon who was noted, in case you didn't know, as one of the most famous English medallists of all time. Not genuine, of course. He told them again and again, and laughed at them—nice laugh he's got—for being so keen on it. Well, they bought it, and I bet it's made them happier than anything they ever bought. They'll never—as you'll never—forget that afternoon in that house, treading, not exactly where the Saints had trod, but where Warwick the Kingmaker had bed and breakfast, and where Monmouth and Katherine Howard slept—not together, naturally, since she left about a hundred years before he rode up. I've seen a lot of historic houses, and I've been taken round them by some elegant people, indeed—but for transporting the jaded human back, right back, out of this atomic age and into a state of mind where peace comes flooding in and you hear the swish-swish of brocade and the twang of the cittern; for merging into the lovely background and, with superb artistry, becoming part of it, give me Major Gray. It's a shop he's got there, and he's a salesman, and what can you find wrong with that?'

'Nothing—much.'

'No. But you find that it leaves a bad taste. And I don't think that's altogether because we're both in love with his daughter. That may have something to do with it, of course, because one of these days, the major'll go too far. These artists have a way of over-reaching themselves. At the moment, our friend's doing pretty well and keeping it nice and legal, but all these confidence boys get over-confident, and then they reach out towards bigger spoils—and then the police rub their eyes and stretch and look round to see where the smell's coming from. And that, I think, is what Cressida's frightened of. She's got a good head, has Cress. She's had to learn a lot these last four years, and she's learnt it fast.'

'I can't see,' said Christopher, 'why he didn't

sell the house.'

'He wouldn't have got his price, and if he had, he wouldn't have got more than about three per cent on his money, like us all. That wouldn't have brought him a tenth of what he makes this way. And, as I said, all tax-free.' Scotty turned in the direction of home, and Christopher fell slowly into step beside him. Neither man spoke for some time.

'I've lowered your spirits,' said Scotty at last. 'I might have kept my mouth shut, but if you're in love with Cressida, you'd better know. You are,' he inquired, wistfully, 'in love with Cressida?'

'Yes,' said Christopher. 'I am.' He glanced at his friend with an expression in which affection, anxiety, and pity were oddly mingled. 'I'd like your comments,' he said.

After a pause Scotty gave them.

'Nobody,' he said, 'can help being in love with her. I was myself, once, and I wouldn't get out of the way for any stray suitor that showed up. But when you showed up I knew it would be all right—why did you think I sent you up that first day? I knew that you ... well ...'

'Well?' prompted Christopher.

'All I want for her,' said Scotty cryptically, 'is the best. You have my blessing.'

146

CHAPTER NINE

Cressida Gray had spent a good deal of time, during the past four years, wishing that her upbringing—excellent though it had been— had been designed with a view to equipping her more fully for the pace and harshness of modern living.

On her mother's death, which had occurred shortly after her eighth birthday, she had been sent by her father to her mother's old school in Lausanne; here the staff, a good many of whom remembered her mother, received her kindly and gave her the same sound education, the same care and attention that they had given her mother. But the principles, which had done very well for a cherished and protected young woman of a generation ago, had not proved so useful in the new world into which Cressida walked; the training she had been given regarding the correct behaviour in polite society was of little use now that society had grown less polite; and the young men and women she had met under the general chaperonage of her guardians had been entirely unlike the uninhibited generation she met for the first time when she came to try her fortune in London.

She had hoped, at eighteen, that her father would change his restless, roving manner of life and settle somewhere where she could live with him and make use of the undoubted gifts of homemaking she possessed. But he had remained abroad, and Cressida stayed on at school in Switzerland and accepted at last a junior teaching post.

When Major Gray learned that Greensleeves had been left to him, he had sent for his daughter, asking her to bring with her Émile and Zoute, an old couple who had worked in her mother's old home near Lausanne, and with whom Cressida had always kept in touch. The three arrived at Grenton; Émile and Zoute took over their duties as gardener and caretaker, but for Cressida there followed a long and painful period of adjustment.

There was no home; it was not long before she saw that her hopes of living at Greensleeves with her father were not to be realized. There were other disappointments in store, the chief being the gradual realization that her father was not the close, understanding guide and companion she had hoped to find. He was what he had always been during his visits to her throughout the years—gay, charming, amusing. He was still gay, he was even more charming, but she found him less amusing. Far from being guide or guardian, she found him entirely free from any sense of obligation or responsibility. He had ceased to pay her school fees when her school days ended, but she had imagined that, since she had given up her work at his request, he would have some suggestions to make about her future. Her future, she found, was to be her own affair. He would maintain Greensleeves; already he was exploiting its possibilities. He would live at his club in London and come down to Grenton now and then. He made his plans calmly and told her of them when they were completed; he made no inquiries about her own.

It was a situation which would have tried a more experienced young woman than Cressida. She had little money; her father intimated, charmingly, ruefully, that he could not give her an allowance. She was virtually a stranger in her homeland, without training, without any knowledge or experience of working conditions, and without anybody to whom she could go for advice.

Her early efforts at settling down were ill-judged and unsuccessful, but during the months of struggle and loneliness, she found one friend—Scotty Linden. It was Scotty who begged her not to undertake the nurse's training, and who paid the bills when she broke down; it was Scotty who, unable to manage his own affairs, showed a cool clear-sightedness when advising her about her own. And it was Scotty, and only Scotty, who supported her in the difficult days when her first love affair came to grief.

It was an ill-starred affair, and Cressida,

looking back upon it, knew that she had handled it badly. She had no regrets, however, about her decision in the matter, and a deep, warm feeling of gratitude towards Scotty for his staunch adherence at a time when everybody else blamed her bitterly. He had stood between her and her most spiteful critics, shielded her from a large part of the abuse, and gone to immense trouble to restore her courage and self-confidence and help her to get work. It was Scotty, finally, who remembered someone who knew someone who was related to someone who had once been a model, and by this tortuous route Cressida had gained the first footing in her present profession. From there she had gone on alone, with growing success; she had gained assurance and poise, and she had conquered the feeling of inferiority that had gripped her when she had seen girls far younger than herself managing their lives with an air of experienced ease. She knew, now, that she had wasted a good many years waiting to be settled in life; a sheltered upbringing was all very well if one did not come too abruptly out of shelter. She had been ill-prepared, ill-equipped; she had waited hopefully to be launched in life instead of using her own initiative and launching herself; she had, she told herself contemptuously, shown all the qualities of a parasite feeling round for something to cling to, and she deserved a good deal less than her present happiness and security.

She was very happy. She liked her work; she had grown to like England; she liked her widening circle of friends. She had a deep affection for Scotty; about her feelings for Christopher, she preferred, at present, not to think.

Mrs Belchamber, examining her from every angle, came to trust her sufficiently to sit with Josette whenever she was too busy to do so herself; the rest of the time Cressida spent obeying orders and keeping up the morale of Mrs Garcia, who declared that the new régime had already taken ten pounds off her weight.

'Fading away, they think I am, at home,' she confided to Cressida. 'If Nero 'imself came back, you and I couldn't be more at beck and call. This is the fourth time I've washed this kitchen floor, and these floors aren't made for it. They're made for rough boots to come in and out of. This is a farm-'ouse, not a smart sort of villa, and I liked it better when it looked like a farm-'ouse. And so did Mr Linden. Mr Linden 'asn't been comfortable since it all got cleaned up.'

'He'll get used to cleanliness,' said Mrs Belchamber, appearing from nowhere with the speed and unexpectedness that made Mrs Garcia feel she had materialized, like a ghost. 'We'll all get used to it.'

Mrs Garcia made no reply. She was satisfying herself, for the twentieth time, that

151

Mrs Belchamber wore ordinary house shoes without rubber soles, and not, as such stealthy approaches argued, felt-soled slippers. She decided at last that there must be a sound-deadening device hidden in the black hat. She rose from her task of scrubbing and surveyed the result of her labours.

'Could eat off it,' was her opinion, as she went outside to empty the bucket.

'I've suspected that Mr Scott does,' commented Mrs Belchamber acidly to Cressida. 'If I ever felt I had a mission in life, I should feel it now—the need to prevent what was once a gentleman from degenerating into a peasant.'

'You mean Scotty?' asked Cressida in surprise.

'Certainly. Have you ever seen anybody who had standards letting them go so completely in so short a time? He was reared as a gentleman; now he dresses like a scarecrow, eats what's thrown at him by that you-know-who outside there, watches his possessions go to ruin under his nose, lives the life of a hind and smells like a perambulating pigsty.'

'Oh—no!' protested Cressida. 'He—'

'You have no nose, my dear girl, but mine is extremely sensitive. No, Mrs Garcia, the bucket is wiped out properly and put over *there*. Thank you. You were late this morning.'

'Madam,' said Mrs Garcia with dignity, 'it's my 'usband. He didn't get back.'

'Back? Back from where?'

'I shouldn't care to say,' said Mrs Garcia darkly. ''E said 'e was going to London in the course of his duty, but there was no need for 'im to take Nellie Crason with 'im and keep 'er there till the last train 'ad gone. It won't be the first time,' said the wronged wife with resignation, 'and it won't be the last. When I married Howsay, they all warned me that 'e was of a roving dispersion.'

'Married who?'

'Howsay, Madam. That's what Mr Garcia's Christian name is, if you can call it a Christian name, my sister says. It's pronounced with a haitch and not a J. 'E don't like to be called Joe, like people call him—he prefers me to call him Howsay. It's a matter of 'ow you say it, like the little girl upstairs. When my sister says it's Josette, I tell 'er it's not. Schozette, I tell her, like in French.'

'Well, don't go away until you've done your full time,' said Mrs Belchamber, coming back to the point. 'Late come, late go.'

'Certainly, Madam.' Nothing could exceed Mrs Garcia's dignity. 'But I can't 'elp having my troubles, and a husband who keeps me short and spends his substance on chambermaids is a 'eavy weight on me.'

'Well, use a heavy weight on him,' advised Mrs Belchamber briskly. 'No woman needs to lie down and let a man walk over her.'

'There's nothing to keep him at home,'

153

mourned Mrs Garcia. 'No little 'ands. If our union had been blessed, 'e would have—'

'—gone off just the same. Now we'll start on those spoons.'

'Was your union blessed, Madam?' asked Mrs Garcia, starting on them.

'It was,' said Mrs Belchamber crisply.

'It was?' Mrs Garcia stared at her. 'You mean you had children, Madam?'

'I mean I didn't. Now sparingly with the polish, if you please, and generous with the rubbing. Cressida, I should like your help upstairs.'

She swept upstairs and Cressida, a little smile on her lips, followed.

'We'll do the boys' beds first. That woman will work better if she has no opportunity to chat.'

'I suppose she doesn't get much chance to chat at home,' said Cressida. 'With four nephews and—'

'She's either grumbling because her own union hasn't been blessed, or because her sister's has. You can't have it both ways, you know. What she ought to do is try and get hold of some of her husband's wages before he's had time to spend them on other women. There are various ways of controlling men, but apron-strings aren't as good for tethering a man as purse-strings are. She rather enjoys being the injured wife.'

'She says she loves him, and—'

'Love!' Nothing could exceed the surprise, the scorn, the contempt Mrs Belchamber put into the word. She whisked off a sheet, shook it and tossed one end to Cressida. 'Love,' she said, 'is the most overworked, the most misrepresented word in the language. The impulse that's called love is given far too much space in the public consciousness. I'm not saying that it doesn't deserve a high place among the emotions, but I do claim that it ought to be presented in a more sane, a less hysterical way. No young person gets a chance to think about anything else ... Every ear is filled with the word; it meets it in verse, in song, at the cinema, on the stage, off the stage. Every schoolgirl, every errand boy learns a hundred worthless songs, all caterwauling on the one theme: love. Love, love, love. If a girls gets to seventeen or eighteen without falling in love, she begins to think she isn't normal. Have you ever been in love?'

'Yes.'

'That's the sort of thing I mean. It's regarded as something that everybody has to suffer, like universal measles. You never hear anybody point out that it isn't necessarily a disease that need be caught by everyone. I myself, I can tell you now, have never—tuck that in more tightly, will you please?—have never been in love.'

Cressida stared at her.

'But-but if you—I mean you were—'

'I was married. Certainly I was; more than once.'

'M-more than...'

'Three times. Twice because I knew what I was doing, and once because I didn't. When I was a young girl,' explained Mrs Belchamber, 'we spent our time either looking for a husband, or waiting until somebody found one for us. I was brought up by an aunt who was well known for finding husbands for girls. She found my first husband for me. He came from Luxembourg and his name was Federico Besnard, and I was no more in love with him than the man in the moon. But everybody insisted that any girl who could look at Federico's wide shoulders and fine moustaches without feeling something, must be very odd. So by looking at them long enough, and hard enough, I managed to feel enough to get married on. Nowadays, of course, girls are more sensible, but the legend still persists. Men, naturally enough, keep it alive; they live and die in the belief that women can't get on without them. Some can't, poor creatures, but then again, some can, and very well, too. Nature gives some women more sense than senses, and I only wish they'd use the sense instead of being influenced by a lot of clap-trap about what women were made for. I hope you'll use your head and not be carried away.'

Cressida said nothing; she felt that her voice would check the flow of reminiscence, and she was longing to learn something of Federico's successors. She smoothed a blanket and waited hopefully.

'When my first husband died,' Mrs Belchamber went on in an unusually dreamy tone, 'I thought of coming back to England—but he had left a great deal of property in one place and another, and I had to see to it; while I was seeing to it, I met my second husband—he and my third husband were both a good deal older than I was, but I buried them both. I thought of settling at Melhampton with Belchamber after we were married, and we came back to England for a time, but the climate got on his nerves, so we went back to Switzerland. People used to say that it was my money they were after, and it may be so, though I had excellent teeth and a good head of hair; if it was my money, they were disappointed, because I don't allow other people to manage my affairs. But it all comes back to what I said—if my aunt hadn't filled my head with nonsense about love, I would have refused Federico and spent my life far more usefully than by listening to a lot of foreigners trying to get their tongues round English. I spoke excellent French, naturally, but I could always express myself better in my own language.'

Cressida bent over her work, unwilling to look at the harsh, wrinkled countenance before her and associate it with a sentiment which, to her, was seemly only in the young and comely. She tried very hard to believe that Mrs Belchamber had once been young, and tried without success to trace the emotions of the long-dead Federico. The wrinkles might not then have been there, but the gimlet eyes, the sharp-pointed nose surely were. She could only suppose that Federico's moustaches had been so luxuriant as to obscure his view. The whole matter was beyond her comprehension, for though her ideas of what a thrice-married woman would look like were vague, Mrs Belchamber fitted into none of them. She put aside, finally, any thought of allure, and decided that the trio, from Federico onwards, had been in search of a home.

Mrs Belchamber, in her turn, was reviewing her impressions of the girl before her, and found herself ready to acknowledge that, as girls went, Cressida had some pleasing qualities. She had none of the fussiness that Mrs Belchamber detested in women; her movements were quiet and graceful, her voice low and musical; animation, the watcher was pleased to see, lay in her eyes and her expression and did not extend, unnecessarily, to over-emphasis in speech or gesture. She was told to do a thing, and she did it. She didn't want it repeated, or explained; she heard the order and carried it out. An undoubtedly good-looking girl, she nevertheless did less to adorn Nature than some of the over-painted hussies Mrs Belchamber could name; and—greatest test of all—though aware of the admiration of Mr Heron and of the odious Mr Scott, satisfied the feminist in Mrs Belchamber by keeping both men at arm's length.

Christopher was scarcely at arm's-length. It would have taken a harder heart than Cressida's to resist the warmth and charm of his wooing. He was impetuous without being importunate; he made ardent and, Cressida realized, expert love, but demanded little response. He brought all the weight of his personality and charm to bear, and Cressida knew that she was giving way before it.

There was no sign, as yet, that any steps were being taken to trace Mrs Belchamber, but Christopher thought it unlikely that those who felt themselves responsible for her would allow her to disappear without making any efforts to find her. She had not gone entirely out of reach; there was, as Scotty pointed out, a slender thread reaching back to the world she had left. Mrs Garcia was a talker; her sister was related by marriage to the village constable; the village constable would carry items of gossip into the wider sphere of Grenton, and, if inquiries were made there, Mrs Belchamber's whereabouts would not long remain a secret.

'And then,' he ended, 'our troubles'll be over.'

'Yours will,' corrected Christopher.

'Mine will. Tonight's my bath night, and

something tells me that the old lady's going to glue her ear to the door to hear me step in and splash.'

'You'll step in and splash,' promised Christopher. 'I'll see to it personally.'

'The skin,' said Scotty, 'has a natural grease, and boiling it off too frequently does the system no good at all. Did you ever hear of a farmer who took a hot bath every night of his life? Why, they'd laugh at you! Why don't you tell this woman that this country runs an efficient sanitary department and doesn't need her as a volunteer?'

'I'll tell her,' promised Christopher, 'when I've finished de-lousing you tomorrow night.'

'De—' Scotty's voice rose to a scandalized yelp. 'Did you say what I thought you said?'

'Yes,' said Christopher.

'Oh. Well, it isn't only our bodies she's taking charge of. Our souls, too,' said Scotty. 'You've got to get the car out at seven-thirty sharp tomorrow morning.'

'What for?'

'To take her to church. St Jude's—that's right away past the town hall. Then you wait there—outside or inside, according to inclination—and bring her home again. Then at ten-fifteen, you take a cargo of boys to *their* church. She asked them what they were, and it turned out they were Holy Romans, so that if it had been left to you, she says, they'd never have got to Mass and their souls would've been

160

damned eternally.'

'But,' protested Christopher, 'they're in quarantine and—'

'I told her that. I told her. But when women start out in pursuit of their Christian duty, don't get in their way, because you only get mown down. I said: "Are you going to send those two boys into that great big church, to breathe germs over the elect?" and she said she'd lived too long in Catholic countries not to understand how they felt about regular attendance and hell-fire, and she said that if their Church is all it sets up to be, the germs won't stand a chance. So you'd better fill up with petrol, son. Oh, and I forgot to tell you. There was a telegram for you.'

'Who from?'

'From *whom*. It was from that place in France. Hautiers something. And it was signed Thérèse Desmoulins. Who's she?'

'Children's nurse. What did she say?'

'Well, I don't want to worry you—'

'Well, come on—out with it.'

'—or to upset you, or—'

'Oh, come *on*, come *on*! Don't take all night.'

'—or to cause you any undue—hey, take your hands off me, you uncouth ruffian!'

'She said?'

'She said that her daughter's still ill, and you can damn well guess what she's got.'

'No!' exclaimed Christopher.

'Yeah!' said Scotty. 'Measles!'

CHAPTER TEN

'"The Gallery,"' read Mrs Belchamber, seated by the window in the sickroom, '"consists of two rooms. In the Salle Chanzy can be found various relics of the Defense Nationale in 1870–1871,"' She paused to peer over her spectacles. 'Do you know about this Defense Nationale?'

'No,' said Josette.

'Oh. Well, I can't enlighten you, but you ought to know your own history. Put that arm inside the clothes, now, before you get pneumonia. "Relics may be seen of General Bourbaki"—if that's a French name, I'm a Dutchman "and General de la Motte-Rouge." Well, that one's French enough. "On the walls are the sword of Miss Antoinette LIX"—now who would she be?—"and the wooden leg of"—good gracious—"the wooden leg of General Louis." Well, if I'd wanted to look for somebody's wooden leg, I shouldn't have thought of looking on the wall, and that's a fact. Now, are you paying attention?'

'Yes, thank you,' said Josette politely.

'It's a pity you never went to Paris. Everybody should know their own capital. Now just think—when you do go, you'll go as a foreign tourist instead of a little French girl, and it won't be the same at all. Well, where was

I? Disgraceful print,' grumbled Mrs Belchamber, peering. '"The Salle des Médailles is at present in transformation." Now what do they mean by that? If they mean they're changing it round, why don't they say so? "The Salle Ney comprises the..."'

Josette lay contentedly in the big bed listening and looking. There was a good deal to look at, for Mrs Belchamber's hat was illuminated on the one side by the shaded light from the window, and on the other by the low flames of the fire; the grey curls were now pink, now black; the reading glasses sent flashes of light darting whenever the reading gave way to comment or question.

There were always, moreover, the spectacles. Mrs Belchamber had six pairs, and Josette now knew them all; the rimless *pince-nez*, used when she did the cooking or carried up hot, steaming drinks, and convenient for taking off and wiping hurriedly; the pair of long-distance glasses; the pair of short-distance glasses; the fascinating bi-focal pair, which had an upper and a lower storey; a pair of elegant lorgnettes, which she had once brought out in order to polish the slender, jewelled handle, and a large pair, three-cornered, horn-rimmed, which she used, she said, when motoring.

When she was tired of reading, she sewed. Scotty's table linen—what there was of it—was in shreds, but Mrs Belchamber grieved less over the condition of the once-beautiful fabric than over Mrs Garcia's crude attempts at repair. Her comments to Cressida on the rapid decline and fall of Scotty's living standards grew even more terse and uncomplimentary.

'It's a matter of soft rearing,' she said, pushing the needle through a patch in a tablecloth. 'Soft surroundings, everything padded, and no discipline. Take this Mr Scott'—she jerked her head in the direction of her host, now crossing the stackyard below. 'His own cowman, if he had one, would have more pride. I don't like shiftlessness, wherever I find it. What are you showing that child? She shouldn't be using her eyes. What's that you've got?'

'It's your pincushion,' explained Cressida, who was sitting at the head of Josette's bed, with Josette watching her hands. 'We're making a spell.'

'You're what?' Mrs Belchamber jerked off her spectacles in order, apparently, to hear better.

'Making a spell.' Cressida and Josette were now holding the pincushion between them, and Cressida was making a new pattern with the pins.

'What sort of nonsense is this,' demanded Mrs Belchamber.

Cressida looked up for a second, eyes mischievous, lips curled in amusement.

'Oh, it isn't nonsense, is it, Josette? We made

a spell yesterday for the spots to go away, and—look—the ones on her arms are going.'

'They are going,' corroborated Josette decisively. 'I counted them yesterday, I counted them today. There are less.'

'Now we're making a spell so's she can eat a custard tomorrow—a great, big custard,' murmured Cressida, her head bent close to Josette's. 'We make *this* pattern—see, Josette?'

'Yes, I see.' Josette took the pincushion and studied it. 'Where shall we put it?'

'You can put it back in my workbasket,' said Mrs Belchamber. 'The spells can work just as well in there, and I'll still have a pincushion. Now then, you boys'—she glared at Robert and Paul, who had clattered upstairs and were peering cautiously round the door—'let me see your shoes.'

'They are clean,' declared Paul.

'Well, that's the first time you've remembered, then,' commented Mrs Belchamber.

'Scotty made us remember,' said Paul. 'He said, "Watch that Madame does not..."' He came to an abrupt stop and, reddening, faced four pairs of eyes fixed expectantly upon him. 'He made us remember,' he ended lamely.

'Ha!' said Mrs Belchamber.

'We made a spell,' said Josette. 'Look.'

Both boys clambered on to the bed and looked.

'What is it?' asked Robert.

165

'A spell. *Une charme*,' explained Josette. 'Tomorrow I shall eat custard.'

'*Tiens!*' Paul handled the pincushion reverently. '*Est-ce-que*'—he stopped and corrected himself—'Is zis good spell, or bad spell?'

'Well, good, naturally,' said Cressida.

'But if it is good, then it can be bad?' persisted Paul.

'Just like a boy,' grated Mrs Belchamber. 'Will it work, will it tick, will it pull, will it come to pieces. Ah-ah-ah ... you mind your feet on that bed, young man. And now who?' she demanded, looking at the opening door, 'Oh, it's you.'

'Yes.' Christopher entered, his manner more conciliatory than the one he usually showed to the enemy. She had the upper hand; if he moved without caution and circumspection, she would dismiss him from the room—and from Cressida's presence. He felt fawning and hypocritical, but he would undergo even this humiliation in order to sit and watch Cressida moving about the room, bending over the bed, performing quiet, graceful services for Josette. He had ready the excuse, the passport without which he was not permitted to enter the sickroom. 'I've had a letter from Thérèse.'

'From Thérèse!' The children were instantly alert. 'From Thérèse? Has Monique,' asked Josette, 'got spots, like me?'

'Lots and lots of spots.'

166

'Read what she says,' demanded Mrs Belchamber.

Christopher gave her a cold, surprised look. It was obvious that she was without the elementary decencies. To wish to hear the contents of a letter which was no possible concern of hers—

She returned his look with as cold a stare.

'I suppose,' she said, 'your French isn't up to it.'

His French was certainly not up to it. Thérèse's writing was all but illegible, her phrasing incomprehensible and her spelling unrecognizable.

'They can read it for themselves,' he said, handing the letter to Robert.

'I will read it for you,' said Robert tactlessly. 'But it is bad to see.'

'Show me,' said Paul, peering over his brother's shoulder. 'I can read it.'

Together, with difficulty, they deciphered the spidery letters. Thérèse, they found, was well; Henri and René were well; Edouard and Josephine were well; Jean and Julien were well, and also Henri, and—

'She's said that,' interrupted Mrs Belchamber, irritably. 'Don't let's have all that again.'

'There are two Henri,' explained Paul. 'One is a boy and one is a'—he groped—'*un furet.*'

'Ferret,' said Cressida.

'Yes. It digs out things,' began Robert, but

Paul stopped him.

'Everyone knows,' he said. 'Go on.'

'—and Nicholas is well, but his brother is not well.'

'He has a brother?' asked Josette in surprise. 'What brother?'

'You know quite well,' said Paul, in rapid French. 'But of course you know. He is the one who came on the horse.'

'Ah ... *ça*!' It was clear that Josette had not, at all events, forgotten the horse. 'Ah, *oui*—'

'*Ong Anglais. Ong Anglais*,' rasped Mrs Belchamber. 'Don't forget that your cousin hasn't lived abroad, as Cressida and I have. It isn't polite to speak in a language he can't follow. Now go on.'

Monique had been ill, very ill, but the doctor was now satisfied that she would make a rapid recovery. A month would have to pass, however—not less than a full month—before she could travel with her mother to England. Henri would arrange the passages.

'Henri the man,' put in Paul swiftly, to the excessive amusement of himself, his brother and sister. Even Cressida, to Paul's gratification, enjoyed the joke very much. When order had been restored, the rest of the letter was read; the children were much missed, and old Jules was saving up in the hope of one day paying them a visit in England. It would not be his first visit, explained Thérèse. He had been before, fifty-six years ago, when he was a

168

lad. She sent a thousand embraces to her charges, and her respectful salutations to Christopher from herself, Monique, Henri, René, Édouard, Josephine, Jean and Julien, Pierre and Siegfried and—

'Siegfried? What's Siegfried doing in with that lot?' inquired Mrs Belchamber. 'Another ferret?'

'He is a horse,' explained Robert. '—And Siegfried and Gautier.'

'That covers the entire population,' said Mrs Belchamber. 'Is that the lot?'

'That is all, and her name is here—Thérèse Desmoulins.'

'Thérèse which?'

'Desmoulins.'

'Oh. What's she coming over for?' asked Mrs Belchamber of Christopher. 'These children are too old for a nurse!'

'Thérèse cooks,' explained Robert, 'and she mends our clothes, and she washes them, and she makes up the beds and sweeps the rooms.'

'I wish Mrs Garcia could hear you,' commented Mrs Belchamber. 'And what does she want to bring over that child for?'

'What child?' Paul sounded mystified.

'This Monique. Isn't that her child?'

'Her child! Ha ha ha ha ha!' Paul threw back his head and gave way to a peal of delighted laughter.

'Her child!' echoed Robert, holding his sides, while Josette, with a giggle, wriggled to

169

and fro in delight.

'All right, all right. When you've finished enjoying the joke,' said Mrs Belchamber acidly, 'we can all share it.'

'Thérèse is—well, she isn't young,' explained Christopher delicately. 'And Monique is—in the children's eyes, I mean—scarcely young, either.'

'She makes the fires,' said Paul, still rocking delightedly, 'and she cleans the windows and she washes the dishes.'

'Well, that's most of the work taken care of,' said Mrs Belchamber folding her work and rising. 'If they were here, I shouldn't be going downstairs to get the tea. You two,' she fixed Robert and Paul with a beady eye. 'Come when I call you. And you, too,' she added to Christopher. 'Cressida, I'll send up the boys with your tea and Josette's barley water.'

She went towards the door and Robert, rising from his perch on the foot of the bed, hurried across and opened it for her, giving her an odd, stiff little bow as she passed him. He shut it behind her and turned to look at Josette's face, puckered in disgust.

'You do not like the barley?' he asked.

Josette, face screwed in distaste, shook her head.

'It'll do you good, you know,' said Cressida, gently.

'I will make a spell,' said Paul, reaching for the pincushion. 'I will make a bad spell for the

170

barley, and then we shall see. Perhaps Madame will not be able to find it when I have put the spell.'

He rearranged the pins carefully, watched by his brother and sister. Over their heads, Christopher's eyes sought those of Cressida, but, after one glance, she dropped hers to Paul's small brown hands and sat quietly watching the spell being prepared.

'There!' said Paul. 'That is a bad spell.'

'It is like a map,' said Robert, studying it. 'A map of France. See how it goes.'

'It is a spell,' insisted Paul. 'See—a bad spell.'

'This is only a game, you know,' put in Cressida. 'It wouldn't be very nice if we could make bad spells, would it?'

'Yes—it would,' said Paul firmly.

'Why not?' asked Christopher. 'There are good fairies and bad fairies; kind witches and cruel witches, bad giants and not-so-bad giants. If there are good spells, there must be bad spells.' His voice dropped to a mysterious whisper, and he looked at Paul with a conspiratorial air. 'But you must put the spell near the fire,' he said under his breath. 'You must warm it; if it isn't warm, it won't work.'

'Near the fire?' Paul, the pincushion held carefully in his hands, walked across the room and laid the pincushion on the fender. 'So?' he whispered.

'So,' said Christopher. 'Now you must say:

171

"Spell, Spell, do your work well."'

'"Spell, Spell,"' enjoined Paul, '"do your work well."'

'Don't,' said Cressida, her voice breaking sharply into the hushed tones. 'Don't. Paul—don't be silly. Christopher's only—'

From below there came a harsh call, and Mrs Belchamber's voice came to the ears of the five in the room.

'Come along, come along you boys!'

Paul's face, rosy in the firelight, lost some of its eager glow.

'She is calling,' he said, his voice oddly hesitant. 'It is—'

Robert, in silence, opened the door and stepped outside.

'Madame?' he answered.

'Come along—Josette's barley water,' said Mrs Belchamber, crisply. 'I can't stand here all day.'

Robert gave a backward glance into the room and his eyes met those of his brother. Paul stood up slowly, his hands still cupped round the pincushion, his eyes wide and incredulous and his lips trembling slightly.

'It—it did not get warm,' he faltered. 'It—'

'Come a-long! Come on, somebody,' called Mrs Belchamber irritably. 'I'm not going to—'

They heard her foot on the lowest step, and then a bump, an exclamation of annoyance and a crash. Robert turned slowly and gazed down over the banisters.

172

'What is it?' asked Paul fearfully.

'It is the barley,' said Robert, slowly, still staring down. 'The glass is broken.'

There was a high, triumphant yell from Paul. Cressida started up, flashing a look of reproach at Christopher as she did so.

'Paul—'

Paul was not listening. He had advanced to meet the outraged Mrs Belchamber, who had come upstairs to voice a strong protest.

'It was!' he shouted. 'It was, it was, it was! It was a spell. I made it! It was a bad spell for the barley! It was a spell, a spell!'

'It was a spell!' shouted Paul, holding the pincushion before the bewildered Mrs Belchamber. 'I made it!'

'I don't know what you're talking about,' said Mrs Belchamber, 'but if you'd stop fiddling with my pins and go downstairs, you can pick up those bits of broken glass. If you'd come when I called you, it wouldn't have happened. Don't talk spells to me. If that bottom stair was the same size as the others, I shouldn't have stumbled. Now put your spells away and stop behaving in that French way. English boys don't shout at their elders, and they don't make spells, either. That's a velvet pincushion made by Mr Belchamber's mother when she would have been better occupied sewing her trousseau. She wasn't a witch, though she looked like one, and there are no spells. Now get downstairs, the two of you, and

173

have your tea. Go along.'

Her flat, matter-of-fact tones would have broken a less tenuous spell. Paul put down the pincushion carefully, with the air of one laying aside a weapon. The three children looked calmly at one another, and then the two boys went downstairs. The first spell had worked. There would be others.

Mrs Belchamber followed them down; the mishap having made her temporarily forgetful of her determination to deprive Christopher of a *tête-à-tête*. Left in the semi-darkness, he relaxed against the head of the big bed, looking now at Cressida, sitting at the foot, and now at Josette, who lay and looked up at him with a smile which grew every moment more uncertain and with eyes which closed gradually in sleep. He stretched out an arm and picked up the pincushion which Paul had left on the table.

'Ssh!' Cressida held up a warning forefinger. 'She's asleep.'

Christopher nodded. He was busy rearranging pins.

'Look, Paul,' said Cressida, 'it wasn't really a—'

'Look,' he whispered, in exact imitation of Paul's accent. 'I am ma-king a spell.'

'Don't be silly,' murmured Cressida. 'Go downstairs.'

Christopher finished his work in silence and held it out across the bed. With a frown, half

174

annoyance, half amusement, Cressida looked down at it.

'Well?'

'Don't be frightened,' Christopher's voice was low, but clear. 'It's a good spell. It's for you.'

'Me?'

'Yes. It's to find you an exceptional husband.'

'Thank you. You're very kind, but I'll manage that for myself,' said Cressida. 'Now go to tea.'

'He's to be tall,' went on Christopher, 'and fair, but not too fair—rather my colouring. He's to be strong, in mind as well as in body— and handsome. Something after my type. He's to have enough to keep you comfortably, but he's to have a profession, too—he could be an architect, for example, to design the House Beautiful for you. He must be kind to orphans. He must look at you—just once—and forget all other women for ever. He must be patient, and humble—he mustn't imagine that a girl like you would look at a fellow like him. He must walk hopefully, and be grateful if you look at him just now and then. He must win you gently, and by degrees, and he must cherish you and protect you and hold you closely in his arms and tell you that he loves you with all his heart and hopes that one day you'll marry him and live happily ever after—'

Josette stirred, threw out an arm and turned

restlessly. In a moment, Cressida had bent over her, murmuring soothing sounds, and bending upon Christopher a look full of reproach and accusation.

'There!' she said. 'See what you've done!'

CHAPTER ELEVEN

It was not long before Mrs Belchamber expressed a wish to go over to Greensleeves, making it clear that the ownership of a fine property of her own gave her a clear right to inspect that of others. She would not, she said, trouble Cressida to show her round; she would leave her in charge of the children and walk round by the long way and tell the caretaker she wished to see the place.

The caretaker, explained Cressida, had no authority to show people over the house; her father made it a rule always to act as guide himself.

'Then it's a very silly rule,' said Mrs Belchamber angrily. 'I don't want anybody following on my heels. If he's afraid of people pocketing anything, he shouldn't leave movable articles lying about. By the time he's down here again, we shall all be I don't know where.'

Christopher heard the last sentence with deep relief; it was the first sign she had ever

176

given of impermanence. So cheering was the thought of a future free from the nagging tones, that, on Cressida's explaining that her father was expected on the following afternoon, he surprised himself by offering to escort the old lady across the fields.

'Well, if it's dry,' she said, without further thanks.

It was dry; Christopher walked beside her, uttered some polite platitudes, dissuading her from waving her umbrella threateningly at the bull and marvelled inwardly at the difference between his enchanted walks along these same paths with Cressida and his present unstimulating march beside this . . . he ran over a score of uncomplimentary epithets and compromised with black crow. The poet who gave it as his opinion that woman

Raises our spirits and charms our ears

had obviously never come in contact with this one.

He wondered whether Major Gray, having been appraised of the visit, would feel it worth his while to put on the entire act. The sight of the tall, handsome figure in the doorway, however, proved to him that the major obviously considered no fish too small; his courtly greeting, while having no visible effect upon Mrs Belchamber, roused Christopher's admiration. He performed the introduction as

177

briefly as possible.

'May I introduce Major Gray? This is Mrs Belchamber who's anxious to see the house. It's very kind of you to—'

'Got a sizeable place of my own,' put in Mrs Belchamber. 'Not as old as this, of course. What date's this?'

'It was begun in 1300 and finished in Edward the Second's time,' began Major Gray, with none of the droning staleness of the guide who has said the same thing a thousand times. 'It's not unique, of course—I've—' He broke off and held out a detaining hand. 'You're not going, are you?' he asked Christopher.

'Well, thank you, yes. I just brought Mrs Belchamber across.'

'Well, stay and take her back when she's ready to go,' urged Major Gray charmingly persuasive. 'There's quite a lot you can see on a second visit—unless, of course, you're anxious to hurry back...'

The words 'to Cressida,' unuttered, hung in the air.

'I'll come round with you,' said Christopher quietly.

He followed them round the rooms, speculating as to why Major Gray did not feel it worth while to change even a word of his patter he had used when showing Christopher over the house. Scotty's words came back to him: there was always Cressida to keep young men from becoming too critical. While the major talked, while Mrs Belchamber directed her long, pointed nose in this and that direction, Christopher tried to analyse his own feelings. He studied Major Gray with the intentness that the circumstances permitted, and was amazed at the bitterness that filled him as he recalled his first response to the attractive figure and the charming voice. It had not, he now knew, been entirely due to the spell that the house had laid upon him; it had sprung equally from the personality of his guide. There could be few men past their first youth who could compel this instant liking and trust, who could be in turn poised, oddly boyish, authoritative, amusing—who could pierce, as it now appeared, even so tough a crust as the Belchamber's. He understood, now, his first capitulation, but what he could not understand was his deep, almost bitter regret that what he had seen was, after all, nothing but a mask. There was no man of the kind he had liked so much; there was only this actor.

It was clear—Christopher's mouth twisted in a wry grin—it was clear that he had hitherto given the psychologists less credit than they deserved. He had regarded a complex as part of the new jargon, and here, in the great hall of Greensleeves, he was prepared to offer an apology, for he had amply demonstrated that he himself had a complex; he was that stock character out of a case-book; the posthumous child looking unconsciously for a father. His middle name, he reflected with a surge of self-contempt, ought to be Japhet.

He brought himself back, with an effort, to realities. The act, he saw, was drawing to a close; they were standing in the hall, looking at a table on which stood a spiked candlestick.

'Anglo-Norman,' explained Major Gray, lifting it reverently. 'It's beautiful, isn't it?'

Mrs Belchamber, looking at it keenly, admitted that it was.

'But not, of course, genuine,' went on the major regretfully.

A flicker of surprise passed across Mrs Belchamber's face and was instantly suppressed.

'Thought not,' she said. 'You can always tell.' She put it down carefully and looked at it. 'You wouldn't I suppose, think of selling it?'

It was amazing, thought Christopher. It never failed. He wondered how many sales had been effected since he was last here. There, upon the wall, was the gun he had bought; no, not the one he had bought, since that had been sent over to the farm and he had posted a cheque to Major Gray's club in London; not the same one, but its counterpart waiting up there for the time when the major's keen and experienced eye would detect in the customer an interest in firearms. Now he was going to remind the old lady, with a teasing laugh, that the candlestick was merely a clever copy.

'You know,' he heard him say, 'it's not the

real thing.'

'Will you sell it?' repeated Mrs Belchamber.

The major gave his delightful laugh.

'If it'll please you to have it. If I were a dealer, I'd have no trouble in calling it a genuine article and asking a pretty stiff price— but I'm not a dealer. I merely—'

Christopher had moved out of earshot. They were coming to terms and he had no wish to hear them. He stood by a window, thinking his own thoughts, looking round the beautiful old hall and regretting—as he felt he would regret to the end of his days—that the place and the owner had not fitted to make a perfect whole.

He was roused by Mrs Belchamber's voice addressing him.

'I'm ready,' she said abruptly.

Their thanks were said; Major Gray had seen them off, charmingly, and they were on their way back across the fields.

'It's a lovely house,' said Christopher.

'It's interesting,' admitted Mrs Belchamber. 'But I didn't want that man treading on my heels all the time. What makes him think I'm as gullible as all his other customers?'

'Gullible?'

'That's the word I used. Did you hear the price he asked for his fake Anglo-Norman candlestick?'

'No. But I thought—'

'No, you didn't. Nobody who had anything to think with would be taken in by all that

181

gentlemanly how-d'ye-do. The man's a dealer, and he ought to have his sign hanging outside.'

'Sign?'

'A corkscrew. I wish you wouldn't keep repeating my words. I suppose you imagined that I was going to walk back to the farm clasping that candlestick reverently in my arms?'

'I thought—'

'You only thought you thought. I suppose he sold you something?'

Christopher was forced to admit, with the utmost reluctance, that he had.

'I knew it. You can always tell,' pronounced Mrs Belchamber. 'And another thing about that major; if he knew his duty as a father, he'd keep his daughter away from that peculiar friend of yours.'

'Scotty,' said Christopher, 'has never hurt any woman in his life.'

'That's not because he hasn't tried, but because they've only to look at him to know what to expect. He's got an animal look.'

'He's your host,' said Christopher briefly.

'Well, he can't hurt me,' declared Mrs Belchamber. 'I know too much about men. The more you know, the less you like. I used to tell Belchamber so.'

'Have you,' inquired Christopher, in his coldest tones, 'have you heard from your friends?'

'Which friends?'

'The friends you were going to when you came to England.'

'Who said they were my friends. They weren't my friends at all. They were simply this body of people I've given my house to, that's all, and that detestable creature they sent to meet me is in charge of it.'

'Have you heard from her?'

'Certainly not. How could I hear from her when she hasn't the faintest idea where I am?'

'That,' said Christopher, 'is a matter I've wanted to bring up for some time.'

'Well, bring it up,' invited Mrs Belchamber.

'I don't want to know anything about your affairs, but I feel that I'm being involved in them—I mean—'

'You mean that you're in an extremely awkward position, and I agree with you,' said Mrs Belchamber. 'You were seen with me on that French train, and on the boat, and in England. Then you got me into your car and drove away with me. I can quite see why you're worrying.'

'I'm not worrying in the least. I'm merely trying to point out that you've left a lot of harmless old people in a very difficult position—you've got some papers to sign and until you go there and sign them, the—'

'—the old people will go on living perfectly comfortably in my house. And papers, my dear young man, can be brought to me—I'm not obliged to make a tedious journey just to sign a few papers. I shall stay here quietly for a little while, looking after those poor children; the Melhampton committee will look for me, and find me—it'll be an interest for them; Melhampton's an extremely dull place.' Mrs Belchamber made a dreadful sound that Christopher realized was a laugh—the first he had heard from her. 'If you take my advice,' she went on, 'you'll forget about my affairs and attend to your own. This Cressida Gray, for example.'

She waited, but there was no reply. Christopher was looking longingly at the bull. If only he had had the forethought to wear a red scarf—if only he were not under a chivalrous obligation to protect women—if only—

'Did you hear me?' she asked after some moments.

'I heard you—yes. But if you don't mind, I'll—'

'You've got those three children on your hands, and what you need is a strong, sturdy motherly sort of girl. This one doesn't look to me at all strong, but she's capable.'

'I heard you telling her that she looked very strong. That was when you asked her to move the furniture.'

'You've got great responsibilities, and you treat them far too lightly. If I hadn't been here to help you out, a fine pickle you would have been in, with one measle case and two more coming on.'

'Robert and Paul needn't get them.'

'Of course they will. They're just at the age.'

Christopher saw, with intense relief, the figure of Scotty coming into view.

'Here's your peculiar friend,' said Mrs Belchamber.

'Hullo, hullo, hullo,' Scotty greeted them. 'Did you have a good tour?'

'We saw the house,' answered Mrs Belchamber frigidly.

'Ah. Interesting,' said Scotty. 'You ought to try and persuade the major to part with one or two of his treasures one day—he's got some nice stuff there.'

'I have all I want, thank you,' said Mrs Belchamber.

'That's a happy state,' sighed Scotty. '"I have all I want." How many people can repeat that after you? Not me. And not Chris. We've never had all we wanted. As soon as Chris gives over mooning about one girl, he begins to moon after another.'

'Open the gate,' ordered Christopher, 'and stop talking through your hat.'

'I'm only thinking of Marie Robson. As soon as you got out of your engagement to her, you—'

'Engagement?' Christopher stared at him. 'What on earth are you—'

'The girl with the hair,' Scotty reminded him.

185

'Oh—her! Good heavens, she was engaged to four of us simultaneously.'

'And Elinor Gateson—remember her? We both—'

'Open the gate,' said Mrs Belchamber, and Scotty pushed it open. She strode through and marched into the house, and the men's eyes followed her.

'Enjoyed your walk?' asked Scotty.

'Why aren't you milking cows?' asked Christopher.

'Would I be milking cows,' demanded Scotty, 'with Cressida by herself in the house? Now would I?'

'You mean y-you've—you've been with Cressida all this time?'

'All this time,' said Scotty with insufferable complacency. 'Now look—keep off, will you?'

'You told me,' said Christopher, 'that nothing ever interfered with milking.'

'Nothing does. Would I leave those poor creatures without attention? No. But when I know in advance that everybody's going off and leaving Cressida alone, then I can get my work done a bit in advance, can't I? Didn't you see the way I bolted down my lunch and went out again?'

'You said you had a sick cow, you liar.'

'I *did*? Then I am.'

'I ought to have known,' Christopher was resigned. 'It isn't the first time. You played your first low-down trick on me when I was six

186

and you've had twenty years steady practice since.'

'Twenty years! Tempus does fugit, doesn't it?' said Scotty wonderingly. 'That makes you twenty-six and me close on thirty. Are you going to send those two boys to the old Alma whatsit?'

'Yes. The fees knocked me back, when I heard them. Do you realize what our parents were paying for us all those years we were at school?'

'To a penny. My father never stopped telling me. He said he wouldn't have minded if they'd only tried to knock some learning into me.'

'They did try. But they were knocking on wood.'

'Bone,' corrected Scotty humbly. 'I never could get the hang of anything. It all seemed so unrelated to my needs, somehow. You remember all those rectangular gardens with paths so many feet wide? And contractors who never finished the job—prophetic, those were. I've never found a contractor yet who— What're you looking at?'

'Those boys. They get dirtier and dirtier, in spite of Mrs Belchamber.'

'They do? I miss their hats,' said Scotty. 'They made a fine touch of the Continental. Those are nice children, Chris,' he said, studying them. 'But French. It'll stick out all over them, a mile, all their lives. You won't make them into Englishmen.'

'I won't have to. They're already English.'

'Oh—on paper, I know. On their passports. But you needn't think that losing their distinctive headgear is going to make much odds. They're their mother's children, and although I'm saying nothing against her, they don't show much of your uncle.'

'They've got his ears, his hands, his build, his cleft chin, his walk, his—'

'Well, I'm not arguing. I'm merely saying that you'll never make them over. You can send them to our excellent old prep and public establishments, and in no time, they'll be saying: "I say, chuck it, you chaps"—but they'll never look anything but Frenchies. You wait and see. All their lives, when they open their mouths and talk faultless B.B.C., everybody'll exclaim: "My, how goot you spik!" Like that Signora Garcia who comes, if you'll excuse the misuse of the word, to clean. When she opens her mouth, you expect a Mediterranean pearl to fall out, and what do you get?'

'Chuck it, you chaps?'

'You get a Thames-side fog, like the girl in the fairytale.'

'What fairy-tale?'

'Don't split hairs—I'm trying to make a point.'

'Well, don't,' said Christopher. 'I haven't time. Look I've got a proposition.'

'Well, what?'

188

'I've got to go up to Town—to the office.'

'Oh, you have an office?' asked Scotty sarcastically. 'I hope they haven't been so inconsiderate as to expect you to work in it?'

'I've got to go and see to some things, and I'm going to take Cressida up with me. We're driving, and we're going to do a show.'

'Over my dead body,' proclaimed Scotty.

'That's what we thought. So we're taking you along. But we're doing the thing, you understand, in the Town and not in the country. In other words, we're dressing.'

'You want me to wear my long dress with the sequins?'

'Yes.'

'Do you know,' said Scotty, putting down his hay fork and gazing across in the direction of Grenton, 'I haven't been to a show for ... well, about eight years, I suppose. Do they still have chorus girls?'

'Not in a line. They spread 'em about over the stage.'

'That involves a bit of eye-strain, doesn't it?'

'Not once you've picked one out. They go in for more individual stuff—some of them hop in one corner and some of them writhe in another and some of them sit on the floor. Sort of ballet idea creeping in.'

'How would I like that?' asked Scotty, hesitant. 'They used to look sweet, all lined up and kicking as one, long, beautiful leg.' He gave a reminiscent sigh. 'All right—I'll come.'

The question of what he was to come in caused some trouble, since he stated, first, that he had never owned evening clothes. Pressed by Christopher to cast his mind back to frolicsome nights when they had both swelled the revenues of night clubs, he agreed, reluctantly, that he must have worn something.

'What I could do,' he offered, 'is to get out the dress clothes from one of the cases I opened under the Belchamber's eye. They're white linen, but with a long cigar I could look like a Brazilian planter.'

'You'll find your stuff,' said Christopher, 'if we have to prise open every single one of those junk-containers.'

Only three had to be opened, however, before Scotty, with a joyful cry, announced that the search was over.

'There!'

There was a scramble to peer in the direction of his pointing finger—Christopher, who had opened the case, Robert and Paul, who had held the tools, Cressida and Mrs Garcia, who had been carrying unpacked articles into the house; Mrs Belchamber, who had assisted in the search in order, she said, to be convinced that Mr Scott had once, even if long ago, owned something fit to wear.

'Yes—those is them,' announced Scotty.

'Those?' Mrs Belchamber, with infinite disgust, drew out a jacket which had once been black and which was now a greyish green, and a pair of trousers with small holes. 'Those?'

'They didn't look like that when they went in there,' complained Scotty. 'Who said those cases were watertight?'

'You're not going in those,' said Christopher.

'Why not?' asked Scotty. 'That coat'll brush up. It's a good one—I got it in Paris, right on Rue de la Paix—through-the-nose. And if I'm sitting down in a dark theatre, a lot of those holes are going to be underfoot, so to speak.'

'You cannot go out with Cressida in those,' said Mrs Belchamber.

'Well, I don't say they're smart, but—'

'She'll be overcome by the fumes. And so will everybody else in the auditorium.'

'If you give them to me,' said Cressida, 'I'll take them home with me and see what I can do.'

She could do little, but with the help of a shirt borrowed from Christopher, a cunningly-draped white silk scarf borrowed from the late Mr Belchamber and a sexless raincoat, which the doctor had left behind by mistake, Scotty was thought by all to be capable of standing up to any but a close scrutiny.

The outing was a complete success. The three drove up to London after lunch, and Christopher allowed Scotty to take charge of Cressida during the afternoon, while he himself attended to the business which had brought him up. They separated after tea—

Christopher and Scotty to change at Christopher's flat, Cressida to change at hers, where the men called for her to begin the evening's celebrations. Scotty enjoyed the dinner, but was dubious about the musical show.

'A chorus,' he told his companions over supper, 'is a chorus. You can't monkey with it. I don't say that all those girls tonight couldn't dance; they could. They did, very prettily, but if they're going to be allowed all this individual treatment, they mustn't be called choruses. They had the right idea when I was a show-goer. The star sang a song, and the orchestra kept out of sight, just doing a twitter of strings. Then crash wallop! Drums and cymbals, noise and fanfare, and in came anything from six to sixteen picked girls; all in a line, all holding each other up. From twelve to thirty-two picked legs, all kicking as one. Twelve to thirty-two silk-clad calves and sweetly—'

'That's enough about that,' put in Christopher.

'I like the new way,' said Cressida. 'Why don't you?'

'It gives me more trouble this way,' explained Scotty. 'With a girl here, a girl there, two more in the middle and a couple in a corner, my eyeballs get tired of rolling round. Besides, I bet you that if we could get hold of a dictionary, we'd find that the word chorus— have you got a dictionary?' he broke off to ask a surprised waiter.

'A dictionary, sir?'

'Please.'

'A—a French dictionary, sir?'

'French? Whatever would I want a—oh, thank you, I see. No, I know about *soufflé* and *vol au vent*, what I'd like is a simple English dictionary.'

'An English dictionary. I'll see, sir.'

The dictionary was some time in coming. It was thought that the manager might have one, but though he had, he did not keep it on the premises. He knew a family in a flat close by... No, they unfortunately could not lay their hands on one, but one of the waiters had an aunt who occupied a room in a block...

The waiter's aunt's dictionary did not mention dancing choruses, but gave Scotty what he wanted. The combination of voices, he read, in one simultaneous utterance. There it was, he said triumphantly, returning the dictionary with a sum which—if it ever reached the waiter's aunt—must have kept her in comfort for some time. It was as he had said. The movement of thirty-two lovely legs in one simultaneous, blood-warming movement.

'Eat up,' said Christopher. 'We're going home.'

'What's the hurry?' asked Scotty. 'It's taken me eight years to get here. I haven't enjoyed myself so much since your mother came down to the school and took us out for half-term—

she used to give us some wonderful times.'

'I don't see,' said Cressida, 'how you two could have been friends at school—four years difference in age when you're at school means you're practically leading separate existences.'

'Only when you travel through school,' said Christopher. 'Most people go *through* school—they go in at the Third or Fourth Form and emerge at the Sixth. Scotty didn't travel.'

'Oh yes, I did—I travelled,' protested Scotty. 'But not perhaps in the orthodox direction. When they got tired of me in one form, they shifted me into whichever one had a spare place. I never had time to get really bored.'

'But didn't you *learn* anything?' asked Cressida.

'Well, somehow—no,' said Scotty regretfully. 'At first I tried, but I found it a wearing process, thinking, and I gave it up. They used to say: "Aren't you ashamed, you big boy, you, sitting with all those fellows half your age and size?" And at first I did feel a bit of a misfit, like swallowing that Alice-in-Wonderland mixture that turned you into an outsize, but I got to like it in time. There was none of the dullness of going right up the school with the same companions, year after year. I always had a fresh lot coming up from below—nice little chaps, some of them, like Chris there. And their mammas used to feel sorry for me, and take me out and treat me.

They were all very kind, bless 'em, but I liked Chris's mother the best of the lot.'

'She treated you more than the others?' inquired Cressida.

'No—well, yes, she did, but it wasn't that I liked. It was the—the *cachet* she gave to an outing. She was lovely to look at, and I used to enjoy the sensation we always made coming into a restaurant. We didn't slink in behind the head waiter, like most, and take what he threw at us in the way of tables. No. Once Chris's mother came to a halt in the entrance, everybody put down their knives and forks— just the way they did when you came in. But you haven't got air—yet. You will have; it's something that comes later in life, and only to lovely women. An air of waiting for something; homage, I suppose. Something quiet and queenly—I could go to the door and show you how she used to come in.'

'You stay where you are,' said Cressida.

'All right. But she was lovely. In fact, Chris comes from a line of lovely women—did you know that?'

'I saw at once.'

'His mother was one of the three famous Lewinter sisters—did you know that? The most photographed trio of the last generation—it was a pity duelling had gone out, because old blades—I speak of human blades—used to call one another out over the question of which sister was the loveliest.'

'Eat up,' ordered Christopher.

'All right, all right.'

'It'll be milking time before we get you home,' said Cressida.

'Home,' repeated Scotty, who was beginning to feel sentimental. 'Home! Home was where I used to be as comfortable as could be, in my—'

'In your unspeakable kitchen,' said Christopher.

'—in my cosy kitchen, with all I needed at my elbow. Home! I shall never have a home again until they come and remove that amateur sanitary inspector from my premises. Why don't they come and get her? Why don't they try to find out what became of her? Why?'

'The car's this way,' said Christopher. 'You're sitting at the back.'

'And if you think I'm going to fall conveniently asleep,' said Scotty, 'then disabuse your mind. My both eyes will be open, and your both hands will be on the wheel. I'll see they are.'

'I'll see, too,' promised Cressida.

CHAPTER TWELVE

Mrs Belchamber's surmise regarding the search that was to be made for her soon proved correct; not long after her conversation with Christopher on the subject, the nose of the law had followed the scent as far as Grenton, and an inspector was sent out from Grenton police station to make preliminary inquiries at the farm. The young man arrived in an official car and Mrs Belchamber, seeing it drive into the yard, drew her own conclusions and went outside to interview the caller.

There was at first some delay, for the inspector, whose idea of his own importance was greater than his knowledge of farmhouses, took the trouble to go out into the road and walk along to the front gate. This, rusty and disused, was somewhat difficult to open, but it yielded at last to a vigorous push and he walked up the weed-hidden path to the front door. Here he seized the knocker, picked it up and replaced it carefully, and then rang the bell. When he had replaced this, he went into the road again, walked through the yard and the stackyard and approached the kitchen door. This was open; within the large, bright and shining kitchen he could see a tall, thin old lady with an apron over her black dress and a black hat upon her head. He stood for some moments at the door, but, finding her too busy to notice him, rapped with his knuckles upon the panel.

'I beg your pardon—' he began.

'Oh.' Mrs Belchamber looked up, took off her *pince-nez* and put on her long-distance glasses. 'You want to see Mr Scott?'

'Mr Scott? Well—no. I thought Mr

Linden—'

'I've never heard of a Mr Linden,' said Mrs Belchamber. 'Mr Scott owns this farm. This is Green Farm—perhaps you've come to the wrong place.'

'No—oh no.' The inspector summoned his official manner. 'It's Green Farm I'm after. Could I see Mr Scott? He could perhaps put me on to Mr Linden. Shall I find him on the farm?'

Mrs Belchamber, glancing over his shoulder, thought it probable; Scotty was at that moment carrying two buckets of water to the horses. The operation, she knew, took about ten minutes. She saw him disappear into the stable and spoke.

'You won't find Mr Scott, I'm afraid,' she told the inspector. 'He's out.'

'Out? Well . . . when will he be back, do you know?'

'Tomorrow.'

'Tomorrow?'

'Yes. He's taken a rather valuable animal to the Show. What Show, I can't tell you.' And neither, she thought grimly, can anybody else. 'Can I,' she asked aloud, 'do anything for you?'

The inspector hesitated. He was almost certain that the odd party before him was his quarry. He only had to ask her name, put a few routine questions, and go and make his report.

'I needn't bother Mr Scott,' he said. 'I really came to ask about a lady who—'

'Do you mean Mrs Belchamber?' asked Mrs

Belchamber.

'Well—yes. Are you...'

'You're too late,' said Mrs Belchamber. 'She's gone.'

'Gone?'

'She left yesterday. Mr Scott drove her to Grenton station.'

The inspector was thinking hard. He had been sure that this—

'Would you very kindly tell me your name?' he asked.

'I am Madame Desmoulins. I came with Mr Christopher Heron from Switzerland to look after his three little cousins. They call me Thérèse, and I have been with them since they were born. May I know why you are asking these questions?'

'I—I'm sorry. I should have explained. I'm from the Grenton police station, and I called to make a few inquiries about a Mrs Belchamber. She was on her way to—'

'To Melhampton. She told us. She left two addresses the Melhampton one and a Swiss one. I can give them to you if you wish.'

'No, thank you. We have them, as a matter of fact. Well...'

'If we hear anything,' said Mrs Belchamber, 'we'll let you know.'

'Oh—thank you. Er—thanks.' The inspector returned Mrs Belchamber's bow and turned towards his car. Coming towards him through the orchard, he saw two small, dusty

199

figures, and eyed them with a revival of hope.

'Those are—'

'Two of the children Mr Heron brought home. A pity they don't know any English yet.'

'Oh—they don't?'

'Not a word.'

She had led him to the car; she stood back to watch him go and Robert and Paul, coming up, sprang forward politely to open the car door for him.

'Oh ... *merci*,' smiled the inspector. '*Merci beaucoup.*'

'It was,' murmured the surprised Robert in French, '*rien. Rien du tout.*'

'*Il fait,*' he said, groping, '*il fait beaux temps aujourd-hui.*'

Robert and Paul agreed, charmingly, that it did.

'Well ... *aur revoir!*'

'*Au revoir, Monsieur.*'

'*Au'voir, Monsieur.*'

He was gone. Mrs Belchamber marched towards the kitchen and Scotty, coming out of the stable, called a question.

'Was that a car?'

'Yes.' Mrs Belchamber did not pause.

'Who was it?'

'He was selling brushes,' said Mrs Belchamber. 'They're always selling brushes. Now you two boys, where've you been?'

'To the big house,' Robert waved a hand in the direction of Greensleeves. 'We saw

200

Cressida's father—Monsieur Gray—and he showed all the inside to us.'

'Oh—he's down here again, is he?'

'Yes—he is here.'

* * *

If Major Gray drew any conclusions from Christopher's frequent appearances at Greensleeves, he gave no sign. He was to be seen on most afternoons standing in his attitude of quiet welcome at the great door; on fine days the sun cast a pattern of light and shade around him, and in inclement weather the flames of a great log fire leapt in the fireplace of the hall behind. Cars drove in, waited for their owners and drove away. Christopher found that the tour of the house, while seeming leisurely, was timed to precision; even those guests who stayed to tea were ushered to their car in good time to be driven away before the next arrivals drove up. The tourist season—Major Gray's season—was at its height, and Christoper saw with unwilling admiration that the warmth of the welcome, the thoroughness of the tour, never slackened; like a sound actor, Major Gray, while playing the same part throughout a long run, gave to each audience the effect of a fresh performance. Though Cressida never appeared, Christopher sometimes waited for her, and Major Gray showed always the same lack of self-consciousness in going through the familiar routine. Christopher knew, without vanity, that he himself fitted well enough into the scene to suit his host's purposes; if he had been less presentable, he was grimly aware that he would have been removed from the framework and charmingly, remorselessly, got out of the way.

He tried, sometimes, to talk of her father to Cressida, but while she answered freely questions relating to the major's career, her replies were merely factual, and never coloured by any expression of feeling. Yes, her mother had died when she was eight, and as her father was abroad, he had decided to send her to Switzerland. No, he did not come home very often—there was, at the time, no home to come to, but at every opportunity he had visited her and spent some time in the neighbourhood of the school. Yes, she had been a little lonely, but not, she thought, as lonely as her father, for he had adored his wife and had never been the same man since her death. No, he had not expected to come into possession of Greensleeves, and they had not been particularly elated at the news. The house was beautiful, and some of the furniture of some value, but there was no money left with the house and, on the major's small income, no possibility of living in it. No, she did not want to go back to Switzerland; she now had more friends here than there; she was in a good job, and would like to keep it. Yes, they had tried to sell Greensleeves, they had tried to let it, but there were no reasonable offers. No, she had never shared a home in London with her father; he was not a man who cared to follow a settled domestic routine, and preferred to live at his club. No, he was not in England all the year round; at the end of the summer, he went abroad.

Christopher did not try to probe her feelings, but he knew well enough what they were. His memory of his first impression of her father was still fresh in his mind; his disillusionment, and the curious pain it gave him, still rankled. He could only too easily conjecture what it must have cost Cressida to go, with far more pain, through the same process. Her demeanour towards her father—as his towards his daughter—was quiet and well-mannered; if there was a lack of exuberance, it could be put down as British.

Christopher was content, for the moment, to leave things as they were. His one fear—that Mrs Belchamber would express, with her usual freedom, her views upon the subject of a wife for him seemed unfounded. He was relieved, but somewhat surprised; sparing people's feelings—even Cressida's—was no part of the old lady's make-up.

Mrs Belchamber, however, had problems of her own. Her dismissal of the inspector, masterly though she considered it, was not likely to end the investigations. Though she boasted that she was a free subject and could do as she pleased, it would become necessary, when she was found, to declare her intentions. If she did not intend to sign the papers and occupy the suite she had insisted should be kept for her, there must be something else she had in mind; the police, having poked so far, would want to poke further. The most she could do was declare her intention of staying with the children until the measles epidemic was at an end.

The same thought had occurred to Scotty.

'When they track her down,' he told Christopher, 'she'll have to show her hand. At the moment it looks as though she's settled here for life. Wouldn't you say?'

'No, I wouldn't when I think about it reasonably,' said Christopher. 'She dislikes you and me, and Mrs Garcia, and the farm and the smells. She misses hot water and indoor comforts.'

'Funny, her passion for cleanliness,' observed Scotty. 'I'm all for being clean, naturally, but on a place like this, you don't have to observe all the rules. You can't take off your boots, for example, every time you go in and out of the house, even here and there, and you can't help a slight—a very slight—odour of toil. This farm—compared with some— shines with cleanliness. Look at the paintwork!'

'That's only the outside. Why didn't you spend a bit of that money on indoor improvements?'

'Because I'm never indoors. If I'd known the house was going to be used as a nursing home, then naturally I'd have put in operating theatres and such. When you've stayed with me before,' pointed out Scotty, 'your standards haven't been so meticulous.'

'For the last eight or ten years,' said Christopher, 'you've been sliding rapidly down the chute from gentleman farmer to hind. Mrs Belchamber's quite right; you look terrible, you smell terrible and you'd be mistaken, anywhere, for your own cowman.'

'But I am my own cowman!'

'But why? You started out as manager and you're ending up as office boy—is that progress?'

'In one direction. It's no use, Chris—I've never been able to come out on the right side financially. I do everything that the other farmers do, and more. I'm willing to work, and willing to learn.'

'You'll never learn. I know a cow when I see one, and look at what you've got here! Good Lord, Scotty, you buy cows for pedigree and performance, not because they look at you as though they want you to buy them!'

'But they do! Nobody else bids for them, and their feelings get hurt. D'you think a cow hasn't got feelings?'

'If you'd put their feelings aside and go for butter-fat and milking records—'

'When I started out,' said Scotty, 'I did all that, and that didn't pay either. Nothing ever pays. I used to employ men who were supposed to know, and they didn't make it pay either. Taking it all round, Chris, I've worked harder and longer with my bare hands, and got less for it, than any man you can name—haven't I, now?'

'You have.'

'I've run through practically what I started out with, one way and another. All that's left now is what the trustees are sitting on, and I shall never get that—except in a starvation-level percentage. But I like this place, and if I can hang on just making ends meet, I'd like to hang on. I like atmosphere, and this place has got it. I know a lot about farms; they put them in the awfullest places. They can be so isolated that, as far as the eye can see, you're occupying a prairie by yourself. They can be low-lying and depressing; they can be way up on a draughty hill where you have to peg the animals down. They can be nasty and bleak and lowering to the spirits. I don't say they all are, but the juicy ones come into the market less often, naturally, than the other sort. Some of those they showed me looked like the fall of man. But this one' Scotty waved a hand— 'Well, you can see.'

'But you didn't see. You bought it blind.'

206

'I did, but I've never regretted it. Even if Gray did see me coming, and doubled the price, I'm glad to be here. It's got good air, good water—even if it doesn't come out of a tap—and a first-rate view. I own a nice bit of shooting and a stretch of river; there's a Hunt handy and two good horses to ride. What more can a man want?'

'Money. Profit. A percentage on his outlay. A return for his work. A sense of achievement. Something to hand on to his sons.'

'Sons?' Scotty shook his head. 'No sons,' he said. 'The only time I ever thought of sons, was when I saw Cress. And I can't have Cress.'

'No,' agreed Christopher. 'But we'll find you someone, some day.'

'You'll have to look a long way, and it'll take a long time, and by then, I'll be too old to appreciate her. I'm a good four years older than you are, remember.'

The words seemed to strike Christopher, and he looked at the speaker with brows knitted thoughtfully.

'Scotty—I've got an idea.'

'It'll have to be a good one. I like them slim and—'

'Listen—it's my birthday soon.'

'It is? I always try not to remember—it saves a lot of trouble.'

'Look,' said Christopher. 'If we've got the Belchamber off our hands by then, or even if we haven't, let's have a party. How about it?'

'A party always sounds a good idea,' said Scotty. 'And there's another thing.'

'Well?'

'It's Cressida's birthday round about now.'

'Then that makes a party imperative. And the kids enjoy it. What do you say?'

'What do I have to do?' inquired Scotty cautiously.

'Nothing. I'll do it all.'

'Oh. Well, in that case, count me in. The place is your own. There's a cakeshop near the Pig and Whistle where they'll make you a cake with pink icing and all the trimmings, if you give them due notice. Don't forget the candles in those ducky little coloured holders, will you? And ices. I'm fond of ices. You can get it in blocks and keep it away from the fire until it's time to use it. And you'll want a few extras like eclairs and meringues and ginger snaps—tell them to send the ginger snaps unfilled and I'll shove some real cream into them. And talking of filling, you don't want to stint the heavy stuff, like sausage rolls and sandwiches with a bit of body in 'em. And don't hold it too early—I don't want to get in and find a lot of chewed fragments and nothing else—I want to be there at the start. You'll have to do things pretty well if it's going to be a double event.'

'Double event?'

'Well—yes. If it's to be your birthday and Cressida's joined. It *is* going to be a double event, isn't it?'

208

'Ye-es.' Christopher's tone was thoughtful, his gaze fixed absently on space.

It could, perhaps, be a double event. If he could persuade her ... If he could make her see that he wasn't after all, so precipitate. Love's arrows flew swiftly. He was twenty-six and Scotty had said that she was twenty-two; they knew their own minds. He, at all events, knew his, and he believed that—lately—she had seemed to be close to him. They had—in spite of Mrs Belchamber—been more in one another's company since they had met than a great many other couples had been after years. She knew that he loved her; he had but to find out whether she loved him...

A double event. He would ask her, and, if she was kind, their engagement and his birthday could be celebrated at one and the same time.

A double event...

CHAPTER THIRTEEN

'"And it is very difficult to get out,"' read Mrs Belchamber, '"for beyond these serpent forests there are great cliffs of dead gold, which form a labyrinth, winding always higher and higher, till the gold is all split asunder by wedges of ice; and glaciers, welded, half of ice seven times frozen, and—"' Do you understand?' she broke off to ask.

'No,' said Josette.

'Neither do I, but it's very good English, so it doesn't matter whether you understand it or not. Now where was I? "—and half of gold seven times frozen—"'

'Why does not Cressida come?' inquired Josette.

'H'm?' Mrs Belchamber peered over her reading glasses.

'Why does not Cressida come today?'

'How do I know?' demanded Mrs Belchamber. 'Ask your cousin Christopher there'—she threw a glance at him as he half sat, half lay on Josette's pillow, one of her hands held in his. 'Ask him; he saw her last, when he took her home last night.'

'Is she sick?' Josette asked, turning to look at him.

'I don't know, Josette,' said Christopher.

'Then ask her,' directed Josette, with the imperiousness of a pampered convalescent, 'ask her why she does not come.'

'If you're not going to listen to me,' said Mrs Belchamber, 'I'm certainly not going to blind myself over this shocking print. Don't you want to listen?'

'Thank you, yes. But I would like that Cressida should come.'

'Not "that Cressida should come." I would-like-Cressida-to-come. Now say that slowly.'

'I-would-like-Cressida-to-come.'

Christopher's lips did not move, but his heart echoed the words. She had not come. Perhaps she would not come again. He had been a fool, and worse than a fool. He had rushed his fences, and he had come down, as he deserved. He had been mad, and worse than mad, to imagine that because her beauty, her calm sweetness, her aloofness and elusiveness had captivated him, he could look for as swift response in her. He was a fool; he was a vain, blundering madman.

But she loved him. She had said so. If he had not been sure that that was all that mattered, he would not have persisted so long, so hotly. But she had loved him, and she had said so . . .

'But if you love me, Cressida, why—why—why not? There's nothing to stand in the way—nothing. Parents, money, prospects, the future as far as anyone can see it there's nothing to stand in the way. I love you, and you love me—you've said so. Then—why won't you marry me?'

She had been white and still. She had freed herself gently from his arms.

'I've told you, Chris. I love you, but . . . it was like this before. I loved him, too.'

'Well, why not? You were young—it was four years ago. We fall in and out of love at eighteen, at twenty, at twenty-one and two. You were—what? eighteen. Every beautiful girl is in love at eighteen. Why not? Her blood's waking up; she's waking up. The world's waking up. You love, and at that age, you forget—that's natural, too. It's a sort of growing process. But now—you've grown. I've grown. We're in love, ready to marry, ready to bring healthy children into the world. What does it matter, this thing that's over and done with? It's finished. You loved a fellow and forgot him, poor devil—but that was yesterday. This is *now!* Cressida—let me kiss you ... Cressida ... Cressida ...'

'But you don't understand, Chris. Listen—please darling, listen! You see, I wasn't eighteen. I was twenty-two—the age at which you've just told me that one knows one's mind at last and for ever. I was twenty-two, and I loved him very much, Chris. He was tall, like you, and young and good-looking and gentle and kind ... like you ... and there was nothing in the way then, either. His parents liked me; I liked them. There was everything ... And then he went away—for a year. Only a year. We could have been married before he left, but we talked it over, and decided to wait—there was such a lot to get, such a lot to do before we were married. He went away—and I felt as though something in me had gone with him. I thought the days would never go by. I looked for him in all the places we had been in together; I thought I heard his voice everywhere, just as I think I hear yours. He was in my mind at every moment of every day, just as you are now. We wrote, we planned, we lived for the day he'd come back ... And before he came back, I knew that ... that, as far as I was concerned, it was ... dead. Whatever it was, had died. I tried to write, but I was ... I was trapped; I was held in by plans, by loving wishes, by everybody's hopes and goodwill. I prayed that, when he came, when I saw him again, everything would be all right. I thought that when I saw him again, heard him again, felt his arms round me again, I'd get back whatever it was that was lost ... I prayed so hard, so hard ...'

'Cressida, my darling, don't cry. Please, please don't cry ...'

'He came back. He loved me; he hadn't changed. He was as much in love as he'd been when he went away. But nothing I could do—nothing, Chris, nothing could bring back the magic. It was gone. He wasn't anybody special any more. I liked him, I admired him, but I couldn't love him. You see—in a year, in just a year, it had died. And now, when I'm in love again, I can't—I can't help remembering. I love you, Chris, but you've got to wait. If you'll be patient—if you'll just wait.'

'A year?'

'Yes. Try to understand, please. If I'd been eighteen, or nineteen, or twenty ... But at twenty-two, it's different. People expect you to know what you're doing. If you're ever going to be sure, you ought to be sure then. And I was sure—so sure. If you'll wait, Chris, and let me prove to myself that I can trust my feelings,

213

that they'll stand up, this time, to any test…'

She would not give in. He had not, in the end, been gentle, and he had left her, at last, shaken and trembling. He had come back to the farm and roamed restlessly round the dark buildings until, in a remote shed, he had found Scotty and sought his sympathy.

'But I *told* you, Chris!'

'You didn't. You never mentioned it.'

'Well, I thought I did. I don't know how it is—I think I've said something, and then you tell me I haven't. You don't listen, that's what it is.'

'You told me she was twenty-two.'

'I didn't! If I did, it was when we were talking about her job—she started that when she was twenty-two. You go too fast for me. I send you over, in the first place, to ask her to come and give a hand with nursing Josette, and you come back looking as though you'd sailed into the sea of love. You don't give a girl time to look you over, and then you rush at her with a proposal and expect her to behave with the same impetuosity as yourself. Girls don't like to be overtaken and passed, Chris—they like to make the pace, and they feel happier when you follow the way they're making you go. This sweeping a girl off her feet is a mistaken idea altogether; she likes to step into love like a bather early in the season—foot by cautious foot. When she's got you sized up, when she's decided you'll do, when she's so sure of herself—and of you—that she's prepared to tell all her other beaux she's suited, then—and only then you can rush her off her feet. It's no compliment to a girl like Cressida to ask her to marry you before you know the first thing about her—her age, her feelings, even her history.'

'All right. You can have all that. I rushed it. But this attitude of hers is ... it's fantastic, but she *means* it, Scotty—she's serious! She loves me; she'll become engaged if I want her to— but, after that, a year's separation. A year! It's—grotesque!'

'Easy, easy. I know. A year's a hell of a long time in those circumstances. But when you take the overall view, it's only one-seventieth of the total span, and—'

'A year!'

'It'll pass, Chris.'

'A year! Does she think a man can—'

'She isn't exactly *thinking* this out, you know, old son. This is a thing she can't help. The burnt child and the fire. She told you all the facts, but not all the trimmings. If it had been just a matter between her and the fellow, she would have remembered it merely as a warning not to trust too much in the keeping qualities of passion. She would have said, like the hare: "Next time, slow time." But you don't know what she went through when—on the eve of the marriage—she handed the poor wight back his ring. He tried to understand. He was a nice guy—I knew him vaguely when I first came here, and liked him. He took it as well as could be expected, considering what he was losing—but his parents went through a series of unpleasant phases, each more vindictive than the last. They weren't bad, as parents go, but he was the only child. Cress might have stood up to it better if she'd had anybody at home to back her up, but her father went over to the enemy. He didn't say much—he isn't the ranting type—but he can do more with a contemptuous eyebrow than most.'

'Why was he—'

'Money. It's his ruling passion—or has been since his wife died. Cress says he was different when she was alive, but I can't really believe it. Well, there you have it. Cressida went through an experience, then, that—there's a word, if you'll give me time to hit on it—yes, seared her. She can't argue rationally now because it all brings back the two shocking months she spent sticking to it that she didn't love him in the least. She was called capricious, heartless, cruel—and worse. A lot worse. A lot of that mud stuck. You won't argue her out of this, Chris. You've taken the cover off something that she's been keeping deep down. This is the first time her feelings have been touched since it all happened, and it's opened up a lot that she thought she'd forgotten. Be patient with her, Chris—it only needs patience...'

Christopher came to himself to find Josette shaking his arm gently. He looked down at her, his eyes still with a faraway look.

'You are not listening,' she said gently.

'No—I wasn't. I'm sorry,' said Christopher. 'Tell me again.'

'What she's been trying to tell you, only you've been off on some dream of your own, is that she's made a spell.'

'Oh.' With an effort, Christopher brought his mind to bear on the pincushion Josette was holding out to him. 'This is the spell, is it?'

'It's for Cressida. To come back.'

'That's all right—she'll come back,' said Mrs Belchamber. 'And without spells, too. If she doesn't, you still won't want spells; your cousin or Mr Scott—one or the other, or both—will be off along that route through the fields. I've watched that path, from this window. It began as a mere thread, and now it's been trodden to a broad highway. Now lie back. If she doesn't come down, they'll go up. Now listen to this nice book; it talks a lot of sense. It wouldn't do both of you any harm to listen. One of you might apply it.'

She adjusted her glasses, held the book, as she invariably did, raised stiffly before her. '"But give up this egotistic indulgence of your fancy: "' she read, '"examine a little what misfortunes, greater a thousandfold, are happening, every second, to twenty times worthier persons".' She peered over her spectacles at Christopher and repeated the words emphatically. '"Twenty times worthier persons; and your self-consciousness will change into pity and humility; and you will know yourself, so far as to understand that 'there hath nothing taken thee but what is common to man'."'

She laid down the book and took off her glasses.

'If you're going to do spells,' she said to Josette, 'then you'd better do one for Mrs Garcia to come back, too.'

'She is not here?' asked Josette.

'She is not. You usually find that, when one support goes, the others collapse too.'

'Where has she gone?' asked Josette.

'I don't know. She hasn't bothered to send word.'

Christopher rose abruptly, smiling down at Josette with an effort.

'I'll go across,' he said, 'and see what's keeping Cressida.'

He went downstairs and was half-way across the stackyard when he heard his name called. He turned and found Scotty coming with unusual speed towards him, wiping his hands on some straw as he came.

'Hey—Chris!'

'Well?'

'You going over to Greensleeves?'

'Yes. Cressida hasn't come, and I want to find out ... I'd like to know why.'

218

'I think I know why.' Scotty threw aside the straw and looked up with a worried countenance. 'I think I know why. If I were you, Chris, old son, I'd wait a bit before going over.'

'Why? There's no reason for her to keep away, is there? I was a fool, but she doesn't imagine, does she, that we're not going to see each other any more?'

'I don't think that's what's keeping her away. I think—' Scotty sent a trouble glance towards the wooded hill—'I think there's a bit of bother up there. Mind you, I'm only guessing—but I'm not sure that you ought to barge in and ... well ... you might worry Cressida.'

'What are you talking about?' demanded Christopher.

'Her father. He's down here, and there are signs that he's staying down. The caretaker's just been along for milk and eggs—I gave her a bit of butter until I heard it wasn't Cress she was stocking up for. She said—as far as I could make out of the lingo—that the major came down early this morning—with luggage. If that's true, it's the first time he's had his things here for four years. Why would he leave London just when the tourists are packing it? I have an idea he's in trouble.'

'Well, there's only one way to find out,' said Christopher, 'and that's to go over and ask. Couldn't you have put one or two questions to

219

the caretaker?'

'Well, if I'd put them in English, she wouldn't have understood them, and, in any case, she and her husband find it convenient to shut their eyes to most of what he does. They don't stay there to suit him, you know; they're there purely because Cress asked them to come. That's why Cress comes down here—to see them and to pay their wages.'

'*Cressida* pays them?'

'Yes—I told you. You didn't suppose her father did, did you?'

'Why not? You said yourself he gets a good income out of the house.'

'So he does, but have you any idea of what it costs to live as he does? The best clubs and the best circles—and he's got to put by enough to keep him comfortably through the winter. Hey, where are you going?'

'To Greensleeves.'

'Wouldn't it be better to wait for Cress?' pleaded Scotty. 'If he's in trouble, she won't want you to know.'

'If I'm going to marry her, which I am, sooner or later,' said Christopher, 'I'll have to marry her father, too. So the more I know about him, the better for everybody concerned.'

He went quickly across the fields, walking with bent head, deep in thought, and taking little stock of his surroundings. The first object his mind registered was Major Gray's black sports car, gleaming in its unaccustomed place in the garage.

The big door was closed; after a moment's hesitation, he turned the heavy handle. If he was not yet past the knocking stage, he reflected, then it was time he was. He pushed open the door and stepped into the hall.

The two figures were standing before an empty fireplace. Cressida was staring into it, and her father was looking at her with no perceptible change in his urbanity. They turned as Christopher entered, and Major Gray raised one eyebrow expressively.

'Sorry not to knock,' said Christopher briefly. 'I was worried about Cressida.'

'Cressida,' said her father evenly, 'is very well ... as you see.'

'We were worried because you hadn't come,' said Christopher, looking beyond Major Gray into Cressida's pale set face. She came forward a step or two, and he waited quietly.

'I ... I was coming,' she said. 'My father came down unexpectedly, and we ... we were talking.'

'Yes. We don't often see each other ... alone,' said the major smoothly.

Christopher spoke as smoothly.

'This isn't perhaps quite the intrusion it seems,' he said. 'One of these days, when Cressida and I have argued over one or two minor matters, I hope she'll marry me.'

'I shall be delighted,' said Major Gray, 'to
221

place her in such good hands.'

There was a pause. Christopher saw that the man before him was watching him; he knew from the amusement in the grey eyes and the slight smile on the major's lips, that he would get no help in whatever he was going to say. It would be better, thought Christopher, to take advantage of the moment and have this thing out. Scotty knew nothing and Cressida would not talk. It only remained for him to put things on a firmer—if less pleasant—footing.

'Scotty didn't want me to come up just now,' he explained, 'because he thought the fact of your being down here meant that you were ... worried about something.'

'Oh—I'm not worried,' smiled Major Gray.

'That's fine. I'm glad.' Christopher's tone had changed; it was very much firmer. 'But if we're to be related, I'd like to feel that Cressida—and you—place enough reliance on me to let me in on anything that did happen to ... to come up. Perhaps I should have talked to you before about wanting to marry Cressida, that is.'

'I don't see why,' said Major Gray, after appearing to give the matter some thought. 'No, I don't really see why. Young people arrange these things for themselves nowadays, and the responsibility of the parents seems to have narrowed down to seeing that the wedding arrangements go off to everybody's credit. I hope, Cressida, you'll have a white wedding. I think it's the greatest pity when girls forgo the opportunity to appear at their loveliest. A white bride ... white velvet. Velvet is so much softer than brocade.'

He was not, then, going to meet Christopher half way. Christopher looked into the calm, handsome face and decided that no good could come of pressing the matter. Cressida, apparently, had come to the same conclusion, and spoke quietly.

'If you wait,' she said, 'I'll come back with you.'

While he waited, Major Gray talked of matters so trivial that Christopher knew that he was being mocked for his impetuous visit. He listened with as much courtesy as he could command, and then was out of the house and walking back with Cressida to the farm.

They walked in silence for some way; Cressida was deep in thought, and Christopher said nothing to disturb her.

'Chris,' she said at last.

'Well?'

'It was ... I was thinking about your coming over just now.'

'I barged in,' said Christopher. 'I didn't mean to be overcurious, but if you're going to marry a girl, you like to know—you like to be there if you feel you can do anything to help her.' He hesitated a moment and added: 'Or to help her father.'

'Father,' said Cressida, 'is a very difficult

223

person to help.'

'Nobody's difficult to help. If they need something, you've just got to find out what they need, and what form they'll take it in.'

'The only form my father will take it in,' said Cressida, 'is in a form which makes it appear that he's doing the giving.'

'Well, I don't mind that,' said Christopher. 'The long-term object is not to please him, but to please you. You're not a girl who tells a man much, and Scotty's idea of imparting information is to wait until you've found it out from some other place and then say: "That's what I told you." All I know is that your father—for reasons best known to himself—uses Greensleeves as a means of exercising his histrionic talents and bringing in some money. I gather that you earn for yourself all the money you handle. There must have been some money once, Cressida.'

'Yes, there was,' said Cressida. 'My father had a certain amount of money when they married, and my mother had rather more. But they saw, soon after they were married that what they had, and what they lived at, were two quite different sums. My mother was a good manager, and between them, with their income and my father's pay, they could have lived very comfortably—but not at the level at which my father wanted to live.'

'Who told you all this?'

'He did. And some of the older mistresses at

the school, who used to see mother from time to time. Father was brought up—as you were—with expectations that never came to anything. He didn't know he was going to get Greensleeves, but he thought he'd get some money. Well ... he didn't, and you can see that the house, without money, was a heavy burden. I don't like my father's way of ... of solving the problem, because it seemed to me that—I can't explain this properly—but it seemed to me that it changed him from what I suppose most people would call a pleasant wastrel into ... into something less pleasant. When I left school and came here, I thought that, with the help of Émile and Zoute, I could perhaps make a corner of Greensleeves habitable ... I thought that my father and I could live here and perhaps even open the place to visitors. But that wouldn't have worked, as my father pointed out. It isn't enough of a show place to have attracted very wide attention, and when the local interest dried up, there would have been nothing. Upkeep was impossible, too, without a good income. So he agreed to undertake the upkeep, and went up to live in London and then began bringing people down more and more, in the way you've seen. He did it, at first, in a more ... a more honest sort of way, and then he seemed to change, too. At first it was rather sad, and then it was ... well ... humiliating, and lately, it's been rather frightening. I don't know why I've been frightened, but I don't think you can mix with the kind of people he's been mixing with lately without coming to some sort of trouble.' She had been walking more and more slowly, and now she stopped and turned, looking at Christopher with an absent, frowning stare. 'It isn't as if he's ... I don't know how to express this, quite, but perhaps you'll understand. He isn't a dishonest man. He's always been gay and charming and pleasant and amusing and what the world calls worthless, because he doesn't accept the ordinary responsibilities. He gave up the Army because it bored him; a settled home bored him; making an effort to make ends meet bored him. I suppose that's worthless—but everybody who knows, agrees that he made my mother very happy, which a lot of worthy men don't make their wives. And although he hasn't one-tenth of the affection for me that he had for her, he never—as it were let me down. He used to come regularly to visit me at school, playing the devoted father beautifully, and always taking care to be sufficiently far away during holidays to make it obvious that I couldn't spend them with him. He may be worthless, or graceless, but he isn't—he isn't really dishonest. Only—if you've seen some of the people who've come down lately, and if you knew how far his sales have come from the small things he used to deal in—then you'd know why I'm frightened.'

'Why did he come down—why's he staying

down here?'

'He won't tell me. But I know he's in trouble; I *know* he is, Chris—I *know*!'

'Well, steady,' said Christopher gently. He took her in his arms, aware of Mrs Belchamber's black hat at a window, and held her in a steady grasp. 'You've nothing to worry about, Cressida. I'm in this as much as you are, you know. If you'd wash out all those silly ideas about not marrying me until you've found you're not in love with me any more...'

He felt, rather than saw, the little shake of her head.

'Give me time, Chris,' she begged.

'I'll give you a little time. We'll shelve the wedding argument for the moment. But I'd hoped to bring off a double. It was to be a double event—our engagement party and my birthday. Well, we can still have the birthday party. Scotty says you've got a birthday this month, too. When?'

'The twenty-seventh,' said Cressida.

Christopher stared down at her, too astounded for speech.

'But ... good Lord!' he cried at last, 'that's my birthday, too. And if you're going to be twenty-six, and I'm going to be twenty-six, then we're—we're—'

Cressida, for the first time that afternoon smiled.

'We're twins,' she agreed.

CHAPTER FOURTEEN

Arrangements for the party proceeded at a smart pace. Josette was to be allowed to put on a dress for the occasion; the festivities were, for her convenience, to be held in a room upstairs; Robert and Paul were to have new grey flannel suits. The only cloud in the sky was the possibility that one of them might develop measles before the great day.

'They will not,' declared Josette. 'I will put a spell.'

The efficacy of the spells was not be doubted. They had cured two puppies of distemper and Scotty of the toothache. The fact that Scotty had pulled out the affected tooth was merely confusing the issue. They had kept the weather dry—too dry, Scotty was beginning to think— and they had, finally, brought back Cressida and Mrs Garcia.

'While you were at it,' complained the latter, 'you might have made it so as I should come back cured. I ought to be in my bed today, instead of straining my constitution coming back before I was strong. I don't feel myself at all.'

'Then I'll make another spell,' said Paul, 'for your constitution. Are there to be two cakes,' he asked Cressida anxiously, 'or only one?'

'There'll be two,' promised Cressida.

'With twenty-six candles each?'

'With twenty-six candles each.'

'That'll take some blowing out,' commented Mrs Garcia. She went on with her task of washing up, but after a few moments her forehead wrinkled in a frown. Her movements became slow and then slower until, at last, they ceased altogether and her hands hung, motionless, in the water. Cressida, watching this process, knew that an idea was making its difficult way to Mrs Garcia's brain, and waited expectantly.

'Miss—' began Mrs Garcia, presently.

'Well?' Cressida polished a knife.

'Miss, about the candles.'

'Well, Mrs Garcia?'

'Just now you said twenty-six candles on each cake. Now, that can't be so. You want twenty-six on Mr Heron's.'

'Well, yes, but on mine, too. I'm twenty-six.'

Mrs Garcia turned her head and ran amazed eyes up and down the slim form standing beside her.

'Twenty-six! You're twenty-six!' she exclaimed. 'Well, I never! I wouldn't,' she said, getting her breath back, 'have credited it.'

'Cred-i-tit-tit. What is that, cred-i-tit-tit?' inquired Robert anxious to learn.

'To credit—to believe. *Croire*,' explained Cressida.

'Well, I wouldn't,' said Mrs Garcia. 'But'— her frown returned—'if *you're* twenty-six and '*e*'s twenty-six ... and if your birthdays are on the same day, then ...'

'They are—*jumeau, jumelle, jumelle, jumeau,*' sang Paul.

'Twins,' said Cressida. 'Yes, we are.'

'Well, now!' Mrs Garcia tried to turn her attention to the washing-up, and failed. 'I can't credit it,' she said again. 'It shows you what life is. When you think of him, born in one place, and you born in another, and twenty-six years later, you both turn up here—twins.'

'It's not really extraordinary, you know,' said Cressida. 'The only extraordinary thing is that we didn't find it out before.'

Mrs Garcia, abandoning the washing up, found her way to a chair and sat down heavily. Cressida saw that the story was going to take first place at future gatherings of the Lower Grenton womanhood.

'Twins!' she gasped. 'It's Fate! Something's going to come o' this!'

'It has come,' said Paul, with satisfaction. 'There will be two cakes, each with twenty-six candles. There will be things to eat.'

'Lots of things to eat!' corroborated Robert.

This attitude of eager anticipation was not shared by everybody at the farm. Mrs Belchamber's mind was not, at present, on the arrangements for the party, and Scotty was not looking forward to the affair with his first eagerness. Christopher, he knew, had wanted a double event—and in a sense, admitted Scotty,

230

he had got it. The discovery that the two were twins was something which he felt should have been uncovered by himself; armed with this splendid lever, he could have used it dramatically and with great effect before Cressida had been able to make her resolve to wait a year before marrying. Talk as he would to Christopher of complexes, he thought her decision wrong and unfair, and did his best to make her change it.

'You're suffering,' he told her, 'from a dog bite. But it healed, long ago, and that once-bit twice-shy talk is pure rot in your case. Take it this way, Cress; you'd just come to England, and you hadn't got readjusted. You came over with a lot of ideas, and they all came to nothing, and that, naturally, upset you. You were lonely, you were disappointed—you shouldn't have been as disappointed as you were, because you would have known, if you'd had more experience, that you wouldn't get a man like your father to settle down into a nice, humdrum, father-daughter setting when he'd been on the loose for twelve years and more. You went too hard at nursing, and you were tired out. So when this man loomed up, you were ready to fall in love with anybody— *anybody*, don't you see? He was something to lean on; he was something nice and solid in a world that wasn't behaving in the nice, settled way you'd expected. Here was something ... well ... clear-cut; love and marriage and a lot

231

of kids to look after. So you fell for it. I don't think, myself, that you ever fell for *him*. You—'

'I did, Scotty. If you're trying to say it was infatuation, then—'

'You're not *listening*, Cress. It was love, all right, but not for the *man*. You were reaching out for what he represented. If you'd been hauled to one of those fellows who read people's bumps and ask you what you used to like to throw out of your pram when you were in one, I bet he'd have said that your chief purpose, four years ago, in wanting to marry that fellow was to get away from your father.'

'I—'

'You needn't walk off. I've never liked him, Cress, and you know I haven't. Chris is different—he gives marks for polish. I don't. And another thing—Chris sees the picture now, with Greensleeves running as a business, with you settled in a good job. He didn't see you as I did, waiting, all lost and bewildered, for your father to give you a lead, or a hand, or—'

'I oughtn't to have needed a hand. I was old enough to take care of myself.'

'No, you weren't. Brought up in the way you were, you weren't. If kids have got to make their own way, you've got to throw 'em out early and let 'em learn. Take me—d'you think I'd be throwing money down cowshed drains if my father had seen that I knew something— something practical. Well, perhaps I would, but your father owed it to you—having brought you over—to settle you into something, and he didn't. So you jumped at the first chance to settle yourself. Cress, you can't bring up that old story and make Chris miserable now! He was a nice fellow, that other one, but he's a dead horse. Let him lie. You and Chris are twenty-six each. Why, in a year you could have quins! Think of it, Cress! Five children, all kept out of the world because you got a bite four years ago. You can't—you can't do it! Why don't you marry him straight away, as he wants you to?'

A tear rolled down Cressida's cheek, and Scotty, fumbling agitatedly among his pockets, pulled out a handkerchief. Discarding it, rightly, as unfit for the purpose, he put out a thick forefinger and gently brushed the tear aside.

'I'd like to, Scotty,' she said. 'I'd like to more than anything in the world. But I can't be reasonable about this. When I think of . . . of all that happened then, I find myself shaking, just as I used to all the time it was happening. Scotty'—she took his hand and held it tightly—'do you remember when we sat, that day, wrapping up wedding presents and sending them back?'

'I—'

'Do you remember his father and mother coming in and . . . Do you remember what they said?'

233

'I remember, Cressida, but—'

'What I can't forget—what I shall never forget—was seeing somebody go to pieces as ... as he did when he knew, at last, that I wouldn't marry him. I didn't know men ... I didn't know they could break up and—and lose all their manhood and ... and ... grovel ... Oh, Scotty...'

'All right, all right, all right,' soothed Scotty tenderly. 'I tell you, Cress my sweetheart, that it's dead and gone, and you shouldn't let it stand in Chris's way. You owe that to him. Whatever you feel is your own affair, but we've all got our dark spots and we have to get used to them. We can't load them on to other people. Chris has nothing to do with anything that happened here or there. What you ought to do is go out one dark night, by yourself, and stand under the stars and go through the whole packet of trouble over again, step by slippery step, not leaving out a bit of it. When you've done that a few times, you'll break the crust that's grown up round it. The first time I lost a cow, I took it hard. I like cows, and this one was a sweet creature. So I went out for a few nights and walked round her favourite meadow, stopping at all the trees she used to rub herself against. It did the trick. I got pneumonia, but that was useful, too, as a counter-irritation. Will you try it?'

'I'll try anything,' promised Cressida.

With this, Scotty had to be content.

234

Christopher, knowing that his friend was doing his best in the matter, tried to be content, too. There was something else in his mind, however, and he took a day or two to come to a decision. When he had reached one, he waited until Cressida was upstairs with Josette, and Mrs Belchamber safely on her own side of the house; then he went swiftly across the fields, passing close to the bull with contempt bred by familiarity. Arriving at Greensleeves, he walked a little uncertainly round the house and then saw the caretaker carrying out a pile of rugs to be shaken. She understood Christopher's question, but he saw that her stock of English did not permit a ready reply. Presently she beckoned and pointed; if he went through the door, he would find her master.

Christopher found Major Gray in the great hall. There was a note-book and a pencil in his hand; he was obviously making a list of his effects. He was in shadow, and Christopher could not tell whether he showed any surprise at the sight of him; by the time he had crossed the hall, the charming mask was in place.

'You must have had a hot walk,' he said. 'There's a storm coming, I think.'

'It's close,' admitted Christopher, and then, without further preamble: 'I walked across to talk to you,' he said. 'Perhaps you could spare me a few minutes.'

'Why, of course. Let's go outside under the trees—there might be a breath of air. Or do you think it would be cooler in here?'

'In here, I think.'

'Just as you like. Sit down, won't you?'

Christopher sat down and then rose, with a feeling that he could say what he had come to say more clearly if he were on his feet.

'It's chiefly about Cressida,' he began. 'I—'

'She told me,' said her father, 'that you're engaged.'

'Yes—we are. I'd like to be married at once, but Cressida's decided to—'

'I know.' The major's voice was sympathetic. 'She's got this fantastic idea that that little affair of four years ago...'

'She prefers to wait,' said Christopher, 'and so,' he lied, 'it's all right as far as I'm concerned.'

'Oh—nonsense!' Major Gray put his cigarette-case back into his pocket and leaned towards Christopher's lighter. 'Thanks. But it's nonsense, you know, and I'm disappointed to find you so ideological. It's a chivalrous attitude, of course, but in this matter I feel it's hardly the right one. I don't care to generalize about women, but when they get a fixed idea, it isn't necessarily a good one. I tried to make Cressida see—when she broke the engagement—that there was nothing extraordinary in feeling cooler about a man after a year's absence. If she'd given herself time—if she'd given *him* time, he—'

'I'm glad she didn't,' said Christopher.

236

'Well, naturally you are. But she's refused more than one offer since then, and I hoped, when I saw you ... Do you know, I liked you extraordinarily, that first day.'

Christopher was silent. He could not bring himself to admit his own feelings on the matter. A glint of amusement came into the older man's eyes, but he continued with scarcely a pause.

'I hoped, thinking about you afterwards, that you wouldn't allow Cressida time to think. You looked impetuous; that was a good start. You had good looks and good manners and an air of knowing what you wanted. And how to get it. I hoped that, at the first hint of hesitation—after Cressida had admitted that she loved you—you would have seen to it that she married first and argued afterwards. My dear Christopher, if I'd waited for her mother to expound all her theories—she was brought up on theories—we should still have been sitting on a bench high up, on a wooded hill above the Lake of Geneva, talking. Women love to talk. But I was very much in love—as you are—and I had, perhaps, less scruples. I had nothing to offer her, so that part of it didn't take long. Her parents showed a disposition to talk, too; she was an exceptionally good dancer and there was talk of her taking it up as a profession. But I used all the ardour of youth—I was just twenty-one—and swept her off her feet and into a marriage

237

that turned out like one of those fairy-tale ones—only mortals aren't permitted the "ever after" clause. The one success I ever made in life was my marriage. I don't take the credit— except to point out that if I'd waited to be convinced, the marriage wouldn't have taken place at all. Everybody would have talked everybody else out of it. Impulses are dangerous, sometimes, I suppose, but it always seems to me that if you obey them, you do at least do something you want to do when you're most in the mood to do it. If I'd known you a little better—if I could have foreseen that you'd allow Cressida to persuade you...'

'I'm quite willing to wait,' said Christopher.

'Oh ... *nonsense!*'

'And that isn't what I came to see you about.'

'No? Then—'

'Last time I was here,' said Christopher, 'you'd just come down—not as you usually come—but in a way that made me feel that things might not'—he had rehearsed the words, and brought them out smoothly— 'might not be well with you. It would be unpardonable of me to pry into your affairs, but I think you know that Cressida ... worries about you. She's going back to London soon, and I'd like her to be able to go with a clear mind, and she can't do that while you stay down here in this...' He stopped on the verge of an unrehearsed 'hole-and-corner fashion,' and went on with less self-consciousness and more firmness. 'I'm in a difficult position,' he pointed out. 'You're not, if I may say so, the ordinary parent. You run your life and Cressida runs hers and yet ... there's a tie, and while I stand in line as your future son-in-law I can't detach myself entirely from your affairs. They don't interest me, except in so far as they affect Cressida. She doesn't know why you've left Town, why you're not bringing people down here any more, what—since that's your only source of income—you'll do about money. I'm sorry to sound officious, but I'm bound, sooner or later, to have to talk this out with you. I shall be going away as soon as I can move the children, so there won't be very much opportunity for me to see you, and I don't like this feeling that something's ... something's hanging fire. Cressida isn't happy—she's uneasy, and, if you'll forgive me for saying so, I'm uneasy too. I feel that you've—this is awfully difficult to say, but I'd like to get it out, sir—I feel that you've run into trouble, and while that wouldn't particularly concern me, in itself, it's bound to affect Cressida—and if I'm taking over her worries, I'd like to take over this one.'

He stopped. He had plunged, finally, and he had no idea whether he had said too much or too little. He knew only that this suave, debonair man, leaning back in a deep chair and looking up as he stood before him, was not

239

going to be allowed to mar his daughter's happiness or her good name. He stood still, waiting, but it was some time before Major Gray spoke.

'Trouble,' he said at last, 'is something that doesn't weigh very heavily on me. And my trouble is a common one—the commonest one, perhaps, of all—and it has been with me all my life. Lack of money. Lack, that is, of enough money. I was brought up to expect it, and it didn't come; but the habits were ingrained, and they were such pleasant habits that I saw no reason to change them. Besides apart from soldiering, I hadn't a profession. I sent in my papers because I felt I could do better as a mild sort of adventurer. Nothing lurid, nothing illegal, even nothing sordid. Greensleeves seemed the answer—but getting money out of people, however you do it, turns out to be a sordid sort of business. But I was doing well—as perhaps you saw. Or perhaps you were prejudiced—your friend Scotty regards me, wrongly, I think, as an outsider. I lived at my club and was well known—and if not well thought of, nobody could really put a finger on anything specific. If you want money, you must move in the golden circle and—until the other day—I was well inside it. Then ... d'you want to hear about it?'

'Please.'

'It was the purest bit of bad luck, as I think you'll agree. I always chose my clients—my

240

victims, if you like—carefully. I found out who they were, and where they came from. They were invariably foreigners, and foreigners of the type who don't come back often. I knew pretty well what levels they moved at, and I worked to ensure that one group of clients would never run up against another group—or if they were likely to, I made sure that they hadn't bought the same article. It wanted organization; that was the part of it I enjoyed. The actual business of coming down here and selling was by far the least interesting side of it. I thought I could go on doing it for a few years and then—when the markets looked healthier, selling Greensleeves and investing the proceeds more profitably than I could do now. But the business—and it was, after all, a business— packed up suddenly, dramatically and, I'm rather afraid, finally, the other day. And this is how it happened. Won't you sit down?'

'No, thank you.'

'Well, I was introduced by a Very, Very Important Person to a South American. It all went off very well; the South American heard about Greensleeves, asked if he could come down, and came, bringing his very charming English wife. It was a profitable afternoon. They bought a Saxon lantern. It was genuine, and one of the most lovely things I ever handled. I bought it in Germany, from an old, old English lady, who told me that it had been in her family for generations. I paid handsomely for it, but I sold it for exactly ten times what I gave. Ten. I was very pleased, and I remained pleased for several days. Then a lot of unpleasant things came about; the charming English wife for whom the South American had bought it, wanted to see as many relations as possible before going back to South America. The old lady, who looked too frail to cross the room, crossed the Channel to see her grand-niece ... I needn't perhaps go on. Taken item by item, it wasn't so bad, but piled, villainy upon villainy like that, I couldn't survive it. I had robbed an old lady; I had robbed a young lady; I had grossly deceived a young man, the South American, and severely humiliated an old one, the extremely Important Person. You can't do that in a golden circle that's really golden; you can't do it in the kind of club I belong—belonged to. I could have dealt with an occasional dissatisfied customer, or an unlucky chance meeting between two sets of customers. What I couldn't stand up to was a blow like that right at the heart of my credit. It was my credit, after all, that I drew on. While I was well-thought-of by those who could provide good contacts, I was all right. But now I must either work from a different centre—which wouldn't amuse me, since I'm most at home in London—or I must bring the business down to a more obviously businesslike level—and that wouldn't amuse me, either. I came down here hoping that the storm would blow over, but I can see now that it won't. I've had to leave the club, and I shan't find myself welcome on the topmost levels any more. And I'm really only at home at the topmost level. So you see, my dear Christopher, that there's nothing for Cressida to worry about. I shall either commercialize Greensleeves—how, I can't yet say—or I shall sell it and live abroad. The most you've got to fear is an occasional begging letter. You can remove Cressida's real fear—that somebody will come down here, one day, and make a disgusting or a violent scene, or denounce me to the police, or cry shame on me through the streets. Girls get exaggerated ideas.'

'I thought—' began Christopher.

'You thought that a timely loan might come in handy, and it was good of you. But the time is not yet. I don't doubt I'll come to it. You've got a disarmingly generous look. All I need is thinking time—and I get a lot of that here.'

There was silence, and after a time Major Gray rose. There seemed nothing more to say, and Christopher found himself being led to the door. Outside, the heat struck like a blow, and the courtyard was hot through Christopher's shoes. Major Gray came out a little way, and the two men stood looking up at the beautiful house.

'Well, there it is,' said the Major affectionately. 'History in stone. The first time I saw it, it revived a longing I hadn't felt for

243

over twenty years—a wish you wouldn't have shared with me.'

'What wish?' asked Christopher.

'That Cressida had been a boy,' said her father.

CHAPTER FIFTEEN

Christopher was wakened at dawn on his birthday by two small pyjama-clad figures bringing offerings to his bedside. He sat up, shook the sleep from his eyes, made an effort to appear enchanted, and looked for suitable phrases in which to give thanks for a leather photograph frame and a box of linen handkerchiefs.

'You can put a photograph into the frame,' pointed out Paul, the donor. 'You can put Cressida.'

'She is your fiancée now, no?' inquired Robert.

'Yes.' It was too early to be conversational, but the two had settled themselves on his bed and were preparing for a chat. 'Yes. We won't be married yet awhile, though.'

'Is she Catholic, like us?' asked Robert.

'No.'

'Will she live with us?'

'Yes, when we're married, we'll all find a nice house in the country, and a couple of ponies.'

244

'Ponies?'

'Small horses.'

'Oh. We shall ride them?'

'Yes—it'll be fun,' said Christopher.

'If there are three, it will be better,' suggested Robert delicately. 'Then there will be one for me, and one for—'

'Yes, yes, of course. Three. What lovely presents—thank you so much! Are you going out to find Scotty now?'

'No—this is your birthday,' said Paul, 'and so we shall talk to you.'

'Oh.' Christopher sought for a topic. 'What's the weather like?'

'It is hot—very, very hot, like yesterday. There will be a storm soon, I think. Mrs Garcia said that.' Paul gave a wriggle of excitement. 'Do you want to see what we have bought for Cressida?'

'Is it a nice surprise?'

'It is a book,' said Robert.

'She'll love that,' said Christopher.

'It is a cookery book,' explained Robert. 'It is to tell about how to cook everything in wine.'

'Oh. Well, that sounds—it sounds interesting. I wonder what Scotty's doing?'

'We shall see later,' said Robert. 'First, you must come to see Josette.'

'Oh—we mustn't wake her yet,' protested Christopher.

'But she is awake—she is waiting to see you, because she has something for your birthday.

You must come and see.'

It was clear that he must. Stifling a series of yawns, Christopher put on a pair of slippers and shuffled in the wake of the two eager figures. Josette was sitting up in bed, her eyes shining, and a large parcel clasped to her chest.

'Ah—*Bonne fête!*' she cried. '*Bonne fête!*'

'Ssh! You will wake Madame! Give him the parcel,' urged Paul.

Josette held out her parcel, and Christopher, bending, kissed her.

'Thank you, Josette. Can I open it now?'

'Oh, yes. It is for that.'

Christopher undid the wrappings and opened a large cardboard box. Inside it was a pair of felt carpet slippers of a pattern he had thought obsolete; they were, moreover, several sizes too large for him and of a shade of yellow that made him feel slightly sick.

'By Jove!' he said, with as much enthusiasm as he could muster. 'My goodness, these are smart!'

Josette gave a laugh of purest joy.

'I made them! I made them!' she cried.

'Ssh! *Tais-toi! Madame dort!*' cautioned Robert.

'I did not make *all*,' Josette's voice dropped to a conspiratorial whisper. 'I made some. Madame showed me, and she gave me the things to make them, because she did not want them.'

Christopher could quite understand that. If

246

they had been intended for the late Mr Belchamber, he reflected, that gentleman must have had a large foot. Two large feet, he decided, lifting out the slippers with every appearance of eagerness.

'You will be able to wear them every day. We shall see them when you put them on,' pointed out Paul.

Yes, there was that. He wondered what his man Merrow would say when he saw them. They would have to be kept on with string or elastic.

'They're lovely—everything's lovely,' he said. 'Thank you all very much. I'm going to have a lovely birthday.'

The children, at any rate, were prepared to enjoy it. In spite of the heat, the boys made several journeys up the lane to see whether the van from the baker's—the van bringing the two birthday cakes—was on the way. They paid an early visit to Cressida with the cookery book, and escorted her back to the farm; they offered to help with the preparations for the party, but were found to be so much in the way that Mrs Belchamber finally sent them out to Scotty with a message that he was to keep them out.

Mrs Garcia worked with even less energy than usual. Howsay, she said, putting on the kettle for her morning tea, was thinking of changing his job.

''E's been offered the Merton Hotel,' she
247

said dolefully.

'Well, is he going to take it?' inquired Mrs Belchamber.

'He says yes one minute, and no the next. He says there's less work for a 'andy man, so there'll be less tips; but 'e says they've got a bigger staff, so there'll be less work.'

'A bigger staff,' pointed out Mrs Belchamber grimly, 'means more chamber-maids.'

'Yes, it does mean more,' agreed Mrs Garcia solemnly. 'But my sister points out to me, she says the more there are, the safer. It's one woman that wrecks a marriage, she says, not several. And there's truth in that. But a man won't stay at home, I pointed out to her, unless there's little 'ands to keep him there. If 'e won't do 'is Christian duty by his wife, 'e'll do it by his children.'

'Rubbish,' said Mrs Belchamber. 'And if you're not feeling well, that black tea won't do you any good. Don't make yourself too comfortable; there's work to be done.'

The work proceeded, and soon the room upstairs began to assume a festive air. As the afternoon drew near, plates filled with delectable home-baked cakes were carried up and placed on the big, round table, the centre being left free for the two birthday cakes. The room was closed during lunch, but, after lunch, Mrs Belchamber, fearing that Robert and Paul would burst with suppressed excitement before

248

they could burst themselves with party fare, permitted everybody a peep into the room. Josette, carried pick-a-back by Christopher, viewed the scene with crows of delight.

'Now back to bed,' he commanded, 'and a good sleep, or no party! Tuck up, now. Eyes shut!'

Josette shut one eye; Mrs Belchamber drew the blanket across the window.

'The telephone is ringing,' announced Robert. 'Please may I go to it?'

'Go ahead,' said Scotty. 'If it's the doctor, say the party's at four, and tell her not to be late. If it's the baker and there's any hitch about the cakes, call me and I'll deal with the monster. I hope they've got initials on, have they?' he asked.

'Yes. They asked, and we told them,' said Paul. 'Why are you C. P.?' he asked Christopher. 'Is it for Paul, like me?'

'Right first time,' said Christopher. 'Christopher Paul. I was going to be Christopher St Armand Robert Paul but my father stepped in and saved me.'

'Who was telephoning?' Scotty inquired of Robert, who had come upstairs, a little breathless.

'I do not know.' Robert frowned with a touch of uneasiness. 'A lady said to me "Is that Green Farm?" and I said "Yes", and she said: "Can you say if Mrs Belchamber is there?"— and I said "Yes, she is here; shall I call her

249

to speak?"'

'Who was it?' inquired Mrs Belchamber, so sharply as to bring all eyes to her face.

'She—she did not say,' faltered Robert. 'She said that she is ... she is coming to see you this afternoon. She is coming in the train, and then she will get a taxi, she says, and come.'

'Didn't you tell her there was a party?' demanded Mrs Belchamber.

'I—I ... There was not time,' said Robert. 'She went away.'

There was a short silence, and an odd air of tension in the room.

'What is she coming for?'

The question came from Josette. She was sitting up in bed, cheeks pale, her eyes fixed upon Mrs Belchamber.

'Coming for? She thinks she's coming to take me away,' said Mrs Belchamber brusquely.

The words, short and sharp, had an extraordinary effect on the three children. Robert was silent, the colour draining out of his face; Paul, too, was silent, but his cheeks grew redder and redder. From Josette's eyes fell one, two tears and then a steady stream. She made no sound, merely staring at Mrs Belchamber with the tears coursing down her face. Cressida sat on the bed and took her gently in her arms, murmuring soothing little phrases.

'You—you will not go?' faltered Robert.

'NO!' It was a shout from Paul, so loud and sudden that Cressida's heart began to thump. 'No!' He stared at Mrs Belchamber and advanced, step by step, towards her. 'I know who this is,' he said, between set teeth. 'I know. She is the one who came here before, on the station—no?'

'There's no need to fuss,' began Mrs Belchamber. 'I can perfectly well—'

'She is that one?' demanded Paul insistently.

'Yes, that's the one,' admitted Mrs Belchamber. 'But—'

'Then she shall not come,' said Paul fiercely. 'You hear me? She shall not! Who is she, to come when we don't want her? Who is she, to think to take you away when you have come to live here? Who is she, this one, who says: "I will come and take you away"? She shall not come. You will see. I will make a spell.' He looked rapidly from side to side, seized the pincushion from the table beside Josette's bed, and tore the pins out of it passionately. 'She will—not—come—to-take-you,' he ground out, stabbing the velvet anew. 'See!' He held the pincushion in a sweeping, dramatic gesture high above his head and spoke in a loud, ringing tone. 'I have made a charm! A bad charm!'

'Steady,' said Christopher.

'There's no need for spells, thank you,' said Mrs Belchamber. 'Put that thing down and try to behave like an English boy instead of Sarah Bernhardt. She won't come today, at all events,

251

if she's got any sense. When this storm breaks, it'll wash all the trains off the lines. Go on— out.' She swept out everybody but Cressida, and drew a chair close to the bed. 'I'll read to you in French,' she said to Josette, 'and you must sleep. Where's that book? Oh—here. Now lie still and listen, or I shall go away. Now I'll read these business letters. I don't suppose they're interesting, but you can learn a bit about commerce. You might be a secretary one day, when you're grown up. Now. "*Monsier*,"' she began, in unrecognizable French, '"*Nous avons appris avec plaisir que vous vous*"—yes, there are two *vous* there. They're always repeating themselves in French. "*—que vous vous interressez à notre* something-or-other. *Notre représentant Monsieur Goguelin*"— there's a name for you, if you can get anybody to pronounce it—"*Monsieur* as-I-said *passera chez vous dans le courant de la semaine, et nous avons en magasin assez de* something or other *pour satisfaire vos besoins.*" Do you understand what they're talking about? I can't keep stopping to translate. "*En sollicitant la continuation de votre*"—oh, well, I suppose that's just ending off politely. Now, here's another. "*Monsieur le Directeur*..."'

'Ssh!' Cressida pointed to the sleeping Josette, and Mrs Belchamber closed the book with an air of relief. 'We'll see about *Monsieur le Directeur* some other time,' she said, ushering Cressida out of the room and closing the door quietly behind her. 'Did you see how excited that boy got?' she inquired on the way downstairs.

'Paul?'

'Yes. Very demonstrative, the French. Bent on fussing all the time. I noticed the difference the moment I married an Englishman. Quiet. None of this hand-waving. God gave people tongues, after all, and the tongue does the talking, not the hand-waving or shoulder-shrugging or eyebrow-raising. It's simply a waste of energy that might be usefully employed in other directions.'

'It makes it more expressive, don't you think?'

'No, I don't. That's what I've been trying to say. If you want to talk, talk; if you want to act, act—but don't do both together unless you're going to make your living at it. I think you'd better put the cream in those things while I mix the scones.'

The party began punctually at four, the first excitement being provided by Josette's appearance in a pretty little white frock; the next by Mrs Belchamber's entrance in a dove-grey creation beneath the usual black hat. She assumed command of the proceedings, welcoming the doctor with an attempt at graciousness, running a keen eye over Scotty's best suit and refusing to allow anybody to get a close view of the cakes which—raised above the lesser fare—waited for their candles to be

253

lit, a ceremony which was not to be performed until the end of the party. She kept a keen eye on Christopher; it was clear that she was going to allow no adult enjoyment to mar what had become, somehow, a purely juvenile entertainment.

As the afternoon advanced, the children reacted in their several ways to the festivities; Josette's excitement was within, showing only in shining eyes and tightly compressed lips, heard only in occasional squeaks of merriment. Robert preserved his usual composure, but Paul became more and more over-excited as the evening went on, until finally Scotty threatened to take him outside and dip his head in the trough.

The threat, on that close, stifling evening, lost a great deal of its meaning, for the thought of immersion in cool water was one which filled every member of the company with longing. The skies had grown so leaden and the light so grey, that it had been necessary, soon after the party began, to bring in lamps and place them about the room. The blanket was brought in from Josette's room and placed across the window, and the party took on every appearance of a night function and added greatly to the children's pleasure.

Games were difficult; Mrs Belchamber was too stiff to play at anything requiring any great degree of mobility. The children knew no English games, and only Cressida knew any

French ones. An attempt by Mrs Belchamber to dance on the Pont d'Avignon came to nothing, and at last a large handkerchief was produced, Mrs Belchamber assumed the position of umpire, and the others—with the exception of Josette—played Blind Man's Buff. The blind man, having caught somebody, could have little difficulty in identifying him, in a company of such varying sizes and shapes, but hints from the umpire and Josette were invariably forthcoming.

'Oho, now who's that big, fat farmer man you've got hold of?'

'There now—don't pull Cressida's hair.'

'Ah!'—a squeak from Josette—'it is not Robert—it is not Paul you have seized!'

There were occasional rumbles of thunder, occasional flashes of lightning, but the company was too merry to notice them. The rain fell, fast and then faster, and soon came dashing against the window pane, but the storm brought blessed relief from the day's closeness, and everybody felt glad of the coolness that now filled the room. The heaviness of the downpour went unheeded as chairs were drawn up to the table and the serious business of eating began.

The ample tea was disposed of and the remains removed; the two birthday cakes still stood, pink-iced, rose bedecked. It was time for Josette to be going back to bed, and Mrs Belchamber called a halt in the proceedings;

she and Cressida would bring up the ices, the candles would be lit, and the ceremony of cake-cutting would begin.

Scotty accompanied the two ladies downstairs—not from gallantry, but in response to Mrs Belchamber's request to 'come and make himself useful for a change.' Christopher settled down to play host, and had organized a game of Hunt-the-Slipper—with one of his birthday slippers, when the door opened and Scotty's head appeared round it. Something in his expression made Christopher uneasy; he left the others to play, and made his way to the door. Scotty took his arm, drew him out on to the landing, and, closing the door, spoke in a cautious undertone.

'You'd better come down,' he said.

'What for?' Christopher's tone was as low.

'Well—someone's come. Don't know who, but I've got an idea it might be Lucy Locket, the jailer's daughter—you know, the one who wants to whisk the old girl off to her suite.'

'Good Lord—you mean she came through this storm?'

'Yes, and she looks it, too. She's all washed out and all washed up. I've put her in the big front room.'

'But—she doesn't want me,' protested Christopher. 'She'll want to talk to Mrs Belchamber.'

'Well, she can't—not just at this moment,' said Scotty. 'In the first place, she isn't fit to talk to anybody—and you can't introduce her into the party at this stage of the proceedings. Look, Chris,' he went on, a serious note in his voice, 'these jollifications are practically over—go down there, settle this bad fairy comfortably and tell her you'll produce the Belchamber as soon as we get the doctor off and the kids out of the way. She can't object to that; explain that it's just a matter of officiating at your own birthday cake-cutting.'

'But—can't she join in?'

'Join in? I've *told* you,' said Scotty, exasperated. 'She looks as though she's walked all the way from Grenton, and she may have done, for all I know. There's no sign of a car anywhere outside, as far as I can see.'

'If you saw her, how is it that Mrs Belchamber didn't?'

'I was going downstairs, and I was just going along the passage to the kitchen, when I saw something at the front door. I thought I'd imagined it—there's a lamp in the hall, and it's a bit murky outside, but I heard a sort of knock, so I went back to investigate. And out there, sure enough, trying to get in, was this she. I got her in—that door took some opening, but I got it open and I got her in. Then when I'd gathered who she was, I took her into the big room and asked her to wait.'

Christopher stood still, thinking swiftly. He came, finally, to feel that Scotty's suggestion was a sensible one; the party was almost over, and the doctor would soon be leaving. The children could be got out of the way, and Mrs Belchamber would then have to be told that somebody had come to see her. Christopher had no doubt that it would be the woman who had borne down upon them on their arrival in England. The search had been long, but it was at an end. They had found Mrs Belchamber.

'All right. I'll go down,' he said.

He turned towards the stairs, but Scotty, putting out a hand, grasped his arm.

'Half a mo!' he said. 'Come with me—wait a minute.'

He went into Josette's room and took from a table a small glass. Holding this, he took Christopher's arm once more and led him across the landing along the corridor.

'Where're we going?' inquired Christopher.

'I told you. I always keep a bottle of the best, against emergencies. Remember the night you arrived?' Scotty took a bottle of brandy from the cupboard and poured a stiff drink into the glass. 'There! Get that down her,' he said.

'Are you out of your mind?' asked Christopher, staring. 'Do you expect me to walk in with a drink and—'

'Chris, old son, don't argue. That woman down there *needs* it.'

'But—good Lord, Scotty! If it's the woman I saw on the station, she's probably never had a drink in her life!'

'Then it'll do her all the more good,' said

Scotty, pressing the glass into Christopher's hand and hurrying him along the corridor. 'If she doesn't drink it, she'll go down with a fine dose of pneumonia—she's soaked to the skin and her teeth are making noises like castenets. Go on—get that down her, ask her to wait—go *on*, turn on the well known charm—and then leave the brandy to do its beneficial, warming work. Go on. Oh, and there's one more thing. I found out what she's called—Cubitt.'

Christopher went reluctantly towards the stairs, passing on the way the over-excited Paul, who, tiring of hunting the slipper, was using up surplus energy by running up to the top floor, poising on the broad, polished banisters and sliding down with outstretched arms and terrifying swiftness. It was a sport normally forbidden, but rules were relaxed today, and the banisters, Christopher acknowledged, were ideal for the purpose.

'See,' shouted Paul, having climbed to the top once more. 'See me!'

Christopher was not looking. He was hurrying, as fast as he could, down the few remaining steps to the hall, where a woman stood at the door of the big room. She had obviously just come out into the hall—one hand still held the large, old-fashioned door-knob; the other was clenched against her chest. She was deathly pale, and her eyes, wide and blank, were staring straight before her, and rested on Christopher unseeingly.

He reached the hall, but her gaze remained fixed on something past his shoulder. Her lips parted in a gasp, and, with admirable promptitude, Christopher placed the glass of brandy on the floor and, stepping forward, was just in time to receive Miss Cubitt's crumpling form in his arms.

CHAPTER SIXTEEN

Miss Cubitt left Melhampton House in good time to catch the train. The day was so unseasonably hot that she put on her thinnest white cotton blouse and then, remembering that she was to have an escort, took it off and substituted her best silk one. Scanning the skies, she felt that she should take a mackintosh, but decided against it; she would look smarter—more *soignée*—without one, and Monsieur Versoix had more than once complimented her upon her *chic*.

She took a last look at herself in the glass; if she was not *chic*, she was at any rate neat. Gathering up her gloves and bag and going on a last round of the rooms before leaving, she found herself musing upon Monsieur Versoix and the changes that—in so short a time—he had wrought at Melhampton House. She had little dreamed, when she saw him that first day, how well, how easily, how rightly he was to fit into the well-ordered routine of Melhampton.

For well-ordered it had been; the rooms all occupied, with the exception of the suite awaiting Mrs Belchamber. The small staff was installed, the list of voluntary duties made and faithfully carried out, the guests feeling settled and at home. She had hesitated, she remembered—more, she had quailed at the thought of coming back, that eventful day, without Mrs Belchamber, without even a coherent account of what had happened to Mrs Belchamber, without anything to show for her journey but a stranger—an unknown Frenchman. It had taken courage to explain the matter to the trustees who had waited, assembled in the drawing-room, eager to welcome the owner of the house and anxious to complete the legal formalities of the change of ownership.

She had begun, she remembered, haltingly. The expression on the stern old faces before her did nothing to assist her explanation. She had seen Mrs Belchamber? Yes, but—She had actually spoken to Mrs Belchamber?—introduced herself, bought Mrs Belchamber's ticket? Yes, but—

It had been Monsieur Versoix, with his extraordinary tact and understanding, who had stepped forward and made matters clear to the committee. He had talked to them, half in French, half in broken English, but with a frank earnestness that had smoothed away,

261

minute by minute, every line of suspicion and disapproval on the faces of his hearers. He had told them of their meeting; he had explained Miss Cubitt's dilemma, and his own. She, distracted at the realization that Mrs Belchamber had disappeared; he, appalled at the thought that she had disappeared with his luggage, his passport, his papers. There was no explanation of her odd conduct, but he could lull their worst apprehensions; with his lifelong knowledge of Mrs Belchamber, he could reassure them. She had no intention of going back on her decision to give them the house; so much he knew. She had talked of it, in the train, on the boat, with every intention of honouring her promise. But she met some friends on the train, and it was with these, doubtless, that she had vanished so abruptly. There were three children, and one of them was obviously unwell; Mrs Belchamber had cared for the child, had looked after her—the trustees murmured their appreciation—and doubtless the old lady, who was, one would understand, known to be impulsive, had made a sudden decision to accompany the child to its destination. She would be unaware of the inconvenience she was causing Miss Cubitt; she had forgotten, no doubt, that his luggage and her own had been carried by the same porter; she could not have paused to imagine his plight, left without anything to show the authorities, left even without

262

adequate means...

His short, portly form seemed to have grown taller as he spoke; nobody, then or since, had withstood his charm. One forgot that he was a stout little Frenchman with a black beard, a figure straight out of illustrations in children's text books; one remembered only the changes that he had wrought at Melhampton House— quietly, gradually, but so steadily that it was now impossible to imagine what old Mrs Pendennis would do without Monsieur Versoix on her walk to the library every morning; what General Oliphant would do without his enlightening comments on the changes in the French Cabinet; what the excellent cook, Miss Lightwater, would do without Monsieur's daily visit to the kitchen, without his demonstrations on omelette-making, soufflé-making, potage-making. How could one think of Thursday afternoons, now, without the French Circle? Who could picture Friday evening without the dinner of *Poisson à la Versoix*? Who had dealt, formerly, with Mrs Obberly's moods and Mr Whiteaway's dyspepsia? Who could have estimated what a leaven this Frenchman would prove? No Englishman could have shown the same interest in the old ladies with such tact and grace; certainly no Englishman who did so would have been accepted by the old gentleman as an equal, and been respected and liked. He fitted everywhere; there was nobody living in the house who could not say that Monsieur Versoix had an especial interest in him or her.

That he himself liked them all, and was happy with them, was not to be doubted. His reluctance, his uneasiness at accompanying Miss Cubitt today was understood and warmly sympathized with. He had found himself with friends, and who knew what today was to bring about? He had hinted that Mrs Belchamber might have certain objections to raise ... certain prejudices against him. He had known, this last week, that the police had traced her; he had expressed his satisfaction at her safety; it was even as he had said—she was with the children. He had at first been strongly averse to going to Grenton, but Miss Cubitt had pointed out the necessity ... the inevitability ...

They walked to the station together, discussing the surprising warmth of the day. The train was a few minutes late and they decided to wait in the shabby, but cool waiting-room. They sat on a hard bench and Monsieur Versoix, oddly silent, gazed at the highly coloured posters displayed on the walls. They invited him to travel to a somewhat glamorized Blackpool and a highly improbable Eastbourne, and offered him a choice of excursion trains to London or Bournemouth.

The train, creaking in, put an end to his musing. They walked outside and got into a carriage; the train jerked into motion, and a hot breeze blew into the compartment. Miss Cubitt looked out and realized that a storm could not long be delayed; she was without any kind of protection, but her suit was of good material and would withstand any but the heaviest shower; in any case, she was not likely to be exposed to the storm, for at Grenton they were to take a taxi to Green Farm; they were to keep the taxi and try to persuade Mrs Belchamber to return to Melhampton at once, and Miss Cubitt had little doubt that the letters she carried from the trustees would make the old lady see how much they all regretted her odd behaviour, and make her realize how much anxiety she had caused them all. In case there should be any difficulty, they had taken the precaution of sending the papers; odd behaviour was the prerogative of old ladies but a firm signature on the papers was the right of every member of the Melhampton household.

Miss Cubitt opened a magazine and tried to read, but the gloom in the carriage was now so great as to make reading impossible without a light, and this the railway authorities seemed unwilling to supply. She closed the book and leaned back, looking out at the scene, which in the strange light looked unreal and unfamiliar. The rain was not far off ...

They were both relieved when the train reached Grenton. Miss Cubitt got out and looked about her, and then, stopping a porter, inquired whether she could get a taxi. She could, he informed her; if she would inquire at the office just outside the station, they would send for one.

The office was small, but easily found. Monsieur Versoix waited in the yard; Miss Cubitt stepped inside and a rubicund man, hot and perspiring, sitting with his shirt-sleeves rolled up, nodded, waved her to a chair and indicated that his telephone call would not last long. Presently he got up and addressed her:

'Good afternoon, ma'am. Sorry to've kept you. You'll want a taxi, I suppose?'

'Please.'

The man opened a greasy notebook and scanned its pages.

'Nothing in at the moment, but there'll be one along in five ... ten minutes. Where're you for?'

'Green Farm.'

'Green Farm!' The man's face assumed a dubious expression, and Miss Cubitt looked at him anxiously.

'Is it very far?'

'No-oo. No, it's not the distance—it's the road. We have a job getting taxi-drivers to go up that last bit of lane. Ruins their cars, they all complain.'

The taxi-driver, arriving at this juncture, complained with a good deal of emphasis, taking off his peaked cap and scratching his sparse white locks in vexation.

'Git you out there, if I'm lucky,' he

promised, 'but I don't fancy the trip. Pot-'oles a yard deep, miss, and the lane the width of me arm. Meet somethink coming the other way, and back you come in reverse all over the pot'oles agin.'

'I—I'm sorry about that,' said Miss Cubitt. 'I wanted you to take us out there and wait for me.'

'Wait 'ow long, about?'

'Well—if you could give me half—at the most, three quarters of an hour...' She stopped as a roll of thunder muttered in the distance and drew nearer.

'Storm's coming,' said the driver. 'You couldn't wait till the worst of it 'ad come down, could you, miss?'

'I—I'd rather go now. Perhaps we could get there before it breaks.'

The driver, muttering something to the effect that he very much doubted it, led her out to the car and opened the door. Miss Cubitt looked at Monsieur Versoix, but to her surprise, he took her arm and drew her aside.

'It is better,' he said in an undertone, 'that I do not go.'

'Do not—' Miss Cubitt gazed at him in dismay. 'But you ... you have as much to say to Mrs Belchamber as I have! You will be anxious to—'

'But yes—I am anxious,' admitted Monsieur Versoix. 'I must see her. But your affairs— those are the most important—you

267

understand?'

'Yes, I see your point, but—'

'Then this will be best,' said Monsieur Versoix. 'First you will go, and she will sign the papers—no?'

'I—I hope so.'

'And then,' continued Monsieur Versoix, 'then you will say: "Come with me," and perhaps she will come.'

'I hope she will. But if she refuses, then I—'

'If she will not come, then you will return in the taxi, and I shall be here. I shall put you in the train to go back to Melhampton, and I shall go myself to this farm and I shall see her, but it is better—it is kinder to her, you onnerstand?—that I shall see her alone.'

'I understand perfectly.' Miss Cubitt took a few moments to consider the matter. 'I go out there now and talk to Mrs Belchamber, and ask her, whatever she feels about returning with me, to sign the papers.'

'That is correct.'

'If she comes back with me, you'll meet us here; if she doesn't come, you're going out there to see her?'

'That is quite correct. It is better,' said Monsieur Versoix with a sage air, 'that we do not do this business togezzer. The business, it is not the same for us—it is better that we should not do it togezzer.'

Miss Cubitt felt the soundness of this. She was on public, he on private business, and whatever the urgency of his affairs, the desirability of obtaining Mrs Belchamber's signature on the papers must be of paramount importance. Satisfied with the arrangement, she left Monsieur Versoix and got into the taxi. It was a large, old-fashioned limousine, and she sank deep into its capacious seat. The driver twisted and turned in the station yard and finally drove off at a speed befitting the age and dignity of the car.

They were not, after all, to miss the storm. The thunder crashed overhead, and, as if it had been a signal, the heavens opened. The rain came down in a steady, sheeting drive, closing in about the car and reducing both speed and visibility to a minimum. They crawled through the streets of the town and out into its suburbs, and then began the drive along the broad main road as far as the turning leading to the farm.

From this point, the journey, for Miss Cubitt, had a nightmare quality. At the beginning of the lane the surface was tolerable, and she had only to grasp the cord-covered strap beside her to steady herself against the car's lurchings. The rain beat an incessant tattoo upon the roof, and Miss Cubitt, listening to the sound, pressed her lips together and looked out for some sign that the farm was near; there was nothing to be seen on either side, however, but the tall, thick hedge. She found the car swaying more and more violently, and heard the driver's muttered imprecations; there could not, she thought, be much more of this.

There was a sickening lurch, and the car came to an abrupt stop, leaning to one side. Miss Cubitt, peering out, saw that the driver was examining one of the back wheels and, with a shoulder against it, was attempting to push the car forward. Finding it impossible, he opened the car door, and shook the water from his face.

'Pot-'ole,' he announced briefly. 'Can't get out. Skidding.'

He banged the door, and she saw that he was tearing twigs from the hedge and heaping them behind the wheel. After a few moments, her nerves racked beyond endurance by the drumming sound of the rain, and moved, too, by the driver's look of age and exhaustion, she opened the car to get out to help him. Remembering her lack of mackintosh, however, she sank back on the seat. The rain beat on the driver as he gathered enough brushwood for his purpose, and presently, wiping a sleeve across his eyes, he opened the car door and pointed down the lane.

'You'd better walk on,' he shouted over the noise of the storm. 'It's only about a hundred yards—if you take it quick you won't get too wet. I'll get the car out and come up for you later. Go on—before it gets worse. First building you come to.'

Miss Cubitt decided to follow his advice; she

got out quickly and hurried along the muddy lane, shaken by the gusts of wind but relieved to have escaped from the noisy imprisonment of the car.

The farm in sight through the trees, not far ahead, but indefinable through the rain's haze. She squared her shoulders, striving, now that her goal was in sight, to call upon the poise and masterfulness that distinguished her. She felt shaken and unlike herself; she could only wish, over and over again, for a swift and satisfactory end to her mission.

She came to the farm's gates, and stood irresolute, and then, like the police inspector, walked on with the intention of finding the front door. She walked rapidly down the lane for a few yards, and, coming to the gate, attempted to push it open. It resisted, as it had resisted the inspector, but Miss Cubitt lacked his height and strength, and, for some time, she struggled with it in vain. Pausing for breath, she made a final effort and, applying a combined pushing and lifting movement, found—too late—that the gate had swung back. Clinging to its iron palings, she was dragged back with it and brought up sharply; her head hit an iron bar and, for a moment, everything swung crazily round her.

She waited for the giddiness to pass and then went, unsteadily, but with an instinctive caution, up the slippery path toward the door. She stood still, gathering her forces, gazing through the glass panels into the wide hall. Someone, she saw, was coming downstairs ... Mrs Belchamber herself ... and a girl ... and someone else ...

Miss Cubitt put up a hand and rapped— whether loudly or not, she could not judge, for her head seemed to be whirling. She waited, and knew that someone was opening the door. A man—a young man, big broad ...

She knew that he had put out a hand and was drawing her inside. In the hall, he still retained his hold, in spite of her faint efforts to release herself, but he closed the door, and the shutting out of the storm, with its surge and confusion, brought a momentary steadiness to her outraged nerves. She freed her arm from his grasp and faced him with an attempt at dignity.

'I've come ... I've come to—'

'Steady!' said Scotty. 'Now, let me give you a hand. Come along, now—come in here and we'll find you a seat and then—'

Miss Cubitt made a strong effort and spoke with more clearness.

'I would like to see Mrs Belchamber,' she said.

'Mrs—? Oh, yes. Oh, yes, yes,' said Scotty, taking in the details of her pallor and dishevelment. 'Well—you shall presently. Now come in here.'

He propelled her, gently but irresistibly, towards the big front room. It was unlighted, and he went back and, taking the lamp from its bracket in the hall, carried it into the room and placed it on a table.

'There—now we can see each other,' he said.

Miss Cubitt, now desperately anxious to fulfil her errand and be gone, found strength enough to speak with a degree of authority.

'Will you fetch Mrs Belchamber, please?'

'Ah!' said Scotty gently. 'What name shall I say?'

'My name is Cubitt. Miss Cubitt. She will know who I am.'

'That's all right. Sit down,' invited Scotty, 'and I'll go straight away.'

Miss Cubitt remained standing stiffly. After a glance at her, Scotty went out and closed the door behind him.

She waited, her giddiness returning with the relief of finding herself alone. She walked to the sofa and clung to it for a few moments. She could hear sounds, and thumping, and a child's voice shouting, but the minutes passed and there was no sign of Mrs Belchamber. It occurred to her suddenly that the man who had admitted her had said that he would fetch her—but she knew that Mrs Belchamber was downstairs—she had seen her come down—and the man had gone upstairs. She had heard his footsteps as he ascended the stairs.

Filled with vague fears, trembling from shock and fatigue, Miss Cubitt walked to the door and opened it. The lamp behind her sent a soft glow into the hall, casting eerie, grotesque

273

shadows. There were sounds from above laughter, and children's voices, raised in chorus. As she listened, she felt the hall swaying dizzily before her. The last vestige of colour left her face and she clung giddily to the door. It was not possible … it was fantastic … she was going to faint. She knew that someone was coming downstairs, and made a last desperate effort to recover herself. Her nerves, however, had given way at last; she swayed slowly and Christopher caught her as she fell.

CHAPTER SEVENTEEN

To carry Miss Cubitt into the room and lay her on the sofa was the work of a moment. Christopher went back for the brandy, shut the door carefully, and knelt beside her. He held the glass to her lips and Miss Cubitt, with a shudder, and a gasp, opened her eyes.

'Oh!' she said. 'I—I—'

'Look—don't try to talk,' said Christopher gently. 'Just drink this and you'll be all right.'

'I don't—thank you, no … I—'

'You're wet through, and you're cold—it's better to save yourself a severe chill,' urged Christopher. 'Please drink this.'

He held the glass and, gulp by gulp, Miss Cubitt drank its contents. He watched a little colour come to her cheeks, and, drawing up a

274

small chair, sat on its edge and waited for her to regain a little composure.

'I'm—I'm—you must forgive me,' she murmured presently.

'You must forgive us,' corrected Christopher gently. 'We've given you a lot of trouble, one way and another.'

'No . . . no.' Miss Cubitt closed her eyes for a moment, and then opened them and fixed them upon him in a sombre stare. 'It wasn't that. No, it wasn't that. It . . . it was the rain.'

'Yes—you shouldn't have come out in this storm, you know.'

'It was the rain,' repeated Miss Cubitt. 'It was—yes it was the rain. And no umbrella—and no mackintosh. I would have brought them, but I thought—I thought they weren't *chic*.'

He looked at her with growing alarm. There was a bruise on one side of her forehead, and it looked to him a recent one. He wished he had disregarded Scotty's advice about the brandy . . . but on second thoughts, it was obviously warming her, and it would stave off a chill. It had gone to her head; she was staring at him with an odd look, and he had an idea that she had forgotten where she was. He hoped she would fall into a doze—it would solve the problem very well; by the time she roused herself, the party would be over. She would have her interview with Mrs Belchamber and—Christopher found himself viewing the prospect with less relief than he would have thought possible—she would arrange for her removal to Melhampton.

'You must rest for a few minutes,' he said.

'Yes ... yes.' Miss Cubitt was still staring at him oddly. He made a movement as if to rise and leave her, and, to his dismay, she put out a hand and made a desperate clutch at him. 'Oh ... don't go! Don't go!' she gasped.

Christopher left his hands in hers, and looked at her a little helplessly. For the first time, he remembered the doctor's presence, and felt a certain relief; he would call her if Miss Cubitt looked like collapsing again. She put out her other hand, so that Christopher's was held tightly in both of hers. He had no idea how long he sat there motionless, watching Miss Cubitt's eyes as they lost their look of terror and began to glaze with sleep. Presently they closed, and after waiting for a few moments more, Christopher released his hands with infinite gentleness and by slow degrees began to edge out of the room. He opened the door soundlessly and glanced back at the sleeping form on the sofa; then he closed the door behind him and made his way upstairs. He paused for a moment outside the door of the room upstairs and then, entering, found himself in instant demand to assist at the cutting of the cake. He glanced at Scotty over the heads of the children, and Scotty, seeing the look, waited until the pieces of cake had been taken round, and then came up to him with a look of inquiry.

'You were a long time,' he said. 'Did you have trouble persuading her to wait down there?'

'No. She's asleep.'

'Asleep? That'll be the drink you gave her. I told you it was just what she needed. The next thing'll be to tell the old lady she's here.'

'Who's here?' demanded Mrs Belchamber from behind him.

'Visitor for you,' said Scotty, unabashed. 'Name of Cubitt.'

'Oh—that detestable creature? Did you tell her to go away?'

'How could we do that?' asked Scotty. 'You've been playing a nice game of come-and-get-me, and now she's come.'

'Well, tell her to go away again.'

'You tell her,' invited Scotty.

'Certainly I'll tell her. Where is she?'

'She's in the big front room,' said Scotty. 'She's asleep.'

'As-leep!' Mrs Belchamber's mouth dropped open in astonishment. 'As-leep! Are you joking?'

'Would I dare?' asked Scotty. 'She was a bit washed out when she arrived.'

'Washed out? Do you mean wet?'

'Well, yes—wet and washed out,' said Scotty. 'I saw her when we went downstairs, and I let her in.'

277

'But my dear Mr Scott, Cressida and I were in the kitchen and not a soul—'

'She came the front way,' explained Scotty.

'I see. And did she ask for me?'

'Yes, she did, but I thought we'd give you time to get the cake-cutting ceremony over—by which time, she'd have pulled herself together.'

Mrs Belchamber gave up the attempt to visualize the situation.

'I shall go down,' she said. 'I don't understand a word you're saying.'

'If I were you,' said Christopher, 'I'd take the doctor down with you.'

'Yes. I think she must have stumbled coming up the lane—I saw a bruise on her head, and she didn't seem herself.'

The doctor, hastily eating the last morsels of her piece of cake, announced herself ready to accompany Mrs Belchamber and examine the visitor. She made her farewells, congratulated her host and hostess on the success of the party, thanked them and followed Mrs Belchamber out. Scotty's eyes followed her with a puzzled look in them, and Christopher eyed him.

'What're you looking at?' he asked curiously.

'The doctor,' said Scotty. 'First time I've seen her when she wasn't wearing her stethoscope.'

'So what?' asked Cressida.

'She's quite feminine, when you see her

behind a bit of birthday cake,' mused Scotty, his eyes still on the closed door. 'And that's the first time I've seen her in a dress you could call a dress—you know—the sort of thing that lets a figure speak for itself. Did you see her figure, Chris?'

'No,' said Christopher.

'You don't look,' complained Scotty. 'She was quite different today. Yesterday I could have told her all my symptoms, and today—well, I'd blush to the roots. How would you explain that?'

'Easily,' said Cressida. 'The symptoms are different, that's all. Who was the visitor? Is she the one—'

'Is she that one?' Paul had come up and was looking up at Scotty eagerly. 'I put a spell for her—a bad spell.'

'Well, I wouldn't play with bad spells or good spells, if I were you,' warned Scotty. 'They've got a way of going off right in your face.'

'But the doctor has gone to look,' persisted Paul. 'That is the bad spell.'

'No, it's nothing of the sort, Maskelyne, old fellow-me-lad. It's the storm and the fatigue of ploughing in and out of all those potholes in the lane, that's what it is. The only people who can make spells in England—I wouldn't know about France, but I can speak for this country—are those peculiar old women with long, pointed noses and long, pointed chins and beady eyes and silly hats and a nasty expression.' He paused, struck by the fact that he was painting a fairly accurate word-picture of Mrs Belchamber.

'No more spells?' said Paul.

'No. No more spells,' said Cressida. 'We've had enough.' She bent over the sleepy Josette and swung her into her arms. 'Bed,' she said. 'Bed for a tired girl.'

Josette made no protest; she allowed herself to be removed, and Robert and Paul followed her, armed with the remainder of the crackers.

'Well, that's over,' said Scotty, viewing the littered table. 'Funny about Miss Cubitt,' he said reflectively. 'I wasn't at all surprised to see her.'

'Well, you knew she was coming,' pointed out Christopher.

'Quite true, but it isn't what I meant. I had a feeling. Oh—incidentally—do you want to buy a house?'

'A house?'

'There's a nice little property on the market—the other side of the town. Not too big, not too small. Nice grounds. I don't know what they're asking for it, but I could find out, if you're interested.'

'No.' There was scarcely any hesitation. 'No, thanks, Scotty. I'd like to be near you, and so would Cressida, but I'd like to put more than a few miles between us and … between…'

'I know—the major. Well, I don't blame you. Be funny to have the farm empty after all this.'

'You won't notice.'

'Yes, I will—for a time, anyhow. And would you have believed, when I first set eyes on—you know who I mean—that I would have felt a pang at the thought of her leaving? But I do. When I think of Mrs Garcia getting back into her big chair with her feet up; when I think of coming in at night with my boots on; when I think of passing the tin bath without having to drag it in, fill it and sit in it, I get a very, very funny feeling—and it isn't relief. If it didn't sound morbid, I'd say I was actually going to miss her. I know you'll be pretty glad to see the last of her, but—'

'I'm not sure,' said Christopher, 'that I will.'

'Will what?'

'Be glad to.'

'To what?'

'What you said.'

'What did I say?' inquired Scotty.

'It doesn't matter. But it's odd, all the same—it'll be difficult to realize she isn't here any more. I shall find myself waiting for orders that don't come; I'll be thinking I hear that voice complaining about the things you smell of.'

'I've already explained,' said Scotty with dignity, 'that farmyard smells are entirely—'

'Yes, I know, but we'd never have convinced

281

her. And although I still deplore her methods, how else could anybody have got you cleaned up so thoroughly? Who else could have flattened that case-hardened Mrs Garcia in one joust? It's incredible, and it's going back on everything I've said, but—I shall miss her.'

'Me too,' said Scotty. 'Ain't Nature wonderful?—And talking of Nature, Chris, I don't find myself feeling too good.'

Christopher gave him a glance of keen anxiety.

'Are you serious?'

'I was never more serious in my life,' declared Scotty. 'I feel all to pieces. I'm going to ring up the doctor and tell her that there's only one thing that can save me.'

'And what's that?'

'The doctor,' said Scotty.

There was a long silence, and they roused themselves at last as Mrs Belchamber entered the room. They saw with surprise that she was dressed in her long tweed coat.

'You going out?' inquired Scotty in astonishment.

'I'm going to the station,' announced Mrs Belchamber. 'I shall put Miss Cubitt on her train, and then come back in the taxi. I hope you two won't stand there idling, and let Cressida do the entire cleaning up.'

'We'll give a hand,' promised Scotty. 'Did the doctor see Miss Cubitt?'

'She did. She was not asleep, as you said she

was. She was sitting on the sofa.'

'Oh. What did the doctor say?'

'The doctor looked her over and said her nerves were shaky, and put it down to the storm and the bump she gave her head on the gate. I didn't disabuse her. After all, she's a doctor and she's supposed to know.'

'Disabuse her?' Scotty stared at her, uncomprehending. 'How?'

Mrs Belchamber drew on a pair of neat black gloves. She took a step backwards and craned her neck towards the door to ensure that she could not be overheard, and then spoke.

'I knew, when I saw that woman down there, that there was something peculiar about her. When I saw her first, I mean to say. I didn't like her manner at all; there was something about it that I couldn't place. But now I know exactly what's the matter with her.'

'Well—what?' inquired Scotty.

'Drink.'

'D-drink?' he echoed.

'You can always tell,' said Mrs Belchamber. 'You might have been taken in with that cow-and-bull story about this and that bump making her feel queer, but as soon as I got into the room, I knew what was the matter with her. She was very dignified, and she said she was feeling better and hoped she had given no trouble. The doctor asked her a few questions, and found that she couldn't remember anything from the time she'd opened the gate until the moment she found herself lying on the sofa. I didn't say a word, but I used my nose, and it never deceives me. That woman had been drinking.'

'But look here—' began Scotty anxiously.

Mrs Belchamber held up an arresting hand.

'No, you needn't fear,' she said acidly. 'I shall say nothing to anybody. I shall put her on the train with a message to the effect that I've changed my mind about living at Melhampton. The house is no longer mine, and I've no wish to interfere with the way in which they run it. If they want to employ women who can't get through a gate when they see one, it isn't my affair. One of these days, she'll take a little too much and somebody with a sensitive nose like mine will smell what's going on. For all I know, all the members of the staff there may spend their entire time drinking; it doesn't matter to me. I don't think this creature is fit to get herself into a train without help, and I don't want it known that somebody who came to visit me went away in a state of intoxication. I shall be back within the hour.'

The door closed firmly behind her. Scotty looked at Christopher and raised his eyebrows expressively. Neither man spoke, but they moved, by common consent, to the window overlooking the road, and saw, presently, the tall form of Mrs Belchamber going towards the taxi. In one hand she held aloft a large umbrella; with the other she held in a firm grasp Miss Cubitt's elbow. Leading her charge to the car, she helped her in, snapped an order at the driver and climbed in beside Miss Cubitt. The taxi turned into the gateway, backed out again, turned and drove away, and Scotty drew a deep breath.

'Well, now what?' he asked. 'Every time they post someone out to fetch her, she posts them back again. First we think we've got rid of her and we feel sad, and then we know we haven't and we feel a lot worse. And we know nothing about anything—why the old girl skipped off, why the French fellow was after her, why anything.'

'We ought to have explained,' said Christopher, 'about the brandy. It wasn't fair to let her get ideas that were right off the mark. We could have explained.'

'No, we couldn't,' said Scotty. 'She can always tell. And I—' He stopped abruptly, staring down at the muddy, puddle-filled road. 'Christ, look down there!'

Christopher looked. A short figure in a dark overcoat had come into view, had paused at the open gate and was obviously looking for a way into the farm. There was no mistaking that build; Christopher gave an exclamation that brought Scotty's eyes to his face.

'That's that French chap you spoke about?'

'Yes. Do you suppose he—where are you going?'

Scotty was at the door and throwing it open.

'I'm going to haul him in, of course,' he said. 'Come on, Chris—get moving before the Belchamber comes back and shuts the council chamber right in our faces. Come on—grab him!'

Grabbing Monsieur Versoix, they led him into the big front room and shut the door.

CHAPTER EIGHTEEN

Scotty's brandy had found its way to a palate that could appreciate it. Monsieur Versoix, rolling it round his tongue, gazed at Scotty with eyes brimming with gratitude.

'Encore?' asked Scotty, and the visitor nodded in solemn agreement. Glass in hand, he faced the two young men across the fireplace, and gave a deep sigh of relief.

'Ah!' he said, on a long breath.

'I know,' said Scotty. 'It's *très bon*. When you've got a bit more down, you can perhaps answer a few questions. *Comprenez?*'

Monsieur Versoix bowed.

'You'd better ask 'em, Chris,' said Scotty. 'After all, this is your show. Ask him why he's been chasing Mrs Belchamber over the Channel.'

'Twice,' said Monsieur Versoix.

286

'Eh?'

The visitor held up two fingers. 'Twice,' he repeated.

'Twice I chase 'er, and each time—' His fingers snapped.

'When you talked to Mrs Belchamber in the train,' said Christopher, 'it was obvious that she didn't want to talk to you. You shouldn't have followed her when she'd made it plain she didn't want to see you.'

Monsieur Versoix leaned forward earnestly.

'*Mais je vous dis, Monsieur,*' he began, '*que*—'

'Whoa!' said Scotty. 'Whoa there! It's no use conducting this interview in anything but basic English. I'm an interested party, after all—it was my house that Mrs Belchamber came to, and it was my habits that she—well, we'll skip that, but we'll begin, if you don't mind, from the beginning. Over to you, Chris.'

'My name is Christopher Heron,' began Christopher, 'and I never saw Mrs Belchamber before I got into her carriage at Hautiers.'

'And the children—are they yours?' inquired Monsieur Versoix.

'No. They're my cousins, but they were brought up in France. I was bringing them home to England. I intended to drive up to London, but one of the children was ill, and so I changed my mind and came here. When I got into my car, Mrs Belchamber was already in it, and refused to get out. But I'm sure she would have gone to Melhampton with Miss Cubitt if she hadn't caught sight of you. I've no right to interfere in Mrs Belchamber's affairs, but I feel that she has put herself, in some way, under our protection, and so we would like to know why you're—if you don't mind the word—pestering her.'

He paused, and Scotty gazed at him in admiration.

'That was a fine inauguration speech,' he said. 'Now we go on to the questions. First, Monsieur, who are you?'

'My name is Versoix—Vairr-soix. Badouin.'

'Bad one?' repeated the puzzled Scotty.

'Ba-dou-in. Badouin Versoix. Forty years ago, my father, who was a widower, married this lady who is now Belchamber.'

'So *that*,' said Scotty, 'is why you called her mommer!'

'*Maman*. But yes—is she not *maman*?'

'If she marries papa, I suppose she is,' conceded Scotty.

'But she obviously isn't keen on owning you—how come?'

'Pardon?'

'Why,' asked Christopher, 'is Mrs Belchamber obviously unwilling to have anything to do with you?'

'It is money,' said Monsieur Versoix simply.

There was a pause; the subject was a large one. At last Scotty attempted to define the position.

288

'Do you mean she's got some of yours, or are you after some of hers?' he inquired.

Monsieur Versoix leaned forward once more, using a thumb and forefinger, pressed together, to give point to his words.

'Messieurs, you shall judge,' he said. 'When my father married, his wife—his second wife, had already money. That is to say, she had enough money of herself, and did not need any more. But for many years, while they were married, she save her money and use my father's; there is plenty, so this is all right. But then my father died. I had then a good business. My father arranged that all his money should be in two pieces—when he died, he said one piece should be for me and the other piece for his wife. We both agreed, and so it was when he died—I have half and she have—has—half.'

'Fair enough,' said Scotty.

'It was then fair—yes. But after that, there is war. My business go, my money goes. I look for my stepmother; I do not know where she is, but I hear that she is again married to a rich man. I say: her husband number one is rich, two is rich, three is rich—also she is rich before she is married at all. I think if I ask her for some of my father's money, she will give it to me. I write to this address, that address, but no answer comes. I see her once—she is coming to England, and I follow her, but she gives me the slip. Now I am here to ask her.'

'Where have you been all this time—in England, I mean?' asked Christopher.

'When you went away and Mrs Belchamber was lost,' explained Monsieur Versoix, 'I did not know what to do. I followed her without thinking—and now she was gone and I had nothing—no papers, no money. There was only one thing—to find the lady who came to take Mrs Belchamber—I see her, I talk to her, I have to say some little ... some what is not true...'

'Some whoppers,' supplied Scotty.

'I explain something—how I can explain everything? It was necessary to make her feel that I was not—'

'Not telling whoppers.'

'Perhaps. I went with her to Melhampton House, and I tell them there that Mrs Belchamber has my passport and my papers. Myself, I had nothing, for when I got on the train, I was going only a little way on business—I am employed by a shoe manufacturer, and I go from here to there in France, in Switzerland, on business.'

'You travel in shoes,' summed up Scotty. 'Did you travel down here with Cubitt?'

'I did—yes. But when we arrive—I was nervous, and also she had papers to be signed. I said it will be better first for you, and then for me. But she was very long—I waited, and I thought perhaps that Mrs Belchamber would ask her to wait for me to come. A car which was

290

coming near took me, and I walked up the muddy lane, but I saw, at the corner, the taxi—I shouted, but they did not see me, and so I came here—it was too far to go back.' He turned from one to the other of his hearers appealingly. 'Gentlemen, I beg you, when Mrs Belchamber comes, if you will ask with me. I do not want her money—I want my father's. If my father had known that my business would not go on, would he not have said: "More than half will be for Badouin?" It is justice. She has much—she will not miss what she gives. I do not wish to work for others—I do not wish to work at all. I have a wound. It is not much, but if I have money, I shall be able to live quietly, slowly, peacefully. Ask her, gentlemen, I beg you. I—'

'Let him do his own asking,' said a voice from the door.

The three men scrambled to their feet and faced her. Mrs Belchamber unbuttoned her coat, took it off and handed it to Scotty.

'Not there,' she said sharply. 'It's damp—can't you feel? Over the back of the chair—that's it. If you care for clothes, they don't go to pieces like yours.' Her nose twitched and then remained screwed in disgust. 'Drink!' she stated.

'Just a *soupçon*,' pleaded Scotty. 'He was wet, poor Bad-One.'

'Who?'

'We've got as far as Christian names,'

explained Scotty, twirling a chair round. 'Won't you come in on this lesson?'

'No,' said Mrs Belchamber. 'This gentleman is leaving.'

'Oh, but look—' began Scotty.

'Couldn't you just—' asked Christopher.

'Thank you, no arguments,' said Mrs Belchamber. 'The taxi is waiting. I could have stopped it on the way in—I saw you cowering in the hedge, of course—but I had something to settle and I didn't want a third person in the car. Give him his coat,' she ordered.

'But *Maman*—' began Monsieur Versoix in heart-rending accents.

'Don't *Maman* me,' requested Mrs Belchamber. 'Put that coat on and leave that drink just where it is. You're going.'

'Going where?' inquired the Frenchman, brokenly. 'Where am I to go, with no money, no papers, no anything? How can I go? Where am I to go?'

'You're going to Melhampton,' stated Mrs Belchamber.

Monsieur Versoix stared at her incredulously.

'To—to Melhampton?' he echoed. 'How can I go there? They kept me there for a little while, but they will not let me—'

'Oh yes, they will,' said Mrs Belchamber calmly. 'Come on, now—put your coat on and get off before I change my mind.'

'Change your mind about what?' asked

Christopher.

'About bothering myself about his future,' said Mrs Belchamber. 'What cow-and-bull story did he spin you?'

'I spin nothing!' cried Monsieur Versoix passionately. 'I spin nothing! I tell them what is true—you married my father, and half the money, it was yours, and half was mine. Why should I not ask for what was his?'

'Because you wouldn't know how to keep it even if I gave it to you,' said Mrs Belchamber. 'It would go where your mother's money went and where your own money went and where your share of your father's money went. Nobody who knows your gift for picking out worthless investments would ever trust you with money. You haven't got the head for it. You've never made a success at anything involving large sums of money and you never will. You've never made a success of anything—until you got to Melhampton, and there you appear to have fallen into your proper sphere. Miss Cubitt is infatuated with you and so, from her account, are a round dozen more. It seems incredible to me, but they like you and you appear to be useful there. Do you wish to remain there?'

'To remain? But yes, I would like to remain,' said Monsieur Versoix. 'Who would not wish that? The house is beautiful, the food—with my help—is cooked well, the people who are there are charming. Who would not wish to remain? But how can I remain? How—'

Mrs Belchamber faced Christopher.

'There's a lawyer in Grenton—not the pompous individual near the Square, but the man called Allen or Allard. Go in with Monsieur Versoix and put this matter into his hands. Monsieux Versoix will be paid an allowance and will have the use, during his lifetime, at Melhampton of the suite I was to occupy. Don't bother me with details, and don't allow Monsieur Versoix to say anything unless he has anything against the project. He is not to mention any relationship—however distant—which may exist between us. And the first time he applies to me for any form of financial assistance, our agreement comes to an end and he can find his way back to wherever he came from. Now hurry along, will you? There's a great deal of work to be done here, and I shall have to do the brunt of it alone, as usual. Mr Scott, what are you doing with that glass of spirits?'

'Toasting you,' said Scotty. He flourished the glass, took a sip and handed it across to Monsieur Versoix. 'To Madame!' he cried. 'To Madame, the human steamroller! Humans rolled over daily!'

'To Madame,' said Monsieur Versoix, and drained the glass.

CHAPTER NINETEEN

The following morning, Christopher rose earlier than usual and took the boys for a walk. They went out towards the hills, followed by a troop of dogs, and returned in time for breakfast, the children red-cheeked, as full of energy as when they went out, and with enormous appetites.

Breakfast was quieter than usual—the boys ate wolfishly, Christopher and Scotty sat with a question trembling on their lips and Mrs Belchamber applied herself to her food with an obvious intention of not answering it if it was asked.

The meal over, Christopher followed Scotty out to the cowshed and leaned against it thoughtfully.

'If she isn't going *there*,' said Scotty, for the twentieth time, 'then what does she intend to do? I couldn't sleep, Chris, I give you my word. She kept coming up to my bed in a bad dream and saying: "Mr Scott, I have decided to remain with you at Green Farm, washing you, cleaning you up, attending to your personal hygiene and making life hell for you until death do us part!"'

'Oh—rubbish,' said Christopher, in a tone in which there was no shred of conviction. 'She—she couldn't.'

295

'Why couldn't she?' demanded Scotty moodily. 'You couldn't stop her; I couldn't stop her. All I'm waiting to see is when her luggage is going to arrive—the stuff that went to Melhampton. You wait and see—it'll be sent here and she'll start unpacking—for ever.'

'Oh—rot!'

'I wish you thought so,' mourned Scotty. 'But you don't—you know she can't leave me. She can't live without a mission, and I'm it.'

'Give her time,' said Christopher. 'After all, it was only yesterday that she gave up Melhampton. She's thinking over her future plans, that's all. She'll decide to live somewhere or other, and then she'll—well, she'll go and live there, that's all.'

Scotty made no reply. Slowly and broodingly he walked over to lift two heavy milk churns and swing them on to a van that had driven into the yard. Christopher waited until his conversation with the driver was over, and watched him come back as thoughtfully as he had gone.

'Come on—brace up,' he urged. 'Only yesterday you were talking about her in terms of deep affection.'

'That's only because I thought she was going,' pointed out Scotty. 'Oh, by the way,' he went on, 'that van driver gave me some news.'

'Well?'

'About Greensleeves,' said Scotty.

Christopher turned and faced him, and

Scotty saw that his face had turned white.

'What did you say?'

'Greensleeves. It's up for sale. That chap in the van just told me.'

Christopher raised his head and stared past Scotty at the wooded hill, at the chimneys of Greensleeves seen through the trees. Something was stirring in him; there was something he wanted to decide, but his mind seemed to be a blank. Somewhere over there, at Greensleeves, was the answer to a question he had never put ... an answer.

He heard himself speaking.

'How did he know?'

'It's in the agent's hands,' said Scotty. 'Gray went down first thing this morning and saw them, and people think he's trying to make the Council raise their bid.'

'What bid?'

'The Council made him an offer—I told you. But he turned it down a few days ago, and now they think he might have changed his mind—or lowered his limit. They think he might—Chris—hey!'

Scotty's cry went unheard. Christopher had begun to run; he had cleared the gate; he was gathering speed; he was over the next obstacle and passing the bull at such close range that sheer outrage kept the animal immobile for five seconds; when he moved in pursuit, Christopher had gained the necessary start and was taking the next hurdle as the bull reached it. He was in the road, and gaining impetus; he was speeding through the grounds and making for the house...

There was no sign of Cressida, and—for once—Christopher was thankful. He went into the hall and stood still to recover his breath; when Major Gray came in he was breathing fast, but evenly.

'You're an early visitor.' The major's voice had all its usual quiet pleasantness. 'Are you looking for Cressida?'

'No.' Christopher plunged without preamble. 'Scotty tells me you're selling Greensleeves.'

The major shrugged, drew out a cigarette case and held it out towards Christopher.

'No, thanks.' Christopher shook his head impatiently. 'Are you selling the house?'

'I am. Grenton Council made me an offer—at last. They won't give me what I want for it, but I've tried all the other likely buyers. It's too big for a house, too small for a school, too expensive for a hospital and not big enough to draw tourists. The Council will give me a quarter of what it's worth, but who else'll buy it?'

'I will,' said Christopher.

He saw, as he said the words, the first unrehearsed expression he had ever seen on Major Gray's face. The two men stared at one another, and then Major Gray had recovered from his surprise. The mask, Christopher saw, was in place; the calculating machine was at work.

'Why you?' he asked curiously.

'Why not me?' countered Christopher.

Major Gray spoke slowly.

'I thought—once—the first time, that you might make an offer. I knew you had the money; I knew you wanted a place, and I knew that you saw the beauty of this one, and even, for a little while, fell under its spell. I might have pressed you—but things were going well enough for me, then, and so I left things as they were. And then, when I decided to sell, I thought your attitude had changed—you didn't look to me as keen as you'd been once.'

'Why have you decided to sell?'

'For the reasons I gave you the other day. I thought I could go on for a bit longer, but my credit's gone. And the game was getting tedious, too, and it was more strenuous, in fact, than it had appeared in planning. I'm not sorry it's over, but I'm sorry the house is to go. If things had been different, I might have had a shot at keeping it somehow, in some way. If I'd had a son, there might have been some point in it—but Cressida will marry and go away.' He paused, walked a few paces and stared out of a window. 'And that, in effect, is what I shall do. Only in reverse order.'

'What?'

'I shall go away, and marry.'

'Marry?'

Major Gray smiled.

'I don't know why I tell you,' he said. 'I've never mentioned it to Cressida, and you can tell her or keep it to yourself—just as you like. There's been a strong attraction taking me abroad for the last few years. To Cape Town to be exact. I don't often look into the future—it doesn't do—but, oddly enough, whenever I did give a glance ahead, I saw nothing about remarrying. But I met another Annette—Cressida's mother, you know, was Annette—and one way and another, I began to see a good deal of her. I tried to persuade her to marry me and come to England, but she's a good business woman, and she didn't see any future for us at Greensleeves. She was right. So when the sale goes through, I shall go and settle out there and hand my capital over to her to look after. I like South Africa—as much as I like any place for long. But one's views change. My feet are getting heavier than they were. Wings fall off, as you grow old, and barnacles begin to form. I don't suppose you know any Kipling—your generation doesn't much but I keep recalling those lines of his about coming with least adventure to our goal—that's very much how I feel about life now. I want it quiet and ordered. Odd, isn't it?'

'No,' said Christopher. 'I don't think it's odd. I suppose I'll feel the same one day.'

The major sighed. 'Well—I'm glad Cressida's going to marry you. If you'll take a word of advice, you'll have one more go at trying to get her to marry you without the delay she's determined to impose—but if she won't, your best plan would be to keep out of the way a bit and see what absence does to make her change her mind. She doesn't like London, and, in spite of what she says, she doesn't like that job she's doing; she'll be near enough to you and those three children to want to know what you're all doing, and, now that you're buying Greensleeves, I have a feeling you'll find her coming round sooner than you know.'

'I hope so,' said Christopher. 'And now—hadn't we better talk about Greensleeves?'

'You're quite certain you want it?'

'Quite.'

'I'm glad. But I want a good price, you know.'

'Name it,' said Christopher.

*　　*　　*

He was going back, not hurriedly, as he had come, but slowly and thoughtfully. He had come with his thoughts in confusion, with his mind astray, and he was returning in peace. Greensleeves was his; Cressida would one day be his. The children would grow up in surroundings that their father and mother would have approved; his own children would grow up with them.

He looked at the farm coming into view. The

301

two boys were playing, high up on the straw stacks. Just below them, Scotty stood cutting the wire that bound a bale of straw, and shaking the golden strands loose. The sun was streaming down on the three figures; above was blue sky. The world was beautiful, and orderly and in tune once more. He would—

He heard the pounding and the low, ominous shuffle, and, without waiting to turn his head, went into a burst of speed that equalled anything he had done in his university days. But to hurry, says the proverb, is not enough; one must start in time, and he had not the five seconds start he had had on the outward journey.

The bull caught him up near the gate; with his assistance, Christopher sailed over it and landed with faultless accuracy on the newly-opened bale of straw at Scotty's feet.

'The last chap I saw do that,' remarked Scotty, looking down at him reflectively, 'was the one on the flying trapeze. But they told me it needed a lifetime's practice...'

CHAPTER TWENTY

Mrs Garcia came late that morning, and Scotty, meeting her in the yard and giving her a cheerful greeting, was greatly taken aback to see her burst into bitter tears. He stood looking at her in dismay.

'I only said good morning,' he said. 'What did you think I said?'

'Oh, sir, I'd rather you didn't talk, reely I'd rather,' sobbed Mrs Garcia, going indoors.

Scotty looked after her in dismay. It could only mean that this time, Howsay had gone off for good. He speculated for a moment as to whether this would deprive the farm of her services, or render them more permanent; he could not decide and, with a helpless shrug, went on with his work.

'I'd rather you didn't talk, reely,' sobbed Mrs Garcia to the distressed Cressida. 'Reely, I'd rather.'

'What's the matter with her?' demanded Mrs Belchamber, entering with a firm tread. 'Is she sick?'

'No, oh, no. Yes—oh, oh, yes,' said Mrs Garcia between gulps. 'If you don't take notice of me, I'll just do my work, madam.'

'Well, you can't do your work in that state,' answered Mrs Belchamber. 'Have you had a fall?'

'I wish I 'ad,' mourned Mrs Garcia.

'Has your husband gone off?'

'Nooo, and now it's too late!' was the extraordinary reply.

A glimmer began to penetrate Mrs Belchamber's bewilderment, and she beckoned Cressida upstairs. Cressida, with a sympathetic pat of the afflicted one's hand, followed the old lady.

'I'll tell you her trouble,' said Mrs Belchamber, facing her in the bedroom.

'Her husband?'

'Well, I only hope so. Her union's been blessed.'

'Her—?'

'Yes. You mark my words—that's what it is. People never know when they're well off—until it's too late.'

'Oh dear!' Cressida made a little sound of distress. 'Do you think the little clinging hands—'

'I can't say what effect they'll have on *him*. They might give him something to stay at home for, and they might not. But she's been so busy posing as a barren fig-tree all these years, that she didn't stop to remember that for the first three or four years, the little hands would cling to her far more than they'd cling to her husband. Now, she's down there, remembering.'

'Are you sure that's what it is?'

'I'm quite certain. You can always tell,' said Mrs Belchamber. 'See if I'm not right. You'd better go downstairs and cheer her up by pointing out some of the brighter aspects of having babies, if you can think of any. I'm going in to see Josette.'

She settled Josette more comfortably on the sofa to which she had been moved, and tidied away some of the toys that had accumulated

304

during her convalescence. Josette watched her with her usual calm complacency.

'Please do not take the little doll,' she said presently. 'I am talking to her.'

'Oh. Well, there you are, then.' Mrs Belchamber handed it over. 'But you want three teddy bears and two woollen dogs all at once, will you, or all those books? Those can go on the table beside you. And so can this—Now *who*,' she demanded, 'broke this nice little paint box?'

'Nobody broke it,' said Josette.

'Nobody?'

'No. By mistake, Robert fell on it when he was fighting.'

'Fighting? You mean fighting with Paul? What were they fighting about?'

'They were fighting because Robert said he had more spots, and Paul said no, he had more.'

'But they haven't got any spots! I looked this morning.'

'Not *now*. Not *this* time,' said Josette, with a shake of her head. 'The other time when they had spots like me.'

'The—' Mrs Belchamber stared at her. 'You mean, they had—are you trying to say that they had measles before?—when you were in France?'

'Yes, then.'

'Well, why didn't they say so? Why didn't they tell us? Why didn't they say something?

305

We've all been waiting for them to get them.'

'You can twice,' said Josette. 'That is what you said. They can have more?'

'They—' Mrs Belchamber gave an exasperated sound. 'They're not likely to get them a second time at their age. If you'd told me, I should have known.'

With this obvious truth, she swept the surplus toys into a neat pile and went downstairs, still making sounds of annoyance. Going into the kitchen, she found that her diagnosis of Mrs Garcia's complaint had been the correct one. The invalid spent the morning between forlorn attempts to work, and even more forlorn attempts to summarize the effects the blessing was going to have upon her life.

'I'll 'ave to go and find a home,' she explained. 'There's room for me and Howsay, but when it come to a baby and my sister's four, then the 'ouse won't 'old us. At my time of life, to start knitting! And pushing a pram all those miles, like those mothers do, day after day, in and out o' the shops and up and down the 'ills! And all that washing, and feeding and doing for! And teething and convulsions! And—'

'Well, don't dwell on it,' said Mrs Belchamber. 'It isn't as though you were expecting quadruplets, you know.'

Mrs Garcia was uncertain what quadruplets were, but when Cressida explained that Mrs Belchamber meant quads, her countenance became so alarmingly pale that it was thought best to send her home to rest. She passed through the yard and Scotty met her with a cheerful smile.

'It *is* a good morning—no?'

Mrs Garcia went by him, deaf and unseeing.

'Oh, goodness me!' she muttered despairingly. 'Oh, goodness me!'

The news was broken to the two men over lunch, in terms designed by Mrs Belchamber to leave the children in ignorance of the purport of her announcement.

'Abigail was out of sorts this morning, as perhaps you noticed,' she said.

'Abigail?' said Scotty, uncomprehending.

'She looked pale,' said Christopher. 'Howsay giving trouble?'

'No. Her hopes are at last to be fulfilled.'

'No!'

'What hopes, and whose?' demanded Scotty. 'Abigail what?'

'And I suppose,' said Christopher, 'she finds that now she's got what she wants, she finds she doesn't want what she wanted when she—'

'Look,' pleaded Scotty, 'can't I join in this?'

'Presently,' said Christopher. 'I've got some news.'

'I knew you had,' said Cressida. 'You look … different.'

'Well, come on,' demanded Mrs Belchamber.

'I've bought Greensleeves.'

'You've WHAT?' Scotty rose from his chair, leaned over the table and gave Christopher a tremendous thump on the shoulder. 'Chris, my old son, say that again! Say it—go on!'

'All right. I've bought Greensleeves.'

'Oh ... Chris!' Cressida's eyes were on his, but he could not read her expression.

'You have bought that house?' asked Paul. 'Have you bought it?'

'Yes.'

'For us to live in?'

'Yes.'

'Shall we all live in it?' asked Robert.

'Yes. Are you glad?'

'I am glad,' said Robert without hesitation. 'I shall be happy. I told Josette it was a good house, and she said why shall we not buy it?'

'Well, you can tell her we've bought it.'

There were exclamations, explanations, suggestions, and a general chorus of congratulations. Cressida's eyes, at first unreadable, began to shine and glisten, and Christopher, looking at her, did not have to wait for her words. She, like Robert, was happy.

Only Mrs Belchamber remained silent, going on with her lunch with a firmness and concentration that left her outside the vociferous circle. She made no comment, and Christopher, after waiting for one of her usual caustic remarks and hearing none, found himself left with a curious feeling—half regret, which he interpreted as pity for her homeless state, and half relief, which he identified without any trouble as the pleasure he would experience when he saw the last of her. He found it impossible to believe that he could actually like her, or feel affection for this combination of soft curl and hard hat, of soft flesh and hard visage. He wondered whether she had made any plans, and, if so, what they were.

He was not left long in doubt. Mrs Belchamber put up a scraggy forefinger as he prepared to follow Scotty outside after lunch, and beckoned him to her side.

'About Greensleeves,' she began at once.

'Well?' asked Christopher, uneasiness creeping over him.

'I'll make you an offer for the West tower. I'll rent it from you on a yearly basis.'

Christopher opened his mouth to speak, but no words came.

'We shan't meet, never fear,' swept on Mrs Belchamber. 'I don't want those children all over my part of the house. I shall keep myself to myself, and I hope you'll do the same.'

'I—'

'But it's a lot of room—too much room—for you and Cressida and three children, and a goodish rent—which I shall give you—won't come amiss, when you start adding up your household bills.'

'As a matter of—'

'I don't want to go back to Switzerland, even if I could get there,' proceeded Mrs Belchamber. 'It's a good deal easier to get out of a foreign country nowadays than it is to get into it again. I shouldn't have burnt my boats, but it's too late to think of that now. I like Greensleeves; it's got what very few houses have: style.'

'Yes, but you see, I—'

'I'm not going to buy myself one of those hideous modern houses that fall to pieces the moment you've moved into them, having paid eight times their value first.'

'No, but—'

'And if I go into an old house, there'll be the expense of getting it up to date and rooting out all the prehistoric stoves—like that one there—and putting in new fittings.'

'I would like to point out that—'

'About servants. I've thought that all out,' said Mrs Belchamber. 'There's a couple there already—Émile and his wife—that's two. I shall get Mrs Garcia to come. She can live in the rooms over the stables, where we shan't hear the baby teething, and I shall get her husband to come. I don't know what he's getting at his hotel, but I shall double it—it's the only way to get servants nowadays. That makes four. Shall you be keeping your flat in London?'

'For the present. But—'

'Well then, your man won't be available. I

310

shall send for my two Swiss maids, and I shall keep one and give you the other. The children will presumably be at boarding school soon, and you'll go up to Town every day, or stay up in Town during the week, so there won't be a great deal except during the holidays.'

'I wonder if you'd let me say a few—'

'The only thing that remains to be settled is the figure for the rent. We can walk over to the house together and decide upon the exact number of rooms I'm to have, and then we shall know where we are.'

'My dear Mrs—'

'I'm glad to have it settled,' declared Mrs Belchamber, beginning to clear the table. 'I don't know why you didn't make an offer for Greensleeves long ago—I should have thought that the plan was an obvious one, but I've noticed that you're a little slow in your reactions. I wonder if you'd mind going outside while I get on with things? I shall work better if you're not here chatting. Take that milk jug out with you, will you, and leave it in the dairy. Did Major Gray tell you when you could have possession?'

'He's leaving for South Africa early next month. But I don't see what difference that makes to me,' said Christopher. 'I can't move the children until Robert and Paul's quarantine ends.'

'What quarantine?' demanded Mrs Belchamber.

He stared at her.

'For measles. If they get measles—'

'Of course they won't get measles! I don't say you can't have them more than once, but those two have had them quite recently. They certainly won't get them again so soon.'

'H-had them? How do you know?' asked Christopher.

'You can always tell,' said Mrs Belchamber. 'Now go along.'

Christopher went along.

* * *

Major Gray left England the day before Christopher began the move to Greensleeves. The leave-taking ceremony was brief; Cressida went up to London to see her father off, and returned the following day to pack her things preparatory to returning to her work. No argument from Scotty, no plea from Christopher, had been able to wring from her more than a promise to do all she could to shake herself free of her fears and marry Christopher at once as he wanted her to. Scotty, like Major Gray, felt that absence would prove a better weapon than argument; Greensleeves, the children and her love for Christopher would all combine to make an irresistible magnet to draw her back.

'I wish I'd rented this farm, instead of buying it,' he complained to Christopher. 'Then you'd have to do all the repairs, at no expense to me. You'll buy butter and eggs and cream and cheese from me, all at top prices?'

'I suppose so,' said Christopher. 'What are you going to use the bath for when we've gone?'

'I need an extra trough. But I have a feeling.'

'Another? Well, what's it about this time?'

'Well—I feel,' said Scotty fearfully, 'that she'll come over here on bath nights, just to—'

'No, she won't.'

Scotty's face cleared.

'But I tell you what she will do,' went on Christopher blandly. 'She's been consulting me—professionally—about putting in a bathroom and etceteras.'

'A—In *my* house?'

'Yes.'

'She can't,' declared Scotty. 'She can't do it.'

'Why not? All she needs is money.'

'And my consent.'

'All she needs,' reaffirmed Christopher, 'is money.'

The gloom that descended upon Scotty lasted until the next day, and was still about him when Cressida came over to say good-bye. He kissed her mournfully and watched her go into the house and say good-bye to Mrs Belchamber. Christopher sat at the wheel of the car; he was to drive her up to London, and Scotty, looking at him, thought that he looked less downcast than he expected to find him.

'I suppose,' he said, propping himself up against the car, 'you think she'll come running back?'

'I don't know whether she'll run,' said Christopher, 'but she's got a kind heart, and I don't feel she'll leave me alone too long with my three orphans—that's all.'

'Perhaps you're right,' said Scotty. 'My own opinion is that she'll come back to protect me from the Belchamber. Cress is the only one who's ever stood between me and that menacing body. Look at me now—clean shirt, dungarees that go to the laundry, and snow-white smocks for milking that make the cows think I'm a surgeon coming in to carve them up. You can see them cringing, poor little things. By the time Cress comes back, I'll be dressed up to kill, like those pictures of cowherds in the old story books.' He paused and then went on thoughtfully: 'Do you remember what I said to you, Chris? I said there was only one thing that could save me?'

'The doctor?'

'The doctor,' said Scotty. 'And I don't know how it is, but ever since I saw her at the party, all sweet and unprofessional, I've had a feeling...'

'Ah,' said Christopher. 'A feeling.'

Scotty sighed. 'We'll just have to pray, Chris old son. Or those two fellows'—he nodded towards Robert and Paul, who were approaching the car—'these two fellows might

314

try a spell.'

'A spell for what?' inquired Robert. 'To bring Cressida back?'

'If she does not come back soon, then we will put a spell,' promised Paul. 'Can we come up the lane in the car, Chris-to-pher?'

'Yes, if you like. What's Cressida doing?'

'She has said good-bye to Josette, and she is saying now to madame.'

Mrs Belchamber glanced up somewhat impatiently as Cressida came downstairs after saying good-bye to Josette.

'I don't see why you're wasting all this time in saying good-byes,' she said. 'You'll be back here in a week or two, to arrange about your wedding. I don't see why you have to go away at all. You could have sent word to those people you work for, and told them you're being married at once.'

'But I'm not,' said Cressida.

'Not what?'

'Being married at once.'

'Oh—well, if you want to be exact,' said Mrs Belchamber irritably. 'In two weeks, three, four.'

'I'm not going to be married for a year,' said Cressida.

If she had suddenly produced an extra head, Mrs Belchamber could not have stared at her with greater astonishment.

'You're not what?' she inquired when she could speak.

'I'm not going to be married for a year.'

'A year?'

'Yes.'

'What's the delay? I thought it was to be soon, from what your fiancé said, and from what I gathered. What does he want to wait a year for?'

'He doesn't. I mean—I asked him to.'

'And why?' demanded Mrs Belchamber. 'I don't believe in long engagements. A lot can happen in a year.'

'I know,' acknowledged Cressida, 'but I'd rather wait.'

'Oh. And that young man out there—is he content to wait?'

'He ... he's agreed to wait.'

Mrs Belchamber gave a sound between a sneer and a snort. It breathed such open contempt that the blood came to Cressida's cheeks.

'Good-bye,' she said. 'I hope we'll—'

'A year!' snorted Mrs Belchamber. 'Twelve months. That'll make you twenty-seven.'

'Yes.'

'An age at which most girls show sense, if they're ever going to have any. Who's going to keep an eye on your fiancé during the twelve months. Have you thought of that?'

'There's no need to keep an eye on him. He—'

It was Mrs Belchamber's turn to redden with anger.

316

'Don't stand there making childish remarks,' she requested. 'I put you down as a girl with a headpiece, and I don't like to find that you're like all the other flutterheads. Now go away and don't irritate me with your waiting a year and not keeping an eye. When you get a man—a young man, a clean-living man, a man with background and money, you don't wait a year. You don't wait a day. You thank God for your plum and you see that nobody else eats it. A year! Faugh! In a year, let me tell you, my over-confident young woman, in a year you'll be looking round for him so diligently that you'll wear yourself out in the process—but you won't find him. You won't find any man you've left lying about for a year. *You* won't, but somebody else will. In a month—a week, your faithful young man will be off.'

'That's a matter for—'

'Off. And I'll tell you exactly where he'll be off to. He'll be off to his Maisie.'

'His—?'

'Maisie.'

'Maisie?'

'Ha. I suppose this is the first you've heard of any Maisie?'

'I—'

'I thought so. I don't suppose you know he was engaged to her?'

'En—'

'—gaged. I'll tell you her full name, if you'll

317

give me a moment. Dobson. Hobson. No—Robson. Maisie Robson. Now go out there and ask him about Maisie Robson and watch his face.'

'I—'

'And I suppose he never mentioned the other one?'

'The—'

'The other one. What did you think he did until he was twenty-six? Don't you know anything about men? He wouldn't mention Elinor to you, naturally.'

'El—'

'Elinor something to do with a gate. Gatesby. Gateson. Yes, Gateson. I could have told you he wasn't a man to waste any time when there were women about. You can always tell. You won't find him again after a year, I promise you. But if you care to try it, you may. I don't care to interfere in any business that isn't mine. Now good-bye. I'm sorry for you, and if I know where to write to you, I'll send you a line the first time he brings either of his women down to Greensleeves. I can't do more.'

'Good-bye,' said Cressida.

Mrs Belchamber adjusted her hat, which had been a little tossed about during her speech, and went into the big front room. Cressida stood where she had left her, in the middle of the kitchen, and stared down at the scrubbed, shining table. After a while, a faint,

318

amused smile touched her lips. She turned and walked slowly upstairs to Josette's room, rumpled Josette's hair absently, and walked to the window.

She looked out on to the yard, and saw the car, with the two boys standing near it and Scotty leaning against it. As she stood, Scotty looked up and saw her, and raised a hand.

'Hi there, Cress,' he called.

Christopher opened the door of the car, and, stepping out, looked up at her.

'Ready?' he asked.

Cressida looked down at him. She saw his tall, strong figure in flannels and a tweed jacket; his pleasant face, his air of lazy strength, his big hands, his fine head; she smiled at him and saw the expression in his eyes as he stood quietly looking up at her. He was twenty-six, and she was twenty-six and their house—she glanced for a moment towards Greensleeves—was there, waiting for them. Here was all she wanted in the world—and she was leaving it calmly, deliberately, for a reason that seemed, suddenly, to be no reason at all. The man down there was hers, and a year ... who knew what a year would bring? The present was here and now; life was waiting for her, standing there and looking up at her ...

'Coming?' said Christopher.

She saw him growing hazy, and then disappearing; she shook her head, whether in answer to Christopher's question, or to shake the tears out of her eyes, she never afterwards knew. When she could see again, there was only Scotty looking up at her, a puzzled expression on his face.

'What's up, Cress?' he inquired. 'Changed your mind?' She might have answered, but an arm—an arm in a tweed sleeve—came round her and swung her out of sight. Scotty, staring, saw Christopher's face at the window, and the expression on it brought a yelp from his lips.

'Chris—isn't she going?'

'No,' said Christopher.

'Has she said so?'

'No,' said Christopher. 'But you can always tell.'